# The Things We Keep

Janet Dawson

Bodie Blue Books

To my mother, Thelma Dawson, and my brother, Roger (Two-Plus Guitars) Dawson, for all their love and support

*The Things We Keep* is a work of fiction. Names, places, and incidents are either the product of the author's imagination or are used fictitiously. Any resemblance to actual events, locales or persons, living or dead, except historical events, is entirely coincidental.

A Bodie Blue Books original

Copyright © 2023 Janet Dawson

Library of Congress Control Number: 2022922512

Cover design 2022 by Interbridge

Sign up for the Bodie Blue Books newsletter at: www.janetdawson.com

All rights reserved.

Without limiting the rights under copyright reserved above, no part of this publication may be reproduced, stored in or introduced into a retrieval system, or transmitted, in any form, or by any means (electronic, mechanical, photocopying, recording or otherwise), without the prior written permission of the copyright owner except for the use of brief quotations in a book review.

ISBN: Paperback — 978-1-944153-26-7

Ebook — 978-1-944153-25-0

# One

"IT LOOKS HAUNTED."

I stood on the sidewalk, looking at the old Victorian house on the corner. Like many others in Alameda, it had been built in that era from 1880 to the early twentieth century, in a style known as the Queen Anne, which often featured bay windows and turrets.

This particular house, however, was a Queen Anne gone rogue, screaming excess. It had a large bay window that jutted out from one side of the front porch, towers and turrets galore, plus a surfeit of roof finials, wall carvings and other elaborate gewgaws. There were several stained glass windows, one above the front door and others on the side of the house.

Dan Westbrook, my fiancé, shut the driver's side door and pressed the key fob to lock the car. "It has a general air of neglect, but I don't see any ghosts hovering in the upstairs windows."

"They wouldn't lurk during daylight hours."

I knew the ghosts were there, lurking, waiting to make their presence known. I had a feeling this old house had secrets, lots of them.

It was the middle of October. Earlier this month, a fire to the north blew smoke into the Bay Area, sending air quality into the unhealthy range and turning skies a dirty orange, the smell of smoke everywhere. The fire had been contained and the wind blew away the smoke and the ash. I had washed off the dirty gray residue that had coated my car and my patio furniture. Today, Saturday, was warm, but not too warm. The sky was bright blue with a dusting of white clouds.

A few blocks away, the Alameda Farmers Market was in full swing. A young couple walked by, the father pushing a stroller containing an infant, the mother with a toddler in tow, telling him they were going to buy apples and grapes at the market. On the other side of the street, a woman headed home, carrying a bouquet of yellow chrysanthemums and a canvas bag with a head of romaine lettuce peeking from the top.

A dog barked. I glanced to my left, where a shaggy brown mutt strained at the leash, eager to go after the fat squirrel that was halfway down the trunk of a nearby oak tree. The squirrel chittered and changed its trajectory, climbing back up into the branches. The dog yipped its disappointment as the man at the other end of the leash tugged it away.

Dan and I crossed the street. He was right about the general air of neglect. It didn't take long for a house to acquire that patina of disrepair. The owner had moved out a month or so ago. But it looked as though exterior maintenance had been deferred far too long. The windows, especially those of stained glass, were dirty and several panes had cracks. The wooden siding had been painted different colors over the years, sometimes several colors at once. Peeling layers showed green, yellow, red and even purple. Right now the exterior was a faded blue, the trim olive green. It looked like the roof could do with some work as.

There were several rose bushes close to the house, all with spent blooms in need of deadheading. The front and side yards featured native plants and succulents instead of grass, with bark and gravel spread out around them to keep down the weeds. But weeds are persistent and they were making inroads. A lemon tree in the front yard had fruit showing bright yellow amid the green leaves. The ground below was littered with fallen lemons, some rotting, which contributed to the house's abandoned look.

At some point in the past the house, like so many of the Victorians in Alameda, had been converted from a single-family home to a multi-unit apartment building, with meters for gas and electricity arrayed on one side of the house, and covered conduits for wiring crawling up the side. A wooden stand at the foot of the front steps held four black mailboxes with locks, each with a brass letter denoting the units, A through D. Two upstairs, I guessed, glancing at the second-floor windows. Maybe two more units on the first floor. But the house also had a ground level unit, its windows shielded by horizontal blinds. I glanced up the cracked and bumpy concrete driveway on the right side of the house. Way at the back, I saw a detached garage big enough for two cars.

On the other side of the driveway, another Victorian house appeared to be empty. It sported a FOR SALE sign. So did the one beyond it, with a smaller sign tacked on above, reading SALE PENDING.

A blue Honda sedan was parked in the Queen Anne's driveway. It belonged to our friends, Noel Benjamin and his wife, Lakshmi Srinivasan. We were here to help them go through the house and inventory its contents. That job had been sweetened by their promise of dinner at the day's end, since their kids were spending the weekend with Lakshmi's parents in Fremont.

Dan and I climbed the steps to the front porch, which was decorated with big terra cotta pots on either side of the front door, both planted with bronze chrysanthemums in need of watering. A small signboard to the left of the door was meant to list the names of the people who lived in the apartments, but all four slots were empty.

Dan pushed the doorbell. A moment later, the door opened and Noel Benjamin waved us into the hallway. He was a wiry man in his thirties, brown hair receding from a high forehead, with a sharp wedge of a nose. Laugh lines crinkled around his hazel eyes as he smiled at us. Like Dan and me, he wore faded jeans and a T-shirt, ready for what would no doubt be a messy task.

"Come in. And let me tell you again how much I appreciate this. Lakshmi's in the kitchen making coffee. We brought pastries, so we'll have a nosh before we get started."

We stepped into the foyer. The hardwood floors were oak, scuffed and stained with years of wear, cracks here and there between floorboards, some of them wide enough to swallow coins or a key. The staircase on the right had a wooden banister and a faded green stair runner. To the left was a closed pocket door. The ceramic plaque on the wall next to it, in bright orange and blue, bore the letter A.

Between the staircase and the pocket door, a hallway led back to another door that opened onto a large kitchen, the walls and cabinets painted a pale green. The vinyl tile on the floor had a green and yellow pattern. In the center of the room was an oval table with metal legs and a yellow Formica top, the kind popular back in the 1950s and now sought by people who liked mid-twentieth century furniture. The countertops were also yellow Formica. There was a built-in dishwasher to the left of the sink. The white refrigerator and the smooth-topped stove looked fairly new, as did the side-by-side washer and dryer in one corner.

Several cardboard boxes sat on the floor, filled with the items common to most kitchens—a set of stainless steel pans, a cookie sheet, several mismatched bowls of varying sizes, and a handheld mixer. An assortment of utensils, everything from wooden spoons to spatulas, filled a smaller box. Donations, I guessed, along with a basket that held placemats, napkins and pot holders. Canned goods and packaged food filled another box.

Lakshmi smiled as she turned to greet us. She was a slender woman in her thirties, casually dressed, her long black hair caught back in a ponytail, her wide eyes brown in an oval face. "The coffee is almost ready. We need to fortify ourselves for the task ahead. I've brought pastries for now, and cheese, fruit and nibbles for later."

On this side of the sink, the counter held a coffeemaker, sputtering as strong black brew dripped into the glass carafe. Next to this were four mismatched ceramic mugs, a pint carton of half and half, and a pink bakery box.

I poured a mugful of coffee and moved to the pastry box, making my selection. "Cheese danish. Works for me."

"I've been picking up lemons. And veggies from the garden out back." Lakshmi pointed at two large paper sacks on the floor near the stove. One held an assortment of squash and tomatoes, and the other bright yellow lemons of varying sizes. "Please, take some home with you. There's no point in letting them go to waste."

"Thanks, I will. I have plenty of squash and tomatoes in my own garden, but I'm always in the market for lemons. I use them in cooking." I pulled out a chair and sat at the kitchen table, which had metal-legged chairs, the seats covered with yellow vinyl that was nearly a match for the table surface.

"Bear claw," Dan said cheerfully, claiming his favorite pastry. He and the others joined me at the table.

Dan writes books about hiking, focusing on different states and regions. Noel and Lakshmi own and operate a small local publishing company. Together they acquire a variety of books. Noel takes care of the financial end of the business, as well as production, while Lakshmi edits books and does the marketing. Their small press is located here in Alameda and so is their home, a bungalow on the East End, where they live with their two children. I'd met them when Dan and I had dinner at their home during the summer.

I glanced across the table at Noel. "This is quite a house. It belongs to your aunt?"

Noel set his coffee mug next to his cherry danish and smiled. "Aunt Gloria, yes. Great-aunt, really. She's my grandmother's sister. We've gotten close over the years, since Lakshmi and I live here in Alameda. As Gloria has gotten older, she's come to rely on us. Older, but not really that old these days. Grandma and Gloria are in their late seventies. Both active and engaged with the world. They're twins, by the way. But nothing alike. My grandmother is quiet and conservative. Gloria, on the other hand, is a character." He laughed. "She's a free spirit. Never been married, and she's had a colorful life, judging from her stories."

As Noel talked, I glanced at Lakshmi. The look on her face told me she had heard the colorful stories too many times. My guess was that Lakshmi didn't much like Aunt Gloria, but tolerated her for Noel's sake.

"Gloria lived in San Francisco in the sixties," Lakshmi said, pulling apart her almond croissant. "In the Haight. Ground zero for hippiedom and the music scene. To hear her tell it, she hung out with everyone from Janis Joplin to the Grateful Dead."

Noel was nodding. "She was lead singer for a band in those days. I don't remember which one. I don't think they ever got to be famous. Then she bought this place in nineteen sixty-nine."

"A move to strait-laced, conservative Alameda?" I chuckled. "After rock 'n rolling in the Haight? That's quite a change."

"I don't know what prompted that move, way back when," Noel said. "Maybe it was chance to do something different. This place was a good investment, still is. It was originally a single family home, then converted to flats during World War Two. Through the years, she rented apartments to sailors from the Naval Air Station and students from the College of Alameda. The base closed, of course, but the college is still here. This is a great location, just a few blocks to Webster Street and several bus lines. Not that far to the ferry terminal either." He paused as he took a bite from his danish and washed it down with coffee. "Around the end of August, six weeks ago, Gloria decided to give up this place and move into a senior apartment. It was a surprise, really. And this all happened really fast."

"What about the tenants?" Dan asked. "The place doesn't look lived in. Did she stop renting out the units?"

"There are no tenants." Lakshmi frowned. "Which is odd, because Gloria always had renters. She priced the apartments on the low side, so she could keep the units full. But the renters moved out, all within the last couple of months."

"That is unusual," I said. "Particularly if she was charging lower rents than market rate. Rents are going up like crazy, all over the Bay Area. I'm glad I bought my house when I did."

Noel shrugged. "People move on. I think the renters leaving at about the same time is just the luck of the draw. Gloria said the man who lived in one of the upstairs apartments moved out of the area. I don't know about the other two tenants."

"I was surprised that the woman who lived in the ground level unit left," Lakshmi said. "She had been here ten years or more. She's the one who created the vegetable garden out back. I thought she was settled in for another ten years, but suddenly in August, she packed up and moved out. I don't even know if she gave thirty days' notice."

"That's strange, given how long she was here," I said. "Maybe she found a better place to live. Or there could have been a problem here."

"If there was a problem, Gloria didn't say what it was. I just . . ." Lakshmi hesitated. "I think there's something odd about the way the tenants left."

So did I. "Did Gloria list the apartments and not get any takers?"

Lakshmi shook her head. "No, it turns out she didn't list them. I asked her why and she said she'd decided to move. That was the first I'd heard of it. Her decision seemed to come out of the blue." She toyed with the handle of her coffee mug. "Gloria always insisted she could age in place here. She's owned this house for decades, living in the first-floor unit and renting out the other apartments. She was vocal about living here until they carried her out. No senior apartment or assisted living for her."

"What changed her mind?"

"She fell," Noel said. "Here in the kitchen."

"That will do it." I thought about my own grandmother, Jerusha. She and Dan's grandmother, Pearl, had been good friends, aspiring actresses living in Hollywood in the forties. Grandma had given it up when she married Grandpa, but Pearl had stayed, making a good living acting in movies and television, a single mother raising her son, who was Dan's father. Grandma was gone now, but she had stayed in her own home here in Alameda, despite suggestions from her children, my father and his sister Caro, that it might be time to consider a different living situation. Pearl was still alive, living with Dan's parents in Lee Vining, in a small apartment they'd added to their house.

Noel got up from the table, poured himself another mugful of coffee, and topped off mugs for those of us who wanted more. Then he returned to the table.

"I don't know exactly what happened, what caused Gloria to fall. I wondered if she'd been up on the step stool," he said. "This place has high ceilings and the cabinets are really high, too."

"I can see that." A glance at the cabinets confirmed that I would need a step stool to reach the upper shelves.

As he spoke, I saw a look on Lakshmi's face that made me curious. Did she suspect that there was more to Gloria's fall than just an accident?

I would like to know more, I thought. Particularly after what Lakshmi said about the abrupt departure of Gloria's tenants.

"I asked about the accident," Noel continued. "But she didn't want to talk about it. She had bruises on her arms and a cut on her head. I was concerned about her. She didn't even see her doctor, just said she was okay. About a week later, she told me the house was too much for her and she would move into this new senior living facility that just opened up here in town. Next thing I knew, she started packing. Her car doesn't have much cargo space, so we helped her move a lot of stuff."

"Her new place is a good-sized one bedroom unit, with a small kitchen and dining area," Lakshmi said. "But the living space is smaller than she had here. She took some of the things she really loves, collectibles that she's acquired over the years. Her bed, of course, and the sofa. She also took a bedside table, a secretary desk, a dresser and a chest of drawers. She wants the bookcases that are still in her bedroom and living room. But we need to empty out the books first, so that's something we'll do today, pack up those books. Then we'll call someone to move stuff. Though I wonder if she might want to donate books as well. I'll let her go through them and then we can go from there."

"What about the rest of the furniture?" I asked. "This retro table and chairs, for example. I know people are really into fifties kitchen stuff."

"I agree," Lakshimi said. "Gloria told us to just get rid of the furniture that's left. Noel convinced her that we should inventory everything in the house, to see what could be sold. I'm sure some of it would fetch a decent price. There's a furniture dealer I know, and a home furnishings consignment store here in Alameda. That may be the best choice for disposing of the furniture. The apartments were unfurnished, but there might be a few things left behind when the tenants moved out. Then there's that double garage outside. Gloria parked her car on one side, and the other side is the place where all the old furniture went to die. I know she had a beautiful oak sideboard that's not in her unit anymore, so I'm wondering if it was relegated to the garage. Or maybe she sold that."

"Kitchen stuff is collectible, too. Dishes, bakeware, that sort of thing." I glanced at the boxes that were already filled with items, then looked up at the cabinets above the Formica counters, wondering what might be on the shelves.

"Absolutely." Lakshmi nodded. "And clothing. Gloria was a flower child back in the sixties. She's got some things that would catch the eye of a vintage clothing dealer."

"Her new place is really nice," Noel said. "They call it a continuing care community. There are several levels, independent living, assisted living, even hospice."

Lakshmi nodded. "Nice doesn't cover it. The place is like a resort hotel, with a price to match. They've got a spa and a salon, outdoor pool, fitness room, all sorts of activities. And a dining room, of course. Gloria says the food is good. She told us she's paid for a year, but if she's going to stay there long term, she needs money."

"She should get it," I said. "Alameda has always been a red-hot housing market. When my grandmother died, my dad and his sister put her house on the market and it sold in less than a week. People were bidding up the price. When Dan and I got here, I noticed the two houses next to this one. Both with 'for sale' signs."

"Prices have skyrocketed all over the Bay Area," Dan said.

Noel nodded. "Especially Alameda. Several houses in this neighborhood have sold recently. Big houses. People who are up in years, whose kids have left home, are downsizing. Anyway, once we clear everything out, we'll put the house on the market. If I can convince Gloria to do that."

I frowned. "She doesn't want to sell the house? Why keep it? Especially if she needs the money for her new living arrangements."

"That's another odd thing," Lakshmi said. "Gloria does want to sell the house, but she doesn't want to put in on the market. She doesn't want to list the house with a realtor. You know how it goes. A realtor would stage the place, get all sorts of bids. Though I'm not sure how that works with a multi-unit place. She could get a really good price for this place. But no, Gloria says she already has a buyer. And she won't say who."

"I'd really like to know who," Noel added. "I'm concerned that someone might take advantage of Gloria."

"Oh, I doubt that." Lakshmi accompanied her comment with an eye roll. "Besides, she could also sell the car."

Noel shook his head. "She'll never part with that. It's a vintage Mustang fastback, a classic." He took out his phone and went to the photos icon, calling up a photo of a candy apple red Mustang.

"Looks like it's in good shape, too," Dan said.

"Yes, she's taken good care of it." Noel set his phone on the table, pushed back his chair and stood up. "We'd better stop talking and get busy."

# Two

I WENT TO THE kitchen sink to rinse my hands, since my fingers were sticky from the pastry. Noel and Lakshmi had brought gloves and masks, warning us that the house was dusty, since it hadn't been cleaned in a while. Dan and I helped ourselves and followed Noel and Lakshmi through a door that led from the kitchen into a short hallway. To the right was a bathroom with a tub and shower combo. The tile floor was turquoise and white, that color motif repeated on the tub surrounds and in the floral shower curtain hanging from the rod. Grab bars had been installed in the tub, as well as next to both the tub and toilet.

The next room had once been the dining room. When the house was divided into apartments, it was turned into a bedroom. The walls were a pale, leafy green and the curtains that covered the tall windows were a muted green and yellow floral, hanging from a cafe rod with rings.

The bed was missing. So were the dresser and chest of drawers. According to Lakshmi, Gloria had moved those furniture items to her new apartment at the senior living facility, along with her sofa. But she hadn't taken the small armoire. It was about five feet tall, made of golden oak with an arched top and a carved leaf design on the doors.

There were two unfinished pine bookcases on the back wall, next to the window that looked out on the backyard. These were about four feet high and crammed with books, both paperback and hardcover. On the floor were several empty cardboard cartons.

"We'll start boxing up the books in here," Noel said. "There are more books in the living room, if you want to tackle that."

"Sure," Dan said, picking up two of the cartons.

Lakshmi grabbed a box, setting it near the armoire. She opened the doors to reveal several shelves containing folded clothing. She reached inside and pulled something from the top shelf, unfolding a long vest beaded with all colors and sizes, and sparkles too. "Look at this. It's gorgeous, and in good condition."

"I know of a vintage clothing store in Lafayette," I said.

"There's one in Oakland, too. I'm definitely letting them have a look at this." She refolded the vest and put it in the box at her feet.

I opened a door next to the armoire, revealing a closet. When the house had been a single family home, and this room a dining room, the closet must have been a pantry, about four feet wide and perhaps six feet deep, with open shelving on the right. A rail for clothing had been added on the left. The rail now held a few empty hangers and the shelves were bare as well. Everything had been removed. I was about to shut the door when I noticed something at the back of the closet. There was a light switch to the right of the door and I turned it on, illuminating the bulb above. Then I walked the length of the closet to investigate what I'd seen. It was a small compartment, with a door about ten by fifteen inches, with a hinged stainless steel hasp that fitted into a fixed staple for a padlock. The lock was gone, the door ajar, and the inside compartment, about a foot deep, was empty as well.

"Did you find something?"

I turned to see Lakshmi standing at the closet door. "I'm curious about this little compartment. I wonder what was inside."

"I don't know," Lakshmi said. "I assume she kept something important there, because it looks like it can be locked. It's empty now. Gloria cleared out some of her papers and took them with her to her new apartment. We took care of the rest. She had a bunch of bankers boxes stashed in this closet, and some loose papers that had been dumped on the floor. We moved those into our storage room at the publishing company. Temporarily, I hope. Gloria needs to go through that stuff and get rid of a lot of it."

I stepped out of the closet and turned off the light. Lakshmi had her hands on the edge of the armoire, now closed. "I thought I saw something underneath," she said. "Would you help me move this?"

The armoire was lighter than I expected. We moved it about a foot away from the wall and Lakshmi bent to retrieve the item she'd seen, which turned out to be a red velvet scarf.

"Want to move the armoire back against the wall?"

"No, just leave it," she said. "I want to take photos for that furniture dealer. See what kind of a price we can get for it, since it looks old."

Dan was busy boxing up the books. I moved from the bedroom to the living room, which were separated by another pocket door, the moving panels tucked into the wall on either side of the wide doorway. The living room looked comfortable and well-used, with wainscoting, panels of oak extending four feet up the walls. Above the wood, the walls were painted the same pale green as the bedroom. The windows here were covered with cream-colored pull-down shades, with scalloped edges and tassels, and white sheers over them.

The exterior wall, to my right, had a fireplace midway between the pocket doors and the bay window. Gloria used the fireplace, judging from the soot on the back of the fire box. A set of black metal fireplace tools, with a poker, shovel, ash broom, and long tongs, hung from a free-standing rack to the right of the mantel. A black mesh fireplace screen fit over the opening. The mantel itself was carved wood, oak that matched the wainscoting, and probably dated to the building of the house. The mantel shelf held a small brass carriage clock and a large Chinese ginger jar, blue with a design of pink and yellow peonies. The carnival glass bowl next to it might have some value. I picked up a green vase decorated with magnolia flowers. Roseville pottery, I thought. The maker's mark on the bottom confirmed it.

Lakshmi had said that Gloria took a number of collectibles when she moved to her new lodgings, telling her great-nephew to get rid of everything else. But art pottery? It was definitely collectible. Why had she left this behind? Both Noel and Lakshmi said that Gloria's decision to leave the house and move to a senior apartment took them by surprise. It looked like she'd moved out in a hurry, taking only what was necessary and leaving a lot behind. Why?

The alcove in the bay window had been turned into a cozy nook for reading, with a comfortable wingback chair in a tapestry print with a matching ottoman. A floor lamp was angled over the chair and the side table held an assortment of books, a box of facial tissues, and a lacquer tray, red and black, decorated with Chinese characters. More books filled a low pine bookshelf opposite the chair. I couldn't see the street from the bay window, just the glossy green leaves and bright yellow fruit of the lemon tree.

Built-in shelves on either side of the pocket doors held books and knick-knacks. Dust bunnies decorated the floor where the sofa once stood, facing another empty spot. From the location and the shape of the dust pattern, I guessed that this had been a stand for the TV and its accessories.

The old piano on the wall opposite the fireplace might be worth something. The dark wood cabinet containing the strings was ornately carved with a rectangle of twining leaves, though scarred and stained in places. Above the keys themselves I saw faded gold letters reading, CHAS.

M. Stieff, Baltimore. I sat down on the wooden chair in front of the piano, my hands moving over the discolored keys. The piano was long out of tune and a plinking sound indicated a broken string or two.

Dan had finished boxing up the books in the bedroom, so we started on those in the living room. That done, we inventoried the contents of the room, from the furniture to the pottery and the pictures on the walls.

An hour or so later, we took a break at the kitchen table, then we moved to the second floor. Both apartments were empty, though a former tenant had left a small rattan table.

"The attic's empty," Noel said, pointing a finger upward. "I went up there before you got here and didn't see anything but dust and insulation. Gloria usually stored things in the garage, so that's going to be a job."

"Let's get to it," Lakshmi said.

We went downstairs, through the enclosed back porch and down the back steps. There was a patio paved with flagstones and the garden was bordered with bricks sunk into the soil. An assortment of herbs and lettuces were overgrown and gone to seed. Tomato plants still held ripened fruit. I saw yellow crookneck squash and Swiss chard. It was a shame to leave all those veggies, but I was sure the birds and squirrels were enjoying them.

The ground floor unit had a letter D on the door. Between the back steps and the driveway was another door. "What's that?" I asked Noel.

"Storage and laundry," he said. "The hot water heater is in there, a big one for all the units. There's a coin-operated washer and dryer for the tenants. The woman who gardened kept potting soil and tools in there."

The double garage had old-style wooden doors that opened out. Noel unlocked the padlock that secured it. He and Dan opened the doors. As Lakshmi had said, one side was empty, the space where Gloria had parked her car. The other side was stuffed with furniture, boxes and old trunks.

"There's that oak sideboard I was talking about earlier," Lakshmi said, hands on her hips as she examined the ornate carvings on the back. "It's in decent condition. Needs refinishing, of course. I'd like to have it. I'll ask Gloria."

"What's in these trunks?" I fiddled with the hasp on a steamer trunk and opened it. "Here's your vintage clothing." I took out a pair of denim pants and shook them, laughing at the sight of the wide bottoms. "Bell bottoms! From the sixties, I'll bet. Look at those patches and the rows of buttons down the legs." I set the trousers aside and pulled out another. "Leather vest, with fringe."

I burrowed deeper and found a tunic made of silk, the fabric swirling with flowers in red, orange and gold. The sleeves and neckline were trimmed with gold braid and sequins scattered across the front. I held it in front of me. I'm sure my brain was playing tricks on me, but I could almost smell a whiff of marijuana. "Look at this. It reminds me of those pictures of Haight-Ashbury back in the Summer of Love days. Should I channel my inner Janis Joplin and sing 'Piece of my Heart?'"

Dan laughed. "No, thanks."

I rolled my eyes as I folded the tunic and put it back in the trunk.

Noel held out a key ring. "Would you and Dan look at the ground floor apartment and the other room? These are the keys. The one with the red dot on it is the apartment and the one with the green dot is the storeroom."

"Sure." Dan and I headed for the apartment first. I opened the front door and walked into a good-sized living room, separated from the kitchen by a counter with cabinets underneath. The carpet was a utilitarian nubby beige, the wall painted the ubiquitous off-white, marked here and there with nail holes and a few smudges and dings.

In the kitchen, the stove and refrigerator were white. So were the cabinets below and above. The tan Formica counter didn't do much to alleviate the bland color scheme. A hallway led to a bathroom and a large bedroom. The windows were covered with horizontal blinds.

There were no human touches, just the residue of the most recent tenant, in a few forgotten items—a yellow notepad with a task list, tissue paper on the floor in the kitchen, a nail file on the hallway carpet, a shampoo bottle in the bathroom.

I opened the bedroom closet. A few empty hangers remained on the rail, but that didn't interest me as much as the door at the back. I pulled the cord that turned on the light bulb hanging from the ceiling. "Hey, there's a door."

"Backs onto that storeroom?" Dan asked.

"Probably." I tried the door handle. "Locked. Let's try it from the other side."

We left the apartment, locking the front door. I unlocked the storeroom and we stepped inside. It was dim, with the only light from the door and a couple of dirty windows. I spotted a light switch next to the door and reached for it. The overhead bulbs illuminated a long narrow room with a concrete floor, an overlay of dust and bare studs on the walls, festooned with cobwebs. To my right were the washer and dryer, with a small table next to those. The water heater was in the opposite corner, to the left of the door. The tenant had taken the gardening supplies, but the earthy smell of potting soil lingered, with a whiff of plant food and fertilizer. An empty metal shelf was splotched with rust. There were a couple of cardboard cartons, both empty. A plastic crate held a large flashlight, a pair of work gloves, and a crowbar.

The door that led to the closet in the ground floor apartment was farther down on my right, a few feet this side of a three-paneled screen that was propped in the corner. I walked over and tried the knob. Locked. Was the key in the collection that Noel had obtained from Gloria?

I moved away from the door, examining the screen in the corner. The dark wood frame held three panels, made of paper, each decorated with cherry blossoms. The colors were faded, the paper torn and ripped, enough for me to see something behind the screen. I moved it aside and saw a big trunk pushed against the wall.

No, it wasn't a trunk. It was a footlocker, large, wide and deep. The black metal surface was coated with dust, and there were a number of dents and scratches on the lid and sides. The metal fittings were rusted. It had a handle on either end. There was a sticker on the top, oval in shape, showing an anchor with a chain and superimposed on this, the letters USN—the symbol of the United States Navy.

I grabbed one handle and tugged the footlocker. The damn thing was heavy but I wrangled it into the middle of the room. Something rattled inside.

"What's that?" Dan asked.

"A footlocker. Like a sailor would have. Gloria rented apartments to sailors from the air station. It must have been left here by a tenant. But the base closed years ago." I tugged the clasps but the lid wouldn't open. Either it was locked or rusted shut. I reached for the crowbar, shoved the end between the lid and the trunk, and applied pressure. It took two tries before something gave way.

I opened the lid. And stared down into the empty eye sockets of a skull.

"Hello," I said. "How long have you been there?"

# Three

Dan stared, at a loss for words. Then he said, "I'll get Noel and Lakshmi." He headed out the door.

I wanted to examine the footlocker more closely, being as careful as possible. I fetched the flashlight from the crate, hoping the batteries still had some juice. They did. I knelt and cast the beam over the contents of the footlocker.

The skull rested on a pile of bones, a second skull visible underneath. The discoloration told me the bones had been buried, probably for a long time. Then they'd been dug up and transferred to the footlocker. I leaned closer, the flashlight beam probing deeper into the footlocker. I saw gravel at the bottom, mixed with dirt and tiny bits of cloth. Those broken bits appeared to be from clamshells. And feathers, white, black, and gray. I counted four of them, of varying sizes.

Dan was back, with Noel and Lakshmi behind him, alarm written on their faces as they crowded into the storeroom. Noel gaped at the skull. "A skeleton?"

"Two skeletons." I pointed. "I see two skulls, a bunch of ribs. An ulna, that's an arm bone. Two pelvic bones, tibias, femurs. And lots of finger bones."

"A skeleton," Noel said again.

Lakshmi took his arm. "We need to call the police."

They went back outside. Noel pulled his phone from his pocket and I heard his voice, sharp with urgency.

"What do you think?" Dan asked.

"People who die of natural causes don't usually wind up in a footlocker." I pointed at the first skull, the one closest to the top. "See that crack?"

"Blunt object?"

"Probably. Somebody killed these people. And went to great lengths to conceal their remains." Once again, I shone the flashlight on the contents of the footlocker. "See that gravel and dirt at the bottom? The remains were disposed of elsewhere, and then moved into the trunk. This is a very cold case."

Dan was looking at the feathers. "California gull." That was the most common gull at Mono Lake, near the town of Lee Vining, where his parents lived. The saline lake was one of the largest California gull rookeries in the United States.

"Could be. Gull feathers and shells, no surprise there. We're in Alameda, surrounded by water. We have several gull species here, including California gulls." I pointed at the largest feather, slate gray tipped in white. "That looks like a wing feather from a gull. But look at the smaller one. It's a lighter gray and there's no white tipping. That tells me it's from another bird. A shore bird."

"Your dad's a birder."

"Yes, he is. And I have several birding books at home. Here, hold the flashlight."

Dan held the flashlight high. I pulled out my phone and touched the camera icon, taking photos of the footlocker's contents. I zoomed in and got several good shots of the feathers. I would send those photos to Dad and consult my own books.

Then I spotted a glint, reflecting light. There was a small bit of metal at the bottom of the footlocker, smeared with dirt, half-buried by some pebbles. Was that engraving I saw on the visible half? With a hole drilled at one end? A pendant from a necklace? A charm from a bracelet? I enlarged the shot as much as I could and snapped several pictures.

"What's that?" Dan asked, shifting the position of the flashlight. The beam highlighted a mass of scratches on the left end of the footlocker. A sharp implement—a chisel, perhaps—had been used with force.

"It looks like an attempt to obliterate something," I said. "A name or some other identifying information."

I moved in for a better look, then raised my phone and focused on the scratches, taking several photos. There were two sets of scratches, one roughly oval-shaped, the size of an egg. The other section was more rectangular, maybe four inches long. In the smaller section, I thought I saw letters. Initials? Or a name, perhaps? I could make out something that could have been a W or possibly an M. Was that other mark a K? Or simply an X? As for the longer section, I was sure I saw digits. Five numbers, possibly six. Could it be part of a social security number?

Guesswork, I thought. The only thing that was truly visible was the peeling sticker with the Navy anchor emblem.

Had the footlocker belonged to a sailor, someone stationed at the now-closed Naval Air Station? Someone who had rented an apartment years ago? Had it been left here for decades? Or brought here recently? I looked at the storeroom floor, checking for any marks that could tell me whether the locker had been dragged to its present resting place. But I didn't see anything.

I took several more pictures, then stood and tucked my phone into my pocket. Noel appeared at the door. "The police are on their way."

We waited in the driveway. Sirens and police cars in this quiet residential neighborhood had attracted a crowd. Passersby stopped on the sidewalks and people came out of nearby houses. Two uniformed officers, a man and a woman, arrived and went inside the storeroom. A few minutes later, a plainclothes officer walked toward us. He identified himself as Lieutenant Bradley Chen. I told him about my discovery of the bones and he and I exchanged business cards. "Your name's familiar. That murder case over on the Oakland waterfront?"

"Yes, I was involved in that. I took a number of photos of the footlocker and the bones. I'll forward those to you."

"Thanks, I would appreciate that."

We answered questions and gave statements as more people showed up to process what was now a crime scene. Finally, the police left, vehicles driving away and taking the bones with them.

By now it was past three. "I don't know about the rest of you," I said, "but I'm not in the mood to continue with this inventory. I think we'd better call it a day."

"Me neither," Lakshmi said. "Let's lock up and have an early dinner."

# Four

THE DISCOVERY OF THE bones was all over the news on Monday. I had a feeling I hadn't heard the last of this. So, I wasn't surprised at the voice mail I got late that morning.

After a client meeting in downtown Berkeley, I walked back to the garage where I'd left my car, checking messages and missed calls as I navigated the crowded sidewalk. I listened to a voice mail from Noel Benjamin. He and Lakshmi wanted to meet with me and I guessed why. I stopped near the entrance to the garage and returned the call.

"We want to hire you," Noel said. "To investigate this whole bones-in-the-footlocker situation."

"The police are investigating. What do you think I can bring to the table?"

"I'd rather have this conversation in person, if at all possible. I prefer talking face to face. I know you're busy, but is there a chance we can arrange a meeting at our office here in Alameda?"

I thought about it. Did I really want to get involved in this? I was up in the air on that one. "I'm in Berkeley. I could be there within the hour."

"Okay, we'll look forward to seeing you."

I ended the call and stood for a moment at the parking garage entrance. Instead of parked cars, I saw that footlocker with the bones. I shook off the memory and walked to the kiosk, where I inserted my parking ticket and paid the tab. Then I took the elevator up to the fourth level where I'd left my Toyota.

Forty minutes later, I drove over the Park Street Bridge into Alameda. I turned right onto Clement Avenue, which ran along the waterfront, near the estuary shore across from Oakland. The publishing company owned by Noel and Lakshmi was on this block, between Park and Oak Streets, in a one-story Victorian-era house that had been turned into offices. Its neighbors were a video production company and an auto detailing shop.

Farther down the street was an auto repair shop, as well as other houses that were still residences. I parked near the repair shop and crossed the street toward the bungalow that housed the publishing company. It was painted light blue with darker blue trim and had a rectangular brass sign giving the company name. The door was locked. I pressed the intercom next to it. Lakshmi's voice greeted me.

"It's Jeri Howard."

"Great. I'll let you in." The buzzer sounded and the door opened. I stepped into a small foyer with a couple of chairs and a table displaying some of the company's travel books. To my right, in what had been the house's living room, was a conference room. The large table was covered with papers, as though someone had been working and had just stepped away for a moment.

Lakshmi appeared in the hallway and beckoned me to join her. "Thanks so much for doing this."

I refrained from pointing out that I hadn't yet agreed to do anything. I didn't know Noel and Lakshmi very well. They were Dan's friends before I'd met them. Plus they were his publishers. For Dan, this was a business relationship as well as a friendship. I didn't want to step on any toes.

When you hire a private investigator, that doesn't necessarily mean you'll like the results. Sometimes people don't understand that.

Still, I could listen to what they had to say, and then make up my mind whether to take the case.

Lakshmi and Noel had offices that had once been bedrooms. In Noel's office, I sat in a chair in front of his desk, while Lakshmi pulled a chair from a nearby work table and sat down near me. Noel offered coffee but I declined.

"Tell me what's on your mind," I said. "I have to get back to Oakland for another appointment."

Noel glanced at Lakshmi, then began. "After what happened this weekend at the house, with you finding the bones, Lakshmi and I had a talk with Gloria, my great-aunt. We told her what happened and that we can't inventory and empty out the house right away. She was upset. I thought at first it was about the bones, but she was concerned about the delay."

Next to me, Lakshmi sighed and rolled her eyes. "She was pissed. She wants to get on with it, clear out the house, and get it sold."

"Not even put it on the market," Noel said. "She keeps saying she already has a buyer. I've been talking with a real estate agent I know here in Alameda. I told Gloria what he told me. If she puts the house on the market she could get multiple offers and have plenty of money to live on for the foreseeable future. But she was adamant that she had already agreed to sell the house to this buyer."

"I see." From what Noel was saying, I gathered that Gloria's attitude was along the lines of—old bones, got nothing to do with me. Did she know something about those bones? Or was something else going on? "I am curious about this buyer for the house. Did she have a name? Or any details about the offer?"

Noel shook his head. "She wouldn't say. I'm guessing she doesn't want to do anything that will sour the deal. On some level, I don't think she took the business of the bones seriously. She acted as though the whole thing was far-fetched. In my opinion, she's showing some signs of dementia."

Or she was using the dotty old lady routine to avoid answering questions. I was being cynical. Though Lakshmi's expression, which she hadn't masked very well, told me she had the same feeling.

This was raising red flags for me. I chose my words carefully. "I have some concerns about taking the case, given your business and personal relationships with Dan."

Noel nodded. "I understand. Will you consider it?"

I glanced at my watch. "I have to go. Let me give it some thought and I'll get back to you about whether I can take this on."

Lakshmi rose from her chair. "I'll walk out with you. I'm heading over to the Little House Cafe for a mocha. Noel, do you want anything?"

He looked up from his desk. "Yeah, a cappuccino would be great."

We left the office. I waited in the foyer as Lakshmi stopped in her own office and came out carrying a small wallet. She tucked it into the pocket of her gray slacks and led the way out the front door. We went down the steps to the street. "Coffee for the road? I'm buying."

"Did you want to talk with me, without Noel listening in?"

She smiled. "Yes. There's something you should know."

"About Gloria?"

"I want to give you my own take," she said as we walked to the intersection. "Which is a bit darker than Noel's view."

"I thought it might be." We crossed the Clement Street and headed up Oak, toward the next corner.

She sighed. "You heard him, when we were at the house on Saturday. He loves Aunt Gloria. He thinks of her as the easy-going free spirit, in contrast to Glenda, his grandmother, who can be a real stick in the mud. But there's a reason those two sisters don't get along. Gloria is self-centered and selfish. Those skeletons you found? She doesn't give a damn about them. She just wants to clear that stuff out of the house so she can sell it and get the money. All she cares about is being inconvenienced."

"That's what you meant about Gloria being pissed about the delay." She frowned. "Something is off about Gloria's reaction. I can't quite put my finger on it. When we told her about the bones, she seemed genuinely taken aback. Then she went into her rant about how inconvenient it is and how she doesn't want Noel involved in her affairs. That's rich. We've been involved in her affairs for years. Gloria glommed onto us the minute we moved to Alameda. For whatever reason, she had already decided that he's her favorite nephew, or rather great-nephew. After Noel and I got married, we bought a house here in town and she was so thrilled to have both of us on call. So yes, he has taken an active role in managing her affairs. And she's okay with having him do that—until she's not. This is one of those times. She wants us to take charge of that inventory, and empty out the house, but anything more than that—"

She didn't finish the sentence. But it was plain that Lakshmi was seriously annoyed with Gloria. Noel's aunt took advantage, frequently.

We had reached the Little House Cafe on the next corner. The small building was teal blue, the windows trimmed in purple. Extending from the front of the structure was a pair of oversize legs in striped black and white stockings, ending at a pair of ruby red slippers.

"Hmm," I said. "Looks like a house fell on a witch."

Lakshmi laughed. "I do get a kick out of that."

We went inside. At the counter, Lakshmi ordered coffees to go, a latte for me and a mocha and cappuccino for herself and Noel.

Outside again, we headed back to Clement Avenue. Lakshmi took a sip of her mocha. "Back to Gloria, when I tried probing a bit deeper, she went into her dotty old lady act. Which she pulls frequently when she doesn't want to talk."

"Selective memory," I said. "Okay, she doesn't want to talk about it. Which makes me wonder if she knows more than she's saying about those bones."

"She claims she doesn't. But—" Lakshmi shrugged. "It's nothing she said, just her reaction when Noel and I went over there to talk with her. I can't explain it, but it bothered me."

"Something else bothered you," I said. "On Saturday. When Noel was telling us about Gloria's fall, there was a look on your face, as though you didn't believe it was an accident."

She nodded. "You picked up on that."

"It's what I do. So, why don't you believe it was an accident?"

"Don't know, can't put my finger on it." She shook her head, her expression frustrated. "That often happens when I have dealings with Gloria. This business about her accidental fall in the kitchen doesn't ring true. I wonder if someone shoved her and that's why she fell."

"Who would have done that? You said the tenants had moved out. Does she have any friends who visit her on a regular basis?"

"A few." Lakshmi shrugged. "Gloria likes to play poker. She has a regular game, once a month, I think. There are some people she goes out with, to lunch, dinner, the theater."

"Any romantic relationships, past or present?" I sipped my latte.

Lakshmi thought for a moment. "Can't think of anyone recently. To hear Gloria tell it, she always played the field. I suppose that's why she never married." She paused. "We saw her having dinner with a man about six months ago. It was quite by accident. Noel and I were going to a concert at the San Francisco Symphony and we had a dinner reservation at a restaurant on Hayes Street. We were outside waiting for our table when I glanced up and saw Gloria outside another restaurant at the end of the block. I was surprised to see her and surprised that she was with a man. She always makes a point to talk about how unencumbered she is, and always has been."

"Did you speak with her?"

She shook her head. "No. Our table was ready and we went inside. And I didn't mention it to her later. In fact, I hadn't even thought of it until now. They seemed to be such a mismatched pair."

"In what way?"

"Gloria is the aging flower child," Lakshmi said. "She was all decked out in colorful gauze, with swirling skirts and sleeves, with lots of dangling jewelry. The man she was with looked like a business executive, tall, silver hair, and wearing an expensive, tailored suit. It was such a contrast. They struck me as being an odd couple. But it was clear they knew each other."

I nodded, digesting all of this, wondering where it fit in. "I really have to go. Don't want to be late for my next appointment."

"Sure, I understand," she said. "I would really like to see what happens when someone like you, an outsider, rattles Gloria's cage. Don't just take my word for it. Talk with Glenda. She will definitely give you a different perspective on her sister."

"As I said earlier, I haven't decided whether I'll take the case. I'll sleep on it and let you know."

"Fair enough."

We had reached my car, parked on Clement Street opposite the publishing company. Lakshmi and I parted company. She crossed the street and I unlocked my Toyota. I took another sip of my coffee and set the container in the cup holder. Then I belted myself into the driver's seat and started the car. As I pulled away from the curb, I mulled over the meeting, and my subsequent talk with Lakshmi.

Taking cases as favors for relatives and friends, yes, I'd done that before. Reluctantly, at times. Gladly, at others. It blurred the line between personal and professional and could lead to trouble.

But I was intrigued by those bones in Gloria's house. I wanted to find out how they got there. And why.

Just curious, I thought. When I returned to my office after my appointment, I did an Internet search with the words "skeletal remains found." I got pages of hits and scrolled through some of the results. Bones had been found in parks, at building sites and in houses consumed by fire. One story told of a family cleaning out their deceased father's house, startled to discover a skeleton in a garden shed. The story about the bones found on the site of a proposed golf course led to a follow-up story saying the bones were identified as part of a Native American burial mound. There were plenty of those in the Bay Area. Bones had also been found in the wreckage of an eighteenth century pirate ship off the New England coast, and in an old Navy ship being dismantled at a ship-breaking yard in the Gulf of Mexico near New Orleans.

A lot of bones out there, I thought. My immediate concern was that footlocker full of bones in Alameda.

# Five

THAT NIGHT, I DISCUSSED the situation with Dan, who told me he had no objection to my taking the case for Noel and Lakshmi. Tuesday morning I called Lakshmi and agreed to investigate the bones in the footlocker. The next step was research, collecting background information.

Gloria's house had been divided into apartments in the forties, when World War II made housing a scarce commodity, especially close to a Navy base. I clicked into the Internet browser and plugged the address into a search engine. I got numerous hits from real estate sites, the kind that showed properties for sale. The house was listed as a multifamily dwelling with four units, not currently for sale, but the various web pages gave me some information, such as when the house was built and how many square feet it had. In some cases, there was data on previous sales and property tax history.

According to Noel, his aunt bought the house in 1969. The real estate sites showed that the most recent sale date was April of 1969 and gave me an Alameda County parcel number. The sale price back then was small by current standards, but probably more than the average for that time. The house had appreciated in value quite a bit. Noel was right. Putting it on the market would garner lots of interest and some hefty offers.

The Alameda County website had a number of resources concerning property taxes and parcels. Property ownership information, while public record, wasn't available online, due to privacy considerations. Obtaining the names of property owners required a visit to the County Administration Building, across the street from the County Courthouse near Lake Merritt. I shut down the computer and left my office. I found a parking spot, always in short supply in this area, and headed for the building entrance. After going through the metal detector, I located the office with property records and settled in to work. I looked up the house and the information on owners in the sixties.

Gloria Rossiter bought the house in April 1969 from Charles Holder, who had purchased the property in 1964 from the Webb Family Trust. The Webbs had owned the house since the late forties. There was nothing unusual about the 1969 transaction that I could see. Though the purchase price made me wonder where a self-professed, free-spirited flower child of the sixties had come up with a down payment, let alone monthly mortgage payments. The original loan had been financed by a bank that was long gone, out of business or gobbled up by another bank over the past five decades.

I needed more information. Perhaps Gloria could provide it. Time to have a talk with her.

I left the building. In my car, I took out my phone. A man in an SUV who was hoping for my parking spot flashed me a look of annoyance, then drove on. I called the number Noel had given me for Gloria.

She answered, her raspy alto making me think "smoker's voice." I identified myself and the reason for my call. There was silence on the other end of the line. When she spoke again, her words had an edge.

"I don't know how I can help you. I know nothing, absolutely nothing, about those bones and how they got there. Besides, I already talked with the police." Her tone told me what she thought about having to do that.

"Yes, I know you spoke with the police. I'd like to get some information on the house itself, though. I'd really appreciate a few minutes of your time. Noel told me where you live. I can be there in about twenty minutes."

Another silence. Her reluctance radiated through every unspoken word. Then came a begrudging, "All right. Fine. Come on over. I'm on the second floor," she added, giving me her apartment number.

It wasn't fine, I thought as I ended the call. She'd made it quite clear that the bones, and my questions, were a major inconvenience.

I started the car and pulled away from the curb. In my rear view mirror, I saw another car pounce on the parking spot.

T HE SIGN IN FRONT of Gloria Rossiter's new home said this was a luxury senior living community, with independent living for seniors as well as an assisted living facility. The building was on the Alameda side of the estuary, close to a shopping center called Alameda Landing, where a number of houses and apartments had been built on land near the old Navy base. On the shoreline were reminders of Alameda's nautical past and present, where Bay Ship and Yacht had a large drydock for repairs and several marine and industrial retail outlets sold everything from propellers to sails.

Noel and Lakshmi had told me the place was expensive, with lots of amenities. Almost like a resort, Lakshmi added. That's why Gloria was eager to sell her Alameda house to fund her new living arrangements.

I parked in a section for visitors and walked toward the entrance. The building was three stories, vaguely Mediterranean in style, beige stucco with brown trim, with two wings protruding from a central building. The entrance itself faced the water, while the back of the building looked out at the parking lot of a marine supply shop.

The front of the building had a covered drive, making it easier for vehicles to pick up or deliver residents. To the right of the lobby door was a bench and a round table, with several chairs grouped around the table. A large planter box contained an assortment of brightly colored geraniums.

I walked into the lobby and paused, looking around to get my bearings. The lobby had a neutral color scheme, off-white walls enlivened with splashes of color here and there in pastel shades such as lavender, peach, and yellow. The low-pile carpet was patterned in beige and brown. The artwork on the walls was a soothing combination of landscapes and florals. Comfortable-looking armchairs upholstered in beige were arranged around a low table that held a bowl filled with an arrangement of white daisies with chrysanthemums in yellow and bronze. Corridors led off in different directions.

On the other side of the lobby, I saw a sitting room with more armchairs. A few of the chairs were occupied by residents. One woman was knitting something soft and fluffy in yellow. Another had a hardback book on her lap, propped up by a pillow. Two men at a small game table were playing dominoes. A sliding glass door opened onto an exterior patio with flowers and shrubbery in ceramic pots and raised beds, with benches and tables for the residents.

According to Lakshmi, there was a dining room for residents on the premises. It wasn't visible, but to my left was a granite countertop with three large urns, one with coffee, another with decaf and a third with hot water. Ceramic cups and saucers were stacked nearby, along with a basket of assorted tea bags, and a metal sugar and creamer set.

The message board on the wall near the front counter listed several announcements. On Saturday at noon, one of the residents was having a party for her hundredth birthday in the third floor meeting room. There would be a trip to the Oakland Museum of California the following week, and residents could sign up at the front desk. Anyone interested in playing bridge should attend a session in the game room on Tuesday afternoons at two o'clock. The mystery book group met every Wednesday afternoon. Residents could take their pick of exercise options, such as a walking group and classes in Pilates, yoga, and tai chi.

I stepped up to the counter, where a sign asked visitors to check in. The middle-aged woman behind it wore a lanyard with an employee ID that told me her name was Mary H. When she ended the call, she looked at me and smiled. "May I help you?"

"I'm here to see Gloria Rossiter. She's expecting me."

"Oh, yes, second floor." She gave me the apartment number and pointed. "The elevator and stairs are that way."

I thanked her. As I walked into the corridor, a man in a wheelchair came out of a TV lounge on my right, a chihuahua nestled on his lap. I glanced inside the room and saw a large screen TV affixed to the wall. A man sat in an armchair opposite the TV set, dozing rather than watching.

Opting for the stairs rather than the elevator, I climbed to the second floor and headed down the hallway. I found a door with a small sign reading ROSSITER and knocked. A moment later, a woman opened the door.

She was tall, her spare frame dressed in denim slacks and a loose-fitting short-sleeved blouse with a bright tropical print of red and yellow flowers amid green leaves. Her narrow face was webbed with wrinkles, framed by curly shoulder-length hair that had once been brown but was now streaked with silver. Earrings made of red and yellow beads dangled from her lobes, matching the brightly colored strands around her neck. She looked me over, blue eyes narrowed over a long thin nose.

"Gloria Rossiter? I'm Jeri Howard."

"Yes. Well, come in."

As she pulled the door wider to admit me, I saw faded bruises on her left forearm, evidence of the fall— the one Lakshmi wasn't sure was accidental.

I stepped into her apartment. To my left was a small kitchen, efficiently designed, with white appliances and gray granite countertops. An alcove to my right had a sliding door that was open far enough for me to see a stackable washer and dryer and shelving for laundry and cleaning supplies.

The living room was separated from the kitchen by a counter. On the other side of the counter were several cardboard cartons that had yet to be unpacked, and a small oak gateleg table with two chairs. She had filled the spacious living room with furniture from the Alameda house. On the wall to my left was a camelback sofa upholstered in a nubby fabric, with a muted pattern in beige and olive green. A crocheted afghan, blue with yellow accents, had been tossed over the back. Next to this was a side table holding a pile of books. Beyond that was a comfortable-looking wingback chair in a tapestry print, with a matching ottoman. The small round piecrust table between the sofa and the chair looked old. It held a slim reading lamp and a cell phone. On the opposite wall was a long low stand topped with a large flatscreen TV. A nearby table held a portable CD player, one that also had a turntable for the LP records that filled several plastic crates nearby. Between this and the window was an antique secretary desk made of dark oak. Pulled up to it was an old wooden office chair on casters, with a pillow in the seat.

The door to my right opened to a large bedroom, furnished with a queen-sized bed covered in a crazy quilt made of odd-sized patches of velvet, silk and taffeta. The square bedside table had a marble top and held a crook-necked lamp. The dresser and chest of drawers were made of a dark wood, perhaps walnut.

The wide living room window was open on this warm October day. I walked to it and looked out at the view, seeing the estuary and the Oakland waterfront. The blue sky held clouds and the sun glinted off the blue-green water. To the left I saw a huge container ship at the Port of Oakland, tall cranes loading cargo. A squat, blunt-nosed tug boat chugged up the estuary toward the bay. Heading the other way was a blue and white catamaran from the San Francisco Bay Ferry, slowing as it approached the Oakland ferry dock, jutting from the end of Clay Street. I heard a whistle and caught a glimpse of an Amtrak train going past on the Oakland Embarcadero, heading south to the Jack London Square station, just a few blocks away.

Gloria sat down in the wing chair and glanced at the cell phone on the piecrust table, as though she was expecting a call. "Tell me again, why do you need to talk with me?"

I took a seat on the sofa. "Noel and Lakshmi asked me to look into the situation at the house. I have a few questions that I hope you can answer."

She shrugged, one finger twirling an unruly curl. "It's sweet of Noel to be concerned. But really, a private investigator? I think he's overreacting. This has nothing to do with me. I'm sure that nice young police detective can figure it out."

Being concerned about human remains found at Gloria's house didn't seem like overreacting to me. Noel had mentioned that he thought his great-aunt might be experiencing some mild dementia. Maybe her air of unconcern was due to that. But Lakshmi had a different view. She didn't much like Gloria and suspected her forgetfulness and other symptoms were a mechanism to avoid things she didn't want to talk about. Which was the case here?

"That old house has a lot of character," I said, skipping over the fact that it needed lots of work. "I'm surprised you decided to move into this place."

"Well, I'm not getting any younger." Her smile was rueful. "I fell, you know. I'm sure Noel told you that. Took a tumble in the kitchen and banged myself up." She showed me the bruises. "I slipped on some water on the floor and down I went."

To me, it looked like someone had grabbed her arm and squeezed hard.

"I even got a little cut on my head." She pointed at her temple and I saw the healing abrasion, about an inch long. "Nothing like falling to make me feel old and clumsy. That started me thinking about moving. And the condition of the house. Well, you've seen it. The place needs a lot of work. More than I could afford. The maintenance and upkeep were just getting to be too much for me."

"You had income from the tenants."

She shrugged. "Well, the tenants left. Moved on. People do."

"They all left about the same time, Lakshmi tells me."

"They had various reasons," she said with a wave of her hand. "It happens."

"So, the tenants moved out and left you with a big house that needs work, and no income," I said. "Still, you've had a good run. I understand you bought the house in nineteen sixty-nine."

"That's right." Gloria narrowed her eyes, as though wondering where I was going with this. "I've had it for over fifty years."

"Noel told me that you lived in San Francisco in the sixties. That must have been an exciting time."

Her expression softened as she smiled. Good. Reminiscing about the old days might get her to open up.

"Oh, yes." She tossed her head, setting her gray curls moving. "San Francisco in the sixties. It was the place to be. I grew up in Oakland.

Boring old Oakland. My sister still lives there. And she really is boring. Hard to believe we're twins. We are so different. Fraternal, not identical, that's for sure." She laughed, a wicked sparkle in her eyes.

"So you moved to San Francisco from Oakland?"

"Well, Berkeley, actually. I was in college for a year or so, living near the campus. But I dropped out. Just wasn't cut out to be Miss Coed. I moved to the city, got a job selling dresses at the City of Paris, if you can believe that."

The City of Paris, a department store, closed a long time ago. Located at the corner of Geary Boulevard and Stockton Street, near San Francisco's Union Square, the store had been quite a showplace in its day. The Beaux-Arts building, constructed in 1896, had survived the 1906 San Francisco earthquake and firestorm, though badly damaged. Rebuilt and reopened in 1909, the building featured a rotunda topped by a stained glass dome. The store, losing money, closed in 1972 and the building was eventually sold to Neiman-Marcus, who planned to tear it down and construct a new store. Despite the efforts of preservationists to save the old building, it was demolished in 1981. The postmodern building that replaced it did retain the stained glass.

"When did you work at the City of Paris?" I asked.

"Early sixties, I guess. I would have been nineteen or twenty."

"I can't picture you selling dresses in a department store."

She laughed. "Oh, that didn't last long. That's when I met Michelle Phillips. She was a model in San Francisco, you know. Then she married John Phillips and a few years later they formed the Mamas and the Papas."

"I understand you sang in a band." No doubt dressed in those funky clothes Lakshmi found in the trunk.

"Yeah. I met a guy, a musician. Monk Guidry." She smiled again, but there was a shadow behind it. That intrigued me. It spoke of unfinished business.

"Monk. That's an interesting name."

"It was a nickname. His real name was Louis, but he said his family always called him Monk. Anyway, I started singing in his band. I had a good voice in those days. Not like now, with my old lady croak."

"What was the band?" I asked.

"One of those bands you never heard of." She laughed. "There were a lot of those way back when. Still are, I'm sure. Three guys with guitars and a drummer. They called themselves the Mad Monks. Like Rasputin. They wore those embroidered Russian shirts. Monk certainly looked good in that shirt."

"Was Monk a local guy?" I was guessing he wasn't. Guidry sounded like a Cajun name.

Gloria confirmed that with a wave of her hand. "Oh, no. He was from Louisiana, Lake Charles. Grew up there, not far from Port Arthur, Texas. That's where Janis Joplin was from. I knew Janis, of course. She was in San Francisco in the early sixties, then she went back to Texas. She joined Big Brother and the Holding Company in nineteen sixty-six, I guess it was. Monk and I were at Monterey Pop in June nineteen sixty-seven. Janis tore the place down." Gloria twirled a finger around one of her curls.

"Monterey. That was a fabulous scene. All the great acts were there. Jefferson Airplane, the Who, the Grateful Dead. Big Brother and the Holding Company, of course, with Janis. Otis Redding, Eric Burdon and the Animals. Laura Nyro, she was wonderful. Ravi Shankar. And of course the Mamas and the Papas, since John Phillips organized the thing. We saw Jimi Hendrix later, in May of nineteen sixty-nine," she added. "That was a festival at the Santa Clara County Fairgrounds. Great lineup. Besides Jimi, Jefferson Airplane was there and so was Canned Heat."

Was she planning to give me the lineup of every rock festival she'd ever attended? Then she veered in another direction.

"I lived in the Haight." She played with her hair again. "Well, that was later. When I first moved to the city, I had a little apartment on Russian Hill, just a block or so from the Hyde and Beach cable car line. That's how I got to work, on the cable car. After I quit the department store job, I moved to the Haight. Moved in with Monk. My parents and sister thought that was just scandalous." She let loose with a ribald chuckle. "We lived in a big old Victorian house that had been converted to flats. We had one on the top floor, with a great view. It was on Ashbury Street, near the Panhandle. It was down the street from where the Grateful Dead lived. Oh, it was a great scene. Crazy, creative people."

The Panhandle was a narrow park, a mile long, that jutted east from Golden Gate Park. It was a couple of blocks north of Haight Street. The district took its name from the intersection of Haight and Ashbury streets, and the memories of the counterculture of the sixties, all the craziness and creativity Gloria was talking about. No doubt she could keep talking about the old days for a while.

But I needed information. "Why did you leave the city and buy a house in Alameda? I mean, if things were so great over in the Haight, why move?"

Gloria hesitated. Then she frowned. "That place we lived on Ashbury Street, the house got sold. All the tenants got evicted. Besides, it seemed like a good time to leave San Francisco. Everything was changing after the Summer of Love in nineteen sixty-seven. In October, there was the Death of the Hippie ceremony. People were leaving. I mean, it just got so commercial after the media discovered hippies. It wasn't the same. People went down to LA, to check out the music scene down there. Others went up north, to Sonoma County, Mendocino County, did that back-to-the-land thing. You know, built their own cabins, raised their own food. Not for me. I'm a city girl. Living in a yurt out in the woods never appealed to me. Anyway, it was time for a change."

I persisted. "But Alameda? Not particularly urban. It's a small town, no matter what the population. And at the time, during the Vietnam war, it was a conservative community with a big Navy presence. That's quite a change. It seems like an odd choice."

She tilted her head and gave me a narrow-eyed look, as though trying to decide what to say next. Then she shrugged. "You know, I really don't remember why I decided on Alameda. It was just—" She paused. "Time for a change, I suppose. I took the first floor unit and rented out the flats. Some of my hippie friends, at first. But they weren't that good about paying rent. After that, I mostly rented to kids going to the College of Alameda. And sailors from the base."

"Did Monk move to Alameda with you?"

She narrowed her blue eyes and stared at me, then she shook her head. "No. Why do you ask?"

"Just curious. Sounds like you were together for several years."

"We'd split up by then. Spring, I think it was. About the time that I bought the house." She paused again. "I didn't see him after that. We didn't keep in touch. The relationship had run its course. Both of us were seeing other people." As she said that last sentence, her voice had an edge to it. I had the feeling Gloria was making this up as she talked. Her story had an improvised feel.

According to the property records, she'd bought the house in April 1969, after the breakup with Monk. If she hadn't seen him after that, why did she imply that the two of them had gone to a rock festival in May of that year?

Then her tone changed, replaced by a smile and a toss of her head. "No skin off my nose. Ancient history. We both moved on. Someone told me the band broke up and Monk left the area. Went back to Louisiana, I heard."

I leaned back in my chair. "I'd like to contact some of your former tenants."

Gloria frowned. "Why?"

"Seems to me the person who left the bones in that storeroom must have had access to the house. A former renter would be a good bet."

She waved away that theory. "Well, I don't know about that. Kind of a stretch, if you ask me. It could have been someone who broke in."

Possible. But why take the trouble to conceal the bones in a footlocker and hide them in the storeroom? I assumed that whoever hid the bones didn't want them to be found.

"I would like to check out the renters," I said. "Noel says the last tenants all moved out recently. I'm sure you have records."

She flashed a look that said she thought I had a lot of nerve pressing the matter. Then the cell phone on the piecrust table began to ring. Gloria jumped, startled by the noise. I glanced down at the same time she did, and saw a name, Lee. Gloria reached for the phone and pressed an icon, declining to answer the call. She slipped it into her pocket. Then her eyelids fluttered. Her sharp expression blurred and her eyes became unfocused. "What were we talking about? I don't remember." She sighed. "I'm so tired. I need to rest. I'm going to take a nap."

She put her hands on the arms of the chair and hoisted herself to a standing position, swaying a bit, as though a wind would blow her over. Then she steadied herself and waved in the direction of the front door, inviting me to leave.

What just happened? Noel speculated that his great-aunt was showing signs of dementia. Was this an example? Or was this what Lakshmi predicted Gloria would do—play the forgetful card to avoid questions she didn't want to answer?

I rose. "Thanks for talking with me."

After Gloria ushered me out the front door, I stood for a moment in the hall, waiting. Sure enough, I heard Gloria's voice, just the other side of the door.

"I've been calling and calling, and you haven't returned my calls, till now— Someone was here, that's why I didn't answer. What? Well, I don't care, we have to talk. It's urgent. You heard about—"

Gloria's voice faded and I guess that she had moved out of hearing range.

What was so urgent? Was this about the bones?

I left the building. Outside, I took out my phone. As long as I was in Alameda, I would check in with Lieutenant Chen, to see if the police had made any progress in their investigation. When I called APD, Chen wasn't available, but the person who answered the phone put me through to his voice mail. I left a message, then made another call, to the publishing company. Noel wasn't there, but Lakshmi was.

"I've been to see Gloria. I see what you mean. I got some stories about the good old days in the Haight. But on the whole, she wasn't very cooperative. Then suddenly she had to take a nap."

"I told you," Lakshmi said. "When she doesn't want to talk about something, she goes into her little old lady routine."

"Listen, you said when Gloria moved to the apartment, you took her records and papers over to your office. Financial, deed to house, taxes—stuff like that. I need to look at the tenant files. I'd like to track down the three who moved out."

"To see if one of them disposed of a skeleton or two?"

"Or is willing to admit to it," I said. "Though I rather doubt that. But whoever left those bones must have access to the house. That could be a tenant who kept a key."

"Makes sense. Yes, we have most of Gloria's records in storage here at the office. Why don't you come over and take a look? Though it would be best to run that past Noel. He's out until later this afternoon."

"Thanks. Let me know when he's back in the office."

I ended the call and sat for a moment, considering my next move. Then I punched in another phone number. When a woman answered, I told her who I was and why I was calling.

"So, you want to talk about my evil twin." Glenda Rossiter Benjamin laughed. "Sure, come on over."

# Six

GLENDA'S FEATURES RESEMBLED THOSE of her twin, long narrow face, thin nose, the same blue eyes. But her hair was short, completely white, and swept back from her forehead, setting off the small silver studs in her earlobes. She wore khaki slacks topped with a blue knit top. On her left hand were a gold wedding band and a diamond engagement ring.

"Coffee? I was just about to have a cup myself."

"Yes, thanks." It was the middle of the afternoon, I was ready for a caffeine boost.

She headed for the kitchen, past an oval dining table and through a wide doorway. I explored the comfortable, well-appointed living room of her house. She lived on Townsend Avenue, south of Park Boulevard, in Oakland's Glenview district. The hilly neighborhood was full of older, well-kept homes, like this two-story Mediterranean-style house, with stucco walls, arched windows and doors, and a red clay-tiled roof. The lawn had been replaced with an assortment of succulents, a customary landscaping solution to the Bay Area's perpetual cycle of drought, more common in these days of climate change. On the wide front porch, large blue ceramic pots stood on either side of the front door, full of more succulents.

I turned to the fireplace, looking at the family photos decorating the mantel. Here was a photo of Glenda with a white-haired man who I took to be her husband. More photos showed other family members—children and grandchildren—and included a picture of Noel and Lakshmi with their two children. I didn't see any photos of Gloria.

I sat down in one of the two armchairs upholstered in a muted blue and gold floral that went with the nearby sofa.

Glenda returned with a wooden tray holding two mugs full of coffee, a sugar and creamer set and several napkins. There was also a plate of chocolate chip cookies that looked homemade. She set the tray on the low round table between the chairs.

Could I eat a cookie? Yes, I could. I reached for one. They were still warm from the oven, chocolate oozing onto my hand. Good thing she brought the napkins. I took a bite and savored it, then chased it with a sip of strong black coffee. "Thanks, this hits the spot. I haven't eaten since breakfast. In my line of work, mealtimes can be erratic."

Glenda laughed as she sat down in the other armchair. "I love to bake. My husband and I get a bit peckish this time of day. He's not home, though. Out playing tennis with friends. So you and I can eat all the cookies." She picked up a coffee mug and a cookie, then leaned back in her chair as though settling in for a long talk. "Noel told me about the bones in the footlocker. And of course, it's in the news. Yet another chapter in my sister's colorful life."

"She took pains to tell me that the two of you are nothing alike."

"I'll bet she didn't say that politely," Glenda said, an edge to her voice. "For all that we're twins, no, we have nothing in common, except a physical resemblance." She paused for a sip of coffee. "She dropped out of college. I finished. Went to graduate school and had a long and satisfying career in administration at UC Berkeley. My sister never married. I did, and quite happily. It's just as well she never had kids. She'd be a lousy mother."

"No love lost between the two of you." I helped myself to another cookie.

Glenda shook her head. "None. I wasn't kidding when I called her my evil twin. Gloria was always up to her eyeballs in some shenanigan. Skating close to edge at times. She got involved in that whole hippie scene over in the Haight. Doing drugs, no doubt. Singing in a band and living with that musician."

"Monk Guidry," I said, wiping chocolate from my fingers. "She told me a little bit about him, but not much."

She took another sip of coffee. "I met him once. Gloria brought him to a family get-together. I suppose some people would think of him as attractive. Gloria certainly did. But not my type. Long hair, bell bottoms and colorful clothes. A little too much patchouli. Probably to disguise the smell of pot." She wrinkled her nose.

"What did he look like?"

She thought for a moment. "I'd say he was about five ten. My husband is six feet tall and Monk was a bit shorter. Dark hair. I think his eyes were brown, but I'm not sure. Why the interest in Monk?"

"Gloria mentioned him, several times."

"They broke up years ago, and Gloria has had many relationships since then. I can't imagine she would be carrying a torch for a scruffy musician after all this time."

"Maybe he's the one that got away."

Glenda sipped her coffee. "As far as I know, they all got away. Gloria never had much staying power in the romance department."

"Where did Gloria get the money to buy the house?"

"I always wondered about that," Glenda said. "How in the world did she come up with a down payment and closing costs? Her employment history was rather sketchy. She worked in a department store and quit that job. Next thing, I hear she's singing in a rock band. Not what you'd call a regular job, the kind where you can actually save any money. I wondered if her musician boyfriend kicked in some cash. But I doubt it. They certainly weren't setting the world on fire with that band. I doubt he had more than a couple of bucks in his pocket at one time. Gloria certainly wouldn't have gotten money from our parents. They weren't forthcoming with any cash for her schemes. She had already been to the well too many times when she was short of rent, things like that. They wouldn't have given her that much money." She paused for another sip of coffee. "I can't help you there. I had a toddler and a job to deal with at the time Gloria bought the house, so I wasn't paying much attention to what my sister was up to."

"Gloria told me she and Monk broke up before she moved to Alameda."

She nodded as she cradled the coffee mug in her hands. "That's right. They were living in an old Victorian in the Haight. She moved out and I recall her saying that he was seeing someone else." She shrugged. "I'm not sure I'm remembering that correctly. Gloria and I didn't really keep in touch. We lived different lives and I saw her from time to time at family get-togethers. We grew up in Oakland. My parents had a house not far from here. We both started college at Berkeley and there our paths diverged. Although you could argue it happened sooner, in high school." She raised her mug. "I'm getting a refill. Do you want more coffee?"

"Yes, thanks."

While Glenda was in the kitchen, I took another cookie. I was halfway through it when I heard the front door open. A man walked into the living room, wearing shorts and a T-shirt under a light jacket. Slung over one shoulder was a blue backpack, with the handle of a tennis racquet protruding from the largest compartment. The side pockets held a cylinder of bright yellow tennis balls and one containing a stainless steel water bottle. He shut the front door and set down the bag, a curious look on his face. "Hi, I'm Ray."

"Jeri Howard."

Just then Glenda returned from the kitchen with our coffee. "How was your tennis date?"

"Won a few, lost a few. Is there any coffee left in the pot? And are those chocolate chip cookies I see?"

"Yes to both questions. I baked a batch of cookies this morning."

"Sounds great." Ray walked back to the kitchen and returned a moment later with his own mug and plate of cookies. He took a seat on the sofa.

"Jeri is a private investigator," Glenda said. "Noel and Lakshmi asked her to look into that business over at Gloria's house."

"The bones in the footlocker." He grinned. "That sounds like a slasher movie playing at the local multiplex."

"As it happens, I'm the one who found the bones. My fiancé Dan and I were helping Noel and Lakshmi inventory the contents of the house last Saturday. I talked with Gloria earlier this afternoon and she seemed reticent with details."

"I'm not surprised." Ray wiped an errant bit of chocolate from his mouth. "Gloria remembers what she wants to remember. The rest of the time, she— Well, let's just say she stretches the truth."

"Jeri is wondering where Gloria got the money to buy that house," Glenda said.

Ray nodded. "We all did, at the time. But it turned out to be a good investment for her. She's lived there for over fifty years and I gather it's provided a decent income."

"It did, until the tenants moved out."

"All of them? At the same time? That's strange." Glenda said. She sipped her coffee. "I must say I was surprised that my sister would do anything so conventional as to move to a senior living complex."

"She slipped and fell in the kitchen. At least that's what she told me." I recalled the bruises on Gloria's arm. I had my doubts about that fall. But I kept that to myself. "She had some minor injuries and she says that made her think it was time for a change."

"That sounds sensible," Ray said.

Glenda was giving her twin no quarter. "I'm not sure sensible is a word I'd use to describe Gloria."

It was time for me to leave. I stood, thanked Glenda for the coffee and cookies, and gave her one of my business cards, adding that I'd be in touch if I had more questions.

Then I left the house, walking down the street to where I'd parked my car. My phone rang as I was fastening my seatbelt. It was Lakshmi, calling to tell me Noel was back in the office.

# Seven

Noel was reluctant to let me search through Gloria's records. As we stood in his office at the publishing company, he frowned. "I don't know what you hope to find. Besides, those boxes contain all sorts of information about Gloria's finances as well as the tenant records. I'm concerned about privacy."

Annoyance flickered on Lakshmi's face. She quickly masked it. They were definitely in separate camps when it came to Gloria.

It's difficult to conduct an investigation when the client won't cooperate. Gloria was already dodging questions and now Noel was throwing up roadblocks.

"Look," I said. "I understand. But you and Lakshmi hired me to investigate this situation. I can't make any progress without your help. I really do need to see the records. Whoever left those bones in the storeroom had access to the house. My best guess is that's a tenant. I also think it's strange that all three tenants moved out in such a short time period."

"So do I." Lakshmi put her hands on her hips as she addressed her husband. "Jeri's right. We agreed to do this. You can't get cold feet now. We need to figure out what happened, and how. Let her look. I'll do it with her. Two sets of eyes are better than one."

Noel's reluctance gave way under Lakshmi's pressure. "All right. Go ahead." He went around his desk and sat down at his computer, retreating into work.

Lakshmi gave me a triumphant look. I followed her out of his office. The building was larger than it looked from the street, extending deep into the lot. One room at the back held another office with two desks and a worktable in the middle, where a man and a woman were bent over several sheets of paper and some photographs, working on a layout.

We went through the small kitchen to what had been a back porch, now holding a large photocopier, shredder and a shelf with a fax machine. Steps led down to the ground level. This house, like Gloria's, was elevated off the ground, high enough so that it had a basement. There was another copier here. I followed Lakshmi into a big room full of printing equipment, where a man knelt in front of an equipment panel, adjusting some dials. He greeted Lakshmi, then turned back to his task.

We stopped in front of a door and Lakshmi pulled out a key, unlocking it. We entered the room, Lakshmi reaching for the light switch to her right. The overhead lighting illuminated a long rectangular room with a table in the middle, the walls painted white. Sturdy metal shelves lined all four walls, all of them stacked with white bankers boxes.

"These days a lot of our files are digitized," she said. "Otherwise, we'd be drowning in paper." She walked toward the back and gestured at a shelf on the left.

"These are Gloria's files, on the two bottom shelves. This is how we found them. Gloria didn't keep things in a filing cabinet. She just had files stuffed in boxes in her closet and on the back porch."

She pointed at seven bankers boxes, all of them somewhat worse for wear, stained here and there with grime and water spots. I was hoping the boxes would be labeled with enough information to tell me what was inside. No such luck. The only label I saw was Gloria's name, written in ink, on the side of each box.

"Are they organized in any way?"

Lakshmi shook her head. "Gloria was never good about being organized. Noel and I helped her pack for the move to her new place. She asked if we could store them here temporarily until she had a chance to go through them. I have a feeling she's forgotten about them. She hasn't mentioned it since the move. Though to be fair, it's only been six weeks."

"So, no order at all. I was afraid of that." I pulled one of the boxes from the shelves, set it on the table, and removed the lid, surveying the file folders inside. They were all different colors and many of them were torn and stained, showing years of use—and reuse. Label tabs had handwritten scrawls in ink and pencil, some erased or crossed out, and rewritten. Some tabs had no labels at all.

"Gloria has a lackadaisical approach to rules, regulations and forms. And taxes." She reached for another box. "I'm surprised she never got audited. Noel and I told her she was going to get in trouble. But she would always say, hey, it hasn't happened yet. She had a simple one-page rental agreement and she would take rent in cash or by check. Tenants would just slip an envelope under her door. When the Navy base was open, she had a lot of turnover, renting to sailors who would get transferred every couple of years. After that, the tenants seemed to stay longer. Anyway, there must be tax stuff and bank records."

"What about house records?" I asked. "The deed? Mortgage documents, that sort of thing?"

Lakshmi frowned. "You know, I'm not sure. That's the important stuff you hang onto. She has checking and savings accounts at Bank of America in Alameda. But I don't know if she has a safe deposit box. Come to think of it, she did have a small fireproof safe. Not large, but big enough to hold that sort of stuff. I didn't see it when we helped pack her things. She may have taken it to the new apartment herself."

"Okay. Let me know if you see anything about the house. I need as much information on that as we can find."

"Why?"

"I'd like to know how she got the money to buy the place. Gloria says she worked at a department store and then sang with the band. With her work history, how did she come up with a down payment and get a bank loan on a multi-unit property?"

"Good question," Lakshmi said. "You don't think—" She stopped.

"What?"

"San Francisco in the sixties. Rock 'n roll. Hippies. And drugs. Lots of drugs. Especially in that scene in the Haight."

"It's possible. But at this point it's speculation."

"Maybe she got the money from that musician friend of hers."

"I doubt it. Musicians, like other artists, don't usually have much money unless they have day jobs. Besides, Gloria told me they broke up about the same time she bought the house."

Lakshmi nodded. "You're right. Musicians, writers and actors, all scrambling to make a living."

I pulled a handful of folders from the box I was working on and laid them on the table. "How did Noel get to be Gloria's favorite nephew? Or great-nephew, to be more accurate."

"I'm not exactly sure. She was already claiming him as her favorite when I came on the scene. That was about twelve years ago. I met Noel at a conference for small, independent publishers. We hit it off, started dating and got married. That's how I inherited Aunt Gloria." She smiled ruefully. "Noel has several cousins. But Gloria glommed onto him with all this talk about how he's her favorite. I think she likes men more than she does women. Which happens. I don't really know how much of this favorite nephew talk is true or if it's just for show. Noel seems to be a soft touch for Gloria. Which is how we wound up dealing with Gloria, her move and the damned house."

I opened folders and sifted through the pages. Here were receipts for the purchase of various appliances for the units—a refrigerator, a stove. Here too was the paperwork for a new water heater. I reached for another folder, this one thicker with receipts and papers, most of them dealing with maintenance. The dates went back several years, showing work on the house—a plumber, an electrician, a handyman to fix a stair banister, a painter, someone to clean out the gutters. It was the sort of day-to-day upkeep any homeowner would have, especially taking care of a rental property. Necessary but not particularly enlightening. Gloria's handwriting was slapdash, wandering all over the page, sometimes difficult to read.

I closed the folder and reached for another. Surely Gloria had kept some sort of records of the people who rented apartments. Or maybe she hadn't. She seemed to be just flaky enough not to. And she'd avoided talking about the issue when I brought it up during our conversation.

Lakshmi shook her head, looking through the contents of another file folder. "Old bank statements. Why keep these? Some of them are twenty years old, or more. I should shred them."

"Hang onto them, for the time being. Just in case I need to take a look." I finished sorting through the box and replaced the lid. "No joy here."

"Me, neither."

We stashed our boxes on the bottom shelf and pulled out two more, setting them on the table. I removed the lid from one. The front half of the box contained a stack of manuals for appliances. The first one was for a coffeemaker and the one underneath it, a blender. "I have a stash of these."

Lakshmi laughed. "So do I. Including manuals for appliances I don't have any more."

At the back of the box were several battered-looking accordion folders made of heavy paper stock, the kind with open tops and pleated sides to allow for expansion. They were covered with smudges, some of them torn. I stuck my hand in the first folder. It was empty. So were the two behind it. I had just slipped my hand into the fourth folder to check it when Lakshmi said, "Hey, here's some rental receipts. But just a few."

I reached for the receipts as she held them out. They were handwritten, the kind that came from a duplicate pad. Surely these weren't the only tenant information Gloria kept, even if she was erratic about recordkeeping.

I would have thought she'd report the property income for taxes. On the other hand, Gloria seemed to be the type of person who wouldn't report that income. But another glance at the box Lakshmi had opened proved me wrong. It contained tax returns.

I heard a chime and Lakshmi pulled her phone from her pocket. "This is something I need to take care of, right now. I'll be back."

"Take your time. This is going to be a slog."

I was tempted to look through the tax returns, and those old bank statements. But my priority right now was the tenant records. I put the lids on both boxes and returned them to the shelves. I pulled out another box and set it on the table.

Finally, tenant records, stuffed into five accordion folders, colors faded and dull. The tabs on the open tops were labeled by years. I pulled out sheets of lined paper, some loose and others held together with rusted paper clips, all of them covered with Gloria's meandering handwriting. I spread them out on the table and glanced through them, looking at tenants' names and the rental prices she charged for each unit, observing how the rents had gone up over the years. In the seventies and eighties, the average tenure was two years, the length of time someone would be posted to the Naval Air Station. After the base closed in the nineties, the tenants stayed longer. And there were gaps. That could mean time periods with no tenants at all—or no records.

The door to the storage room opened and Lakshmi came in. "Sorry about that. I had to deal with a situation involving a distributor. Any luck?"

"Yes. I found the rental records." I gestured at the papers I'd spread out on the table. "Believe it or not, they were in chronological order. Well, sort of."

She joined me at the table and scanned the pages. "Wow, look at what she charged for rent back in the seventies."

"Salaries were much lower then, remember. And you could buy a car for pennies compared to what one costs now." I shook my head. "This is a rough time line, from the time Gloria took possession of the house in nineteen sixty-nine, to the present. But there are holes. Missing records. Maybe they're in one of the other boxes."

"Maybe whoever owned the footlocker wasn't a tenant," she said.

"Access." I tapped a finger on the table. "Whoever left the bones in the house needed access."

"Okay, then. Maybe he knew someone who did live there, or maybe he lived with Gloria. That wouldn't surprise me. She's had a lot of relationships through the years."

"Any of those scenarios you outlined would work, though I still think it must be someone who lived there. I located the records for those last three tenants." I had set those aside. I pointed at the papers. "Andrew Vogel, moved in June. Graham Costa, in July. And Peggy Slocum, in August."

Lakshmi nodded. "Peggy lived in the ground level apartment. She was the gardener."

"And she lived next to the storeroom, where I found the footlocker. I've got phone numbers now, so I'll contact them. I'd like to talk with all three of them, to find out why they moved. Can I have copies of these records? Not just these three, but all of them, back to nineteen sixty-nine. I've got a hunch that I might need to take a closer look and I don't have time right now. I know it's a lot of paperwork, but I haven't looked at every single sheet of paper and it would help to be able to go through them when I have more time."

"If it will help get to the bottom of this, absolutely. Let's split them up and get started."

Lakshmi and I divided the tenant records and she carried her stack upstairs, while I set to work at the downstairs copier. It was slow going, since I had to copy both sides of the sheets of paper. Finally, I finished. Lakshmi returned with her stack. We carried the originals and copies back to the storage room. I put the originals back in the box where I'd found them.

"You need something to carry that stuff," Lakshmi said, indicating the copies. "I can get another box."

"Wait," I said. "There were several empty accordion folders in that box with the appliance manuals. That would work."

I retrieved the folders from the box. There were five of them, just enough for the copies. That done, I carried them out of the basement. Lakshmi let me out a side gate and I walked to my car, stashing the folders in the trunk.

# Eight

Ordinarily I would have left Alameda by the Park Street bridge, since the publishing company was nearby. Instead, I drove the other way, down Clement to Grand Street, then up Lincoln Avenue to the West End. I wanted another look at Gloria's house.

The windows on the west side of the house reflected the afternoon sun. I parked at the curb and got out, leaning against my Toyota as I gazed at the house on the corner, willing it to reveal more secrets. The lemon tree in the front yard was still full of bright yellow fruit, the weight of it pulling down the branches. More fruit, some rotting, scattered the brown grass at the trunk. The neglected flower beds beside the house added to the forlorn look.

I glanced down the street, at the nearby houses, all looking better kept than the one in front of me. The first two houses were the ones I'd noticed when I was here last Saturday, both with FOR SALE signs in front. Only now, both sported additional signs that read, SALE PENDING. And there was a new FOR SALE sign on a house just beyond those two. That one hadn't been there before, I was sure of it.

Three houses in a row, all for sale, on the same block? Why?

It was the middle of October. The real estate agent I'd used when I bought my own house once told me that the best time of year to sell a house was around the beginning of May. She added that listings at the end of spring and in early summer tended to sell faster, and for higher prices. April to June, she added, those are the best times. The weather is great, buyers are checking out the open houses.

Of course, that varies from location to location. Here in the Bay Area, we have pleasant weather in the fall, as well as a lower housing supply. And real estate was always hot in Alameda.

This needs looking into, I thought, twirling my car keys on my finger. Maybe I was being overly suspicious, but I wondered if there was some connection between the number of houses for sale in this neighborhood, Gloria's mysterious and unnamed buyer, and the three tenants who had moved out of the house. I had to find it.

Taking out my phone, I took photos of all the FOR SALE signs. That told me which real estate companies and agents were selling the houses. Then I got in my car and called the real estate agent who'd handled the purchase of my house.

"Hey, Emma, I need a favor."

"What? You're putting your house on the market? With all the improvements you've made, I could get you a great price."

"No way. I'm staying where I am. I'm quite comfortable there. Actually, I need information. It's about a house. I'd like your best guess as to what it would sell for in the current market."

"What's the address? I can look it up." I gave her the street address of Gloria's house and heard her humming on the other end of the line. "Okay, Queen Anne Victorian, corner lot, detached garage, multi-unit building with four apartments. The exterior has some good architectural features and I'll bet the interior does, too. Last sold in nineteen sixty-nine. I'm looking at a picture right now. Looks like the place needs a lot of work. A new roof and some foundation work, maybe. Still, it's an income property, in Alameda. Have you been inside?"

"I have. It does need updating, It has some drawbacks, mainly deferred maintenance. But yes, there are lots of those charming Victorian details. High ceilings, hardwood floors, pocket doors."

"Is this house going on the market soon? I'd definitely be interested, if the owner is looking for an agent. And I have clients who would bid on the place."

I didn't answer her question, instead asking one of my own. "How much do you think it would sell for, in its current condition?"

"Well . . ." She drew out the word, thinking about her answer. "Okay, here's my best guess." She named a figure.

"Wow. That's a lot of money."

"Is the house going on the market? If so, when?"

"It's not going on the market. But it's going to be sold, eventually. You know that story that's been on the news about the skeletal remains?"

"That house? Details, please."

I gave Emma a brief overview of the situation, adding that Gloria claimed she already had a buyer lined up. Then I told her about the real estate signs sprouting in that neighborhood. "I've got a feeling the buyer who is supposedly buying this house is the same person, or persons, who is buying other houses nearby. I do have a list of the agents, from the signs in the yard."

"Never mind," Emma said. "I can get that information from the listings. You could be right about whoever is buying those properties. Let me check through the databases and see what I can find out. I'll get back to you as soon as I have something."

"Thanks, I appreciate it."

---

MY OFFICE WAS LOCATED in a neighborhood called the Valdez Triangle. The building was owned by a law firm, Alwin, Taylor and Chao. The second law partner, Cassie Taylor, was a good friend from the days when we both worked as paralegals. She had moved on, to law school, while I'd gone to work for private investigator Errol Seville, setting up my own business after he retired.

Until recently, the law firm, and my business, rented space in a building on Franklin Street in Oakland's Chinatown. The last time the landlord raised the rent, the increase had been too much for my budget, and that of the law firm. Cassie and her partners decided it would be more cost effective, in the long run, to buy their own building. Once the transaction was complete, they did a remodel, then made the move. So had I, since they had offered to lease space to me at a reasonable rate. There were several other tenants as well. Plus I had my own reserved parking space in the lot at the back of the building. That was great, because I'd been paying for parking at the other location.

I punched my code into the keypad at the back door. Inside my office, I locked the copies of the rental records in the lower drawer of a filing cabinet, for safekeeping until I could look through them again. Once my computer was on, I worked my way through a series of emails and returned several phone calls. I had a report to finish for a client I was seeing later in the week, so I set to work on that. When I finished, I printed out the report, proofread it, and stuck it into an envelope, ready to deliver to the client. My phone rang again. It was Dan.

"How soon will you be home?" he asked. "I'm cooking dinner."

"Half an hour." I turned off the computer, locked my office and headed out to my car.

The bungalow on Chabot Road in Oakland's Rockridge neighborhood was nearly out of my price range when I bought it a few years ago, but I lucked out, since I'd just received a big fee from a client. I forked over a large down payment and now I had my very own mortgage and property taxes, instead of paying rent. My home was a comfortable place to live and I had a backyard and a vegetable garden.

I also had a garage with a studio apartment above it. My current renter was Madison Brady. She was the daughter of Cal Brady, who'd been a fellow investigator for the firm where I'd worked before starting my own business. He'd fallen on hard times, due to his drinking, but he got sober and reinvented his life—only to be murdered while working as a security guard on a waterfront construction site. Madison came to me looking for help and I had the satisfaction of finding out who killed her father.

That was about the time my former tenant had moved out, so Madison moved in. It worked well for both of us. I had someone living there to keep an eye on things and look after my cats when I was out of town. Madison was a graduate student in City Planning at the University of California. It was a good location for her, as she could walk to nearby College Avenue and catch the bus to campus.

For years I'd lived alone with my cats, Abigail and Black Bart. Then I met Dan while on a case. We dated for over a year and had decided to think about marriage. We'd been spending so much time together it didn't make sense for Dan to continue paying rent on his North Berkeley apartment, especially after his landlord upped the rent. Still, I'd hesitated when the subject of marriage came up. Dan and I were in our late thirties and we'd both been married before. Dan had children from his earlier marriage who lived with their mother. My brief foray into matrimony with an Oakland detective named Sid Vernon had left me wary about marriage, reluctant to commit again. Even living together was a big step.

It was, however, great to have a roommate who cooked. When I opened the front door, the dining room table was set and delicious smells wafted from the kitchen. I detected the presence of garlic, lots of it.

"Smells wonderful." I crossed the living room as the cats ran up the stairs from the lower level, where the bedroom was located. They trotted toward the kitchen door and Black Bart meowed as I joined him in the doorway. Abigail strolled regally to the large tray that held the cat dishes and water bowl. She sat, pointedly staring at me. "There's food in your bowl," I told her.

"Don't pay any attention to those cats," Dan said as he turned from the stove, waving a large wooden spoon. "They're performing their usual song-and-dance about not having any food, but I dished it up less than an hour ago."

I checked out the contents of a big stainless steel pan on one of the stove burners, seeing chicken, whole tomatoes, onions, bell peppers, mushrooms and who knew what else. "Chicken cacciatore?"

Dan nodded and stirred the mixture. "I made a big salad and there's garlic bread in the oven. Dinner in about ten minutes."

"Okay. I'm going to get out of these clothes and into something more comfortable."

I headed downstairs to the bedroom and exchanged the slacks and shirt I'd been wearing for stretchy gray lounge pants and an oversized T-shirt. When I returned to the dining room, the salad and garlic bread were on the table, along with an open bottle of merlot. Dan appeared from the kitchen, carrying two plates filled with chicken cacciatore. It was delicious. I cleaned my plate, sopping up the tomatoey juices with garlic bread.

During dinner, we talked about Dan's current project. While I was in New Orleans on a case several months ago, he'd been traveling around New Mexico, researching a book on hiking in that state. Now the book was written and he was reviewing the copyedited manuscript and selecting photos to appear in the book.

"What state are you going to explore next?" I asked.

He took a sip of his wine. "Noel and Lakshmi suggested Arizona, as a companion to the New Mexico book. Doing the American Southwest and all that. But I'm thinking Colorado. And I'd like to visit Big Bend National Park."

"So would I. Maybe when my schedule empties out a bit."

"In the meantime," he said, "I'm also thinking whenever you're done with this case, we should take a few days off and go up to Mendocino. After all, you have a birthday at the end of the month."

"I'd like that." Mendocino was one of my favorite places. I always enjoyed a visit to the small coastal community about three hours north on Highway One. "Speaking of this case, me looking into the bones situation, are you sure you don't mind me doing this? It does have the potential to bring bad news to Noel and Lakshmi, at least to their family. I don't want to mess things up, either your friendship with them or your professional relationship."

Dan swirled wine in his glass. "I am sure my friendship with Noel and Lakshmi can withstand whatever you find out about the bones." He smiled. "Besides, I know how you are when you get into a case and you're already into this one. You won't be happy until you figure it all out."

"That's true."

We finished dinner and I cleaned up the kitchen, since Dan had cooked. I had just finished loading the dishwasher when the phone rang. I dried my hands on a dishcloth and picked up the kitchen extension, recognizing the number on the caller ID. "Hi, Dad. What's up?"

"I'm calling about those pictures you sent me," he said. "The larger feathers are from a California gull. The smaller feather is definitely from a least tern."

I pulled out a chair and sat down. "I thought it might be."

My father had become an avid birder since he retired. He was active in his local chapter of the Audubon Society. He continued, warming to the subject. "As you know, there's a least tern colony on the old air station. It's between a couple of airstrips. The birds showed up there in the seventies and it's become the most productive breeding site in the state. Both Audubon and the Friends of the Alameda Wildlife Reserve have been working to protect those birds for years."

"My guess is that the bones were buried somewhere on the base," I said. "The feathers got mixed in when they were dug up and put in the footlocker."

"Good theory," Dad said. "The bones are discolored and those photos you sent showed some dirt and gravel. But if they were buried, why dig them up?"

"I don't know, but I intend to find out."

# Nine

GARY MANVILLE WAS A former Navy officer who started his own security company after leaving the service. We'd met while I was investigating the death of Cal Brady, Madison's father, who at the time of his murder had been working as a guard for Manville Security. In fact, he and Gary, both former Navy officers, had known each other during their military service. At first Gary and I had clashed. But we'd worked our way through that initial antagonism. Now our relationship was cordial. In fact, he called on me for help during a recent case involving arson at building sites here in Oakland.

Now it was my turn to ask for help.

I arrived at my office Wednesday morning and called his number before making my first pot of coffee. When he answered the phone, I heard a lot of background noise. I guessed he was outside rather than in his office. "Can you talk?"

"I'm at a job site. Heading downtown now. I haven't had breakfast. How about Sweet Bar in twenty?"

"You're on. See you there."

The Sweet Bar Bakery was on Broadway, halfway between my office at 27th and Valdez and his office on Telegraph Avenue. It was an easy walk, which was good because street parking in that area was a problem. I got there first and joined the queue that formed at the counter and straggled out the door. The bakery was popular, especially in the morning, with people who worked nearby stopping to purchase coffee and pastries on the way to the office. I was nearing the counter when Gary showed up.

"This is on me," I said.

He grinned. "You must want information. Fine, I'll have a large regular coffee and a ham and cheese croissant."

I ordered that, plus a latte and a lemon blueberry scone for myself. Gary stepped away from the counter and looked for a table. He found one near the back, snagging it as someone else got up. I carried our coffee and nosh to the table.

I nibbled on my scone and sipped my latte while Gary demolished half his croissant. He paused and swallowed a mouthful of coffee. Then he leaned back in his chair, wiping his hands with a napkin. "Wow, I was hungry. I've been on the go for hours. I just took on a contract at a site near the Port of Oakland, so I'm being hand's-on with my crew." He paused for another sip of coffee. "What's up?"

"I need information on someone who may be a former sailor, possibly at the Alameda Naval Air Station. I know there are all sorts of databases, but I'm not sure I can access those sources. I'm hoping you have a contact who can get me where I need to be, fast."

"That's a lot of maybes," Gary said. "As for fast, that depends on how far back this guy was in the Navy. I'm assuming it was a guy. And of course, the Alameda base has been closed for years."

"I'm guessing it's a guy. As for how far back, could be decades, maybe the sixties."

"Now I'm intrigued." Gary drank more coffee. "What's this about?"

"Did you hear about the skeletons found in an old house in Alameda?"

"Saw something on the news. Two sets of bones. Are you involved?"

"I found them. Long story, short version. Dan and I were helping friends inventory the contents of the house. I found an old footlocker, pried it open, and it was full of bones."

That got his attention. "A Navy footlocker? Did it have any identification on it?"

"A Navy symbol on an oval sticker, with an anchor and chain and the letters USN. There were scratches on the side. It looked like an attempt to get rid of identifying marks, such as a name or number. I took pictures." I pulled out my phone and found the photos I'd taken of the footlocker. "In this shot, I'm seeing letters. I think one of them is an M or a W. And that section looks like numbers. Maybe it's a social security number. Or part of one. I think I can make out several numbers."

Gary took the phone and examined the pictures, using his fingers to enlarge each photo in turn. "I'll give you a short history of service numbers," he said. "That's what various branches of the military used up until the late sixties and early seventies. As I recall, they had six digits. And in some cases, a letter prefix for enlisted ranks during the Vietnam era. Then they phased those out and used social security numbers instead. I think the Navy did that by nineteen seventy-two. So, if these numbers turn out to have a letter in front of them, that might give us a possible date. As for the letters, I'm seeing AM. That's an aviation structural mechanic. It's a Navy rating. Job specialty, for you civilians. Aviation structural mechanics maintain aircraft, everything from doors, decks and seats, to the mechanical and hydraulic systems. Landing gear, wheels, tires and all that. You get the picture."

"I do. You don't see a W?" I peered at the photos. "Here. That looks like a W."

Gary squinted. "Yeah, I see it now. An initial, maybe. Or the first letter of a name." He handed back my phone. "Are you sure the footlocker is connected to the bones?"

"Not entirely sure. But it's possible. It could be the footlocker was already there in the storeroom, and whoever was hiding those bones just grabbed the most convenient receptacle. But I've got a hunch that whoever owned that footlocker has something to do with this."

"Well, sometimes you've got to go with your gut." Gary paused. "Do we have a time frame? You said the sixties. Any idea how old the bones are?"

"Right now I don't have an answer to that question. The house is in West Alameda. The woman who owns the place bought it in nineteen sixty-nine. It had been divided into apartments before that. She rented to sailors from the base, while it was open. My impression from looking at the bones is that they were buried in the ground for a long time. There were pebbles and dirt on the bottom of the footlocker. Also feathers, seagull and one from a least tern. There's a least tern colony on an old airstrip at the Alameda Naval Air Station."

Gary was working on the other half of his croissant. Now he nodded. "Okay, the bodies were buried on or near the base. But was that before it closed? Or after?"

"At this point, I don't know. The feathers could have gotten mixed with the bones when they were dug up. But why dig up a couple of skeletons, transfer them to a footlocker, and stash them at the house?"

"Beats the hell out of me." He chased the last bit of his breakfast with coffee. "Just the kind of puzzle you like."

I smiled, breaking off a piece of my scone. "Yes, it is. Whoever left the bones in that footlocker had access to that house. That's not random. There must be some connection. The footlocker was in a part of the basement used for storage. Maybe it was left there by a renter."

"What does the current owner say?"

"Not much. Could be a case of selective memory, or she could be hiding something. She has a way of changing the subject when she doesn't want to talk. She just moved to a very fancy senior living facility, which is why Dan and I were helping her nephew and his wife inventory the furniture and other stuff. She needs the money in order to afford her new digs, so she wants to sell the house, as soon as possible. She even has a buyer lined up. But finding those bones puts a stick in the spokes. I asked to see her rental records. She didn't want me to look. But the nephew and his wife have all her papers and I persuaded them to let me see them. Didn't find anything conclusive. In fact I spotted several gaps in the records, which could be deliberate, or poor record keeping." I took another sip of my latte. "Can you help me out with the Navy contact?"

He nodded. "I know a guy. He's retired now but he used to be an investigator for the Naval Criminal Investigative Service, otherwise known as NCIS. I'll call him when I get back to the office. If he's amenable to talking with you, and I think he will be, I'll send you his contact info."

"Thanks, Gary, I appreciate it."

"Hey, you can buy me breakfast anytime."

---

CLIENTS AND CASES DEMANDED my attention when I returned to my office. I spent the next few hours going through the work that had piled up on my desk—making phone calls, answering emails, writing reports, and searching databases.

I opened the file drawer where I'd stashed Gloria's tenant records. The top folder contained information on the most recent tenants. I pulled out that one and shut the drawer, then I arranged the papers on my desk surface and examined them.

Andrew Vogel had been the first tenant to leave. He'd rented apartment B, the smaller of the two upstairs apartments, for nearly three years. On the rental application, he listed a job as a graphic designer for a financial services company in downtown Oakland. He'd given Gloria thirty days' notice in late May and moved out in June.

Graham Costa had rented apartment C, the larger of the two upstairs apartments, for two and a half years. According to his rental application, he worked for a tech company in San Francisco. I didn't recognize the name of the company, but there were hundreds of them in the city, proliferating like toadstools after a rainstorm. This one was located on Mission Street, south of Market Street and not far from the Embarcadero and the waterfront. He had moved out at the end of July.

I was particularly interested in Peggy Slocum, since she lived in the ground level unit, apartment D, adjacent to the storeroom where I'd found the bones. She'd also created the garden that was now going to seed in the backyard. I suspected she would be dismayed to see how neglected the place looked since she'd moved out in August.

She was the tenant with the longest tenure, twelve years. According to Gloria's rental files, Slocum worked in the human resources department at the Peralta Community College District, which oversaw the operations of four colleges in the East Bay, including the nearby College of Alameda and Laney College in Oakland, where the district office was located.

Gloria's income came from renting out those three apartments. After losing three tenants in a short time, she didn't have any money coming in, except for the social security payments Noel said she was drawing, a small amount given her work history and self-employment status as a landlord. Or was there another source of money? I made a note to start a background check, to see if she had any investments or sums of money stashed somewhere.

Then there was the accident in August. Gloria told her nephew and his wife that she fell in the kitchen, slipping on water spilled on the floor. Noel was fine with that explanation. But Lakshmi suspected there was more to it. She wondered if Gloria had in fact fallen, or if there was something else going on. So did I. Those bruises on her arm aroused my suspicion. Did it have something to do with all those FOR SALE signs in the neighborhood? The accident, and probably the loss of the tenants, had led to Gloria's decision to give up the house and move to her new apartment in the independent living complex for seniors. An expensive place, which is why she was eager to sell the house to her mysterious and unnamed buyer.

I had phone numbers and email addresses for all three tenants, taken from their rental applications. It was possible that contact information had changed over the years. But it was a place to start.

I put in a call to Andrew Vogel, leaving a message on his voice mail. Then I called the other two tenants, getting voice mail for both. I worked at my desk a while longer, then walked to a nearby deli, where I got a salad. I had just finished lunch when Vogel returned my call.

"I'm sorry to hear about Gloria," he said. "She was really nice. I liked her. She had that old hippie vibe going on. The stories she used to tell about living over in the Haight, singing with a rock band and hanging out with Janis Joplin."

After talking with Gloria, I wondered how much of what Gloria had told her tenants about the old days was embellished. "Why did you leave?" I asked.

"I got laid off."

"That's rough. Happens a lot these days."

"Yes, it does. Recessions and downsizing, boom and bust. It's not the first time it's happened and probably won't be the last. I got severance pay. But it wasn't much. I was out of a job and looking in the Bay Area, going on interviews and not getting any callbacks. Worrying about my finances and hoping I didn't have to dip too far into my savings."

"Couldn't afford the apartment?"

"No, come right down to it. With no salary coming in, it was all I could do to come up with the rent. Oh, I had savings, but I didn't want to drain that account while I battled my way through the job market. Believe me, the rent on that apartment was reasonable. Gloria probably would have let me skate for a couple of months. But I really hated to ask. In the end, I didn't have to. A buddy of mine moved to Portland last year. He told me, come on up to Oregon, you can stay with me as long as it takes. That worked for me. I gave Gloria notice that I was moving. Then I sold most of my furniture, packed everything I owned into a cargo trailer, and hauled it up Interstate 5."

"I hope it was a good move for you."

His voice was cheerful. "It was. It didn't take long to find a job, the salary's a little better and the cost of living up here is way better. I might get a place of my own eventually but so far, living with my friend is working out." He hesitated. "You know, I gave Gloria notice. She didn't say anything at the time. I didn't realize there was a problem."

"Not a problem, exactly. It's just that all three of the tenants moved out in a short time. Graham Costa left the month after you did, and Peggy Slocum in August."

"Really? Graham and Peggy left? Graham moved into the house a couple of months after I did. I didn't see him all that much. He was always out, doing something. He works in San Francisco, rode his bike over to the ferry terminal every morning. Said it was a great commute. He rode his bike a lot. Kept it locked up in the storeroom next to Peggy's apartment." He paused. "Peggy moved out, too? That surprises me. She'd been there a long time. She loved to garden and kept me in tomatoes and squash all summer long."

"I haven't talked with her yet," I said. "Graham either. Neither of them has returned my calls. But as I told you, I'm curious as to why all three of you left around the same time."

"In my case, just one of those things."

"Thanks for getting back to me. I appreciate it."

After I ended the call with Andrew Vogel, I tried Graham Costa's number again. The call went straight to voice mail. I left another message, then I called Peggy Slocum's number. Same result again. After leaving a message, I looked up the number for the Peralta Community College District, called and asked to be transferred to the Human Resources office. The man who answered said, "She's out of the office, due back on Monday. Do you want to be transferred to her voice mail?"

"No, thanks." I ended the call, pushed aside my notes, and turned my attention to another case. Then my phone pinged. It was a text from Gary, transmitting a name, Lloyd Humphrey, an email address, and a phone number with a 707 area code. If it was a landline, that could be anywhere in the northwest part of California, from here to the Oregon border. If it was a cell phone, all bets were off. I called Humphrey.

The voice on the other end of the line was gruff. "Lloyd Humphrey."

"This is Jeri Howard. I got your number from Gary Manville. He told me you were with the Naval Criminal Investigation Service."

"Yes, I've been retired for a while. Gary called me. He says you're a private eye in Oakland, and you found some human bones in a Navy footlocker."

I leaned back in my chair. "That's right. The footlocker was in a storage room in a house in Alameda, near the old Navy base. There are scratches on the side, as though someone was trying to obscure letters and numbers. I think I can make out some letters. One of them is a K, maybe. Or it could be an X. Then a couple of letters that I saw as M and possibly W. Gary saw them as an A and an M. He tells me that an AM is a Navy rating, an aviation structural mechanic."

"It is," he said. "I worked in the Bay Area for a while. Spent some time at the air station. But the base closed in the nineties. How far back are we talking?"

"I don't know. My guess is that the footlocker was left there by a tenant. If that tenant was a sailor, I would assume that would be before the closure. The house had been divided into apartments. It's in West Alameda, close to the base, so could be a lot of sailors lived there over the years. The current owner bought the house in nineteen sixty-nine. The bones look like they were buried and dug up again. They're discolored and there was dirt and gravel mixed with them."

"You say there are some numbers?" Humphrey sounded thoughtful.

"Five, maybe six. The rest are obscured. I thought it could be part of a social security number."

"Or part of a serial number. The Navy used those for years before switching to social security numbers. So, you want me to use my resources to see if this combination of letters and numbers leads you to a sailor who was stationed at NAS Alameda some time before the base closed?"

"That's about the size of it."

"A big size. A lot of sailors were stationed there over the years. It would be helpful to have a name, even part of one. But maybe I can come up with a few leads. If this person was in fact an aviation structural mechanic, that might narrow it down a bit. So would some numbers." He chuckled. "I like a puzzle and this one intrigues me. Send me the pictures you took of the footlocker. I'll see what I can find out and get back to you."

We ended the call. I had downloaded the photos I'd taken at the house to my computer, and I sent those to Humphrey.

Peggy Slocum called me an hour later. "You've been trying to reach me. What's this about?"

"The house where you used to live."

Wariness radiated over the phone line. "I saw the news. But I don't know anything about those bones."

"I'm more interested in why you moved out of Gloria's house." Silence. "Look, can we meet somewhere? You name the time and place."

"I guess it couldn't hurt," she said. "Tomorrow morning, ten o'clock. At Julie's in Alameda."

# Ten

Julie's Coffee and Tea Garden on Park Street in Alameda was a popular spot, with a menu of breakfast and lunch items, and baked goods. In addition to selling coffee and tea by the cup and pot, it had bins of loose tea, and things to put tea in, such as colorful teapots and tins.

I parked on a side street. As I rounded the corner and approached the cafe, I looked for Peggy Slocum. She told me she would be wearing a green shirt. I spotted her immediately. Lime green it was, with short sleeves, worn over a pair of loose-fitting khaki slacks. She appeared to be in her fifties, with a head of curly, shoulder-length brown hair.

"Peggy Slocum?"

She looked at me over the rims of her glasses.

"That's me. You're Jeri Howard?"

"Thanks for agreeing to talk with me." I handed her my business card.

She glanced at the card, then slipped it into her pocket. "That's okay. I need to get it off my chest. I am so upset about what happened. Something needs to be done. Maybe you can get to the bottom of it."

I didn't know what happened but I wanted to find out. I gestured at the front entrance. "Let's get some coffee."

We went inside and queued up at the counter. When our turn came, I ordered coffees for both of us, a latte for me and a cappuccino for her, and two currant scones to go with them. We stepped away from the counter and I led the way to the garden in back of the building. We settled at a table near a blue ceramic pot full of orange marigolds.

"Where are you living now?"

She sipped her cappuccino and broke off a piece of her scone. "I have a one bedroom flat in an old Victorian, a couple of blocks from here. It's smaller than the apartment I had in Gloria's house, not as much space or storage. But I feel safe."

Why hadn't she felt safe in her old apartment? I sipped my latte and figured she'd tell me.

"The new apartment is closer to Park Street and the downtown businesses," she continued. "Which I really like. But it's farther to my office. I work in HR over at Peralta. At least my new place has a backyard with a garden. I do like to garden."

"So do I. You created a wonderful garden at Gloria's house. Unfortunately, it's been neglected. A lot of weeds and dead plants."

She shook her head. "I'm not surprised. That's what I figured when I moved out in August. It's the middle of October now, but it doesn't take long for things to go bad. I drove past the house a week or so ago. Well, after I heard the news about those bones. The place looks abandoned. As for the yard and the garden, terrible. I really hope the people in the neighborhood are taking the vegetables."

Peggy took another sip of coffee and sighed. "I put in so much work over the years. I'm the one who planted all those rose bushes and perennials. Gloria wasn't interested in any of that. She did like the way the place looked with all my hard work. But she never offered to help with money to buy plants or potting soil."

I cupped my hands around my latte. "How long did you live there?"

"Twelve years," she said. "I moved in after my divorce. Before that, I lived in San Lorenzo. The apartment was so convenient to work. Through the Tube and over to the Peralta district office. I'd planned on staying in that apartment until I retired. I was so upset when that man told me the house was being sold and I had to move."

I hadn't heard this before. "What man?"

"A thug." She shuddered. "A creep."

"Can you describe him?"

She frowned as she sipped her coffee. "A young guy. I'd say he was in his twenties. Muscles, like he worked out, but he had a beer gut, too. Dirty blond hair, shaggy. He had blue eyes. Mean little eyes. Like I said, a creep."

"When did this guy show up?"

"Early August," she said. "It was a Saturday. I was on the patio at the back of the house repotting some flowers. I saw him get out of a funky looking car. He walked up to the patio. I thought he was going to ask me for directions or something like that. Instead, he told me the house was being sold and I had to move."

I recalled what Lakshmi said—that Peggy had left in August, and that she may not have given the usual thirty days' notice.

"Did he threaten you with eviction?" California had laws about that sort of thing.

Peggy shook her head. "No, he didn't. Not with eviction. I'm aware of the law. I pay my rent on time, always have. And I certainly didn't violate anything in my rental agreement. Gloria was really easygoing, loose with the rules and so forth. I've always had a cat and she was okay with that. It wasn't in the rental agreement, it was just understood that it was okay for me to have a cat. And she was certainly happy to let me take over the gardening."

She paused, reaching for the coffee mug. "But he did threaten me. Not at first. When I told him I didn't want to move, he tried bribing me, saying he'd make it worth my while. I told him no, I wasn't interested in leaving. He kept coming back. He must have approached me two or three times. By then it was the middle of August and I kept trying to talk with Gloria, to find out what was going on. She wasn't returning any of my calls. The two guys who lived upstairs had already moved out. That left me alone in the house and I was really feeling vulnerable. Then the vandalism started."

I leaned forward in my chair. "What sort of vandalism?"

"Little things at first," she said. "Plants in the garden damaged. Pots broken. At first I didn't want to believe it. Kids in the neighborhood, that's what I thought. It happens. But it kept getting worse, over a couple of weeks. Then the guy showed up again. Asked if I'd changed my mind about moving. He made it clear he was responsible for the vandalism. I threatened to call the police. Then he said that wouldn't be a good idea. Or something bad might happen to my cat."

Son of a bitch. The cat lover in me was clear on that. Anyone who threatened my two cats would be in serious trouble.

"I still hadn't been able to communicate with Gloria," Peggy continued, a grim look on her face. "I thought, okay, this guy has me over a barrel. My cat is strictly indoors, I never let her outside. But she likes to sit in the window, where she's visible to anyone who walks by. It would be so easy for someone to break that window. I started packing. I even thought about moving in with a friend in Oakland, on a temporary basis, just to get away from there. I didn't feel safe. Fortunately I found this new apartment right away. You can see how the whole thing has me spooked. Then when I read about those bones being found in the storeroom, I wondered if it had something to do with that."

So did I. "I'm sorry you had such a horrible experience. Did you report the harassment to the police?"

"I did. I gave them a description of the man and his car. It was a sedan, though I couldn't tell what make or model. I think it was dark gray and I didn't see the plates. But there was a big ding on the passenger side door. So yes, I reported it. But nothing happened that I know of."

"Let's go back to what you said about Gloria being easygoing concerning rules for the rentals. What's your take on her, both as a person and a landlord?"

Peggy hesitated. "Well, as a landlord, she was okay. She was iffy on maintenance. She'd let that slide, or put off small problems until they got to be big ones. I'm good with tools and minor repairs, even painted my apartment myself. But the big stuff, well, I'd have to nag Gloria to get anything major done. We were having some sewer line problems and I kept after her until that got taken care of. I don't think she had the money for any huge projects. So she let them go, for too long. That roof was way overdue to be replaced."

She paused, shrugging. "But Gloria didn't raise the rent every year, like some landlords who are only interested in making money and could care less about maintaining their property. And she let me create my garden. We did have fun. We'd sit out on the patio in the evening. I like to bake, so I'd always have cookies on hand. I'd be drinking iced tea and she'd be drinking something stronger. And telling stories about her wild and crazy days back in the sixties. If only half of what she told me is true, it sounds like she had quite the life."

"I was told that one reason Gloria decided to move into the senior apartment was that she fell in the kitchen and injured herself. That would have been sometime in August. Do you know anything about that?"

The mystified look on Peggy's face told me that this was news to her. "I never heard that. Maybe that's why I couldn't get in touch with her. Was she hospitalized?"

"Not to my knowledge," I said. "The other two tenants had already moved out. Did you have much interaction with them?"

"From time to time, saying hello around the place. Andrew, the one who moved out first, he was nice. I would give him produce from my garden. I know he got laid off and that's why he moved. Portland, he said. I hope he found something there."

"I talked with him, and he did find a job that he likes. What can you tell me about Graham Costa?" I asked.

Peggy made a face. "I didn't much care for him. He's one of those entitled techies. It's a cliche to say it, but it's true. He just rubbed me the wrong way. He used to leave his bike in the storeroom, not tucked away in the corner, but out in the middle where you'd have to step around it all the time. Or blocking the way to the washer and dryer. And I know this sounds like a small thing to anyone who doesn't garden. But he used to help himself to my tomatoes. Now, if he'd asked, I would have given him some, just like I gave produce to Andrew. But to take them without asking?"

"I garden," I said. "And I understand completely." Those who pilfered my homegrown tomatoes would have a permanent black mark on their record. "I've been calling and leaving messages, but he hasn't responded. I'll have to go look for him."

"He works for one of those tech companies over in the city," she said. "I can't remember the name of the company, though. It must be located close to the Ferry Building, because he made a big deal about being so fit and environmentally conscious, riding his bike over to the Alameda ferry terminal every morning and then riding to work."

"I don't know what he looks like," I said, hoping Peggy could rectify that situation.

"Graham is about thirty," she said. "Maybe five ten. He has a skinny build. His hair is somewhere between brown and blond, longish. He wears it slicked back from his face. His eyes are—" She thought for a moment. "I guess I'd call them hazel. Dresses casually most of the time, you know, khakis and jeans. I don't think I ever saw him in a suit. And he has a thing for Hawaiian shirts. You know, the kind with palm leaves and flowers. The gaudier the better."

"Thanks. That's helpful." Next up, a trip to San Francisco. I needed to run Costa to ground. "Did Gloria get visitors on a regular basis?"

"There was a young couple, well, younger than me. I'd say they're in their thirties, with two kids, grade school age. They drove a blue car and they would come over from time to time. Gloria once told me he was her great-nephew. Those kids would try to climb the lemon tree and sometimes they'd throw lemons at each other." She smiled. "I don't remember anyone else. Well, wait. There was a distinguished looking older gentleman, about Gloria's age. Late seventies, I would guess."

Distinguished. That was the word Lakshmi had used when she mentioned seeing Gloria with a man outside a restaurant on Hayes Street in San Francisco. An older man with silver hair, tall, wearing a suit.

"Can you describe him?"

Peggy thought for a moment. "Tall. Silvery hair, fair-skinned. Really light eyes. Blue, I think. Expensive suits and a fancy watch. He always looked very formal. He drove a silver BMW. He had money, that's for sure. Made me wonder what he was doing with Gloria."

That sounded like the man Lakshmi had seen in the city.

"I only saw him a couple of times when he was there visiting Gloria," Peggy continued. "I never spoke to him. With that ground floor apartment, I had my own entrance, didn't go into the main house all that often. But I would get my mail from the boxes in front of the house. That was when I saw him getting out of his car."

I shifted direction, asking the question that had nagging at me. "The bones were in an old Navy footlocker. Do you remember seeing that in the storeroom?"

She shook her head. "I don't recall seeing anything like that. Of course, there was a lot of stuff in there. It was storage for all the tenants, over the years. Bikes, luggage, equipment, that sort of thing. And I'm sure some of that stuff had been in there for a while." She paused. "I sometimes heard noises in the storeroom. But I thought it was Andrew or Graham, the other tenants. And once we had raccoons get in there, through a broken window. But no, I'm not sure that footlocker was there when I moved out. I left at the end of August and you found the bones last week. That's six weeks that the place was empty."

And someone could have put the footlocker there during that time.

---

WHEN I GOT BACK to my office, I checked messages and returned phone calls. I also called the Alameda Police Department, to verify that Peggy Slocum had reported the vandalism she'd told me about. She had.

Then I made another call, this one to New Orleans.

"A musician in South Louisiana." Antoine Lasalle laughed, his warm voice and characteristic good humor radiating over the miles. "That narrows it down—not."

Antoine was a private investigator in NOLA. I'd met him several years ago at a convention. When I was in the Big Easy on a vacation that turned into a case, I called on Antoine for help and he'd delivered. Now I was asking him for another favor.

"We got musicians thick as mosquitoes down here," Antoine continued. His own sister Daisy was one of them, a singer with a band that performed regularly in clubs all over NOLA. "You say this guy's name is Guidry? That's a common name in Cajun country."

"Yeah, Louis Guidry, otherwise known as Monk. Supposedly from Lake Charles. Played guitar and had a band called the Mad Monks. I know it's a long shot. And a long time ago, more than fifty years."

"How old is this guy? Do you know when he was born? And where?"

"I'm not sure. The information I have is that he was in San Francisco in time for the Summer of Love in nineteen sixty-seven. So he probably arrived in the mid-sixties. I'm guessing he was in his twenties. I'm getting this information from his former girlfriend, a woman named Gloria Rossiter. I get the feeling they didn't part on good terms. So I don't know how much of what she told me is true. Taking it with several grains of salt. As for age, she is in her late seventies. I'm guessing they were about the same age. If he's still alive, he'd be—"

"Old," Antoine said, finishing my sentence. "Or he's dead. In which case I can check some databases to see if there's a death certificate to go with the name."

"Great. Really appreciate your help. Let me give you some background." I told Antoine how this investigation started, with me finding the bones in the footlocker. "Gloria recently moved to an upscale senior living facility. She needs to sell the house to pay for it and says she has a buyer lined up for the house. Her great-nephew and his wife are going through the house, to get it ready to sell, which is how Dan and I got involved, helping with the inventory. Then came the bones. I've talked with Gloria. It's clear there are things she doesn't want to discuss. She'd rather talk about the good old days in San Francisco in the sixties. I think she's trying to steer me in another direction. Which makes me wonder why." I paused for another sip of coffee.

"Maybe there were some bad old days in the sixties," he said. "You think this guy Monk has something to do with the bones?"

"I don't know. She says they broke up in the spring of nineteen sixty-nine, then she bought the house. Supposedly Monk went back to Louisiana later that year. She swears she hasn't heard from him since they split, but I'm not sure. I just get a feeling when she talks about him, that there's more to their story. Unfinished business."

"Okay. You got a gut feeling and have to go with it," Antoine said. "Could be Monk didn't go back to Lake Charles, wound up in Lafayette or New Orleans. Lafayette's a hub of Cajun musicians and NOLA, well, you know the music scene here. I'll nose around. We've got a lot of organizations in NOLA providing help and services to musicians. I'll see if this guy turns up on someone's radar. And I have contacts in Lake Charles."

"Thanks, Antoine. I'll look forward to hearing from you."

As we ended the call, I sat back in my chair, thinking and trying on a few "what ifs."

What if Monk Guidry had something do with those bones in the footlocker?

What if he'd put them there?

And what if those were Monk's bones? Monk and someone else?

# Eleven

I HAD A MEETING with a prospective client in downtown Oakland, a few blocks from my office, which resulted in the client hiring me. On the way back, I grabbed a quick lunch at a taqueria. When I returned to my office, I turned on my computer and located the California Department of Justice website.

I had found the skeletal remains of two people. Had they been reported missing in the state of California? If they had, I could find a trail here. The DOJ site has a missing persons search component, with a database I could search by name. But I didn't have any names. I clicked on the link marked DETAILED SEARCH. This allowed me to fill in details, such as name, sex, eye color, hair color, date of birth range, and current age, and county where the person was reported missing. The website also included a disclaimer, noting that the listings in the database were persons reported missing by law enforcement in California. If the two skeletons I'd found hadn't been reported missing, I was out of luck.

County name was all I had. I assumed the skeletons I'd found in the footlocker belonged to people who had gone missing from the city of Alameda. I selected Alameda County from the drop-down menu. My search returned over a hundred-thirty missing persons.

The faces of the missing stared back at me. So many people, their lives and those of their families interrupted. Birthdays and anniversaries uncelebrated, questions unanswered.

The photographs were displayed on the web page—children, teenagers, young adults, older people, male and female, of all ethnic groups. In some cases there were multiple photos, some of those computer-generated to show what the person would look like now. As I scrolled through the pages, I recognized two names, because of the intense news coverage these cases had received. Here was thirteen-year-old Ilene Misheloff, last seen on January 30, 1989, as she walked home from school in the East Bay suburb of Dublin. Here, too, was Michaela Garecht, snatched from a grocery store parking lot in Hayward on November 19, 1988.

The other names I didn't know. The missing persons were displayed in alphabetical order, according to the person's first name. On the right side of the screen was the name of the agency investigating the missing persons report. I scrolled down the list, looking for persons reported missing by the Alameda Police Department.

Midway down the first page, I found the name of Ann Marie Lombardi. I clicked into the listing and studied the photograph of a smiling, pretty girl with long dark hair. She was 20 years old, last seen on the evening of October 4, 1969, near the South Shore Twin Theatre in Alameda, California. That old two-screen movie theater had long since been torn down. She had been with Edward Charles Baldwin, age 22, who was also missing.

I printed out the listing and highlighted the case number. Then I went back to the list of missing persons. Baldwin's name was listed right below Lombardi's. The photo showed a young man with short, sandy hair and a friendly smile. Last seen near the movie theater, with Ann Lombardi. I printed this listing, then opened another web page and searched for a 1969 calendar. October 4 that year had been a Saturday. So, Ann Lombardi and Edward Baldwin were a pleasant-looking young couple in their twenties, out for a movie date. And then they vanished.

The missing persons database kicked up three additional listings of people reported missing in the city of Alameda. One was an elderly man who had disappeared in the mid-eighties. Another was a teenaged boy who went missing in in the nineties, listed as a possible runaway. Also listed as missing—and a possible runaway—was an 18-year-old girl named Martha Post. She had disappeared on June 24, 1969.

Interesting, I thought, to have three people reported missing in Alameda the same year, in a five-month period. Coincidence? Maybe. But it certainly called for further research.

I didn't have any idea as to how long those bones had been in the footlocker but the dirt, gravel and feathers mixed in with them told me the skeletons had been in the ground at some point. Why would someone bury a couple of bodies and then dig them up? I kept asking myself that question and as yet had no answer. I had a hunch that the bones were old. But did they date back to 1969?

Now that I had some names, I could do further research. Martha Post had disappeared first. I looked at the black-and-white photo that accompanied the listing. It showed a girl with long fair hair. A search on her name plus the town netted a few hits that led to short articles. Martha had disappeared from the Naval Air Station in Alameda, where her father, a lieutenant commander, was stationed. He and his family had lived in officers' quarters on the base. Martha turned 18 in April and she'd graduated from Encinal High School a few weeks later. Her parents told the police that Martha may have run away. She had done it before, her father said. Another article quoted an Alameda PD investigator as saying the girl was known as a chronic runaway. After one disappearance, she'd been located a week later in the Haight, hanging out with hippies. A wild child? But the last time she went missing, she stayed missing.

I turned my attention to Ann Lombardi. This time, my search returned thousands of hits. I stared at the screen, taking in list after list of websites, processing what I was seeing.

The Zodiac Killer.

The infamous serial killer who was the focus of so many websites and articles had been active in the 1960s and 1970s, mostly in Northern California. He wrote letters to newspapers, starting with the phrase, "This is the Zodiac speaking." In those communiques, he claimed to have murdered 37 people. And the websites I was seeing told me that when Ann Lombardi and her boyfriend Edward Baldwin vanished on October 4, 1969, lots of people assumed Zodiac was responsible. After all, the timing was right. The year and the month were in the middle of the Zodiac's killing spree.

I had read Robert Graysmith's book *Zodiac*, one of the best-known books on the case. But that was years ago, and I needed to refresh my knowledge.

Typing "Zodiac Killer" into the search bar returned more than 15 million hits. I clicked into web pages, reading about the serial killer whose rampage baffled Bay Area law enforcement for years.

The killer's first confirmed victims were David Faraday, 17, and Betty Lou Jensen, 16. The teenagers were shot and killed on December 20, 1968, on Lake Henry Road in the Solano County town of Benicia. Six months later, on the Fourth of July, 1969, Michael Mageau, 19, and Darlene Ferrin, 22, were shot in the parking lot of Blue Rock Springs Park in Vallejo. Mageau survived, Ferrin didn't. The next attack took place on September 27, 1969, at Lake Berryessa in Napa County. Bryan Hartnell, 20, and Cecelia Ann Shepard, 22, were stabbed by a masked assailant. Hartnell survived, Shepard died two days later. On October 11, 1969, cabdriver Paul Stine picked up a fare in downtown San Francisco. A short time later, he was shot and killed at an intersection in the Presidio Heights neighborhood.

The press was in full cry. A man phoned the Vallejo Police department in the early hours of July 5, 1969, taking credit for the attack on Mageau and Ferrin. He also claimed he had killed Faraday and Jensen. On August 1, 1969, letters arrived at the *Vallejo Times Herald*, the *San Francisco Chronicle* and the *San Francisco Examiner*. Whoever wrote the letters again claimed credit for the murders. Each of the letters included one-third of a cryptogram with 408 symbols, which became known as the 408 Cipher. The killer claimed the cryptogram contained clues to his identity and demanded that they be printed on each paper's front page.

Otherwise, he wrote, he would "cruse around all weekend killing lone people in the night and then move on to kill again, until I end up with a dozen people over the weekend."

More letters followed, including one on August 7, 1969 where the killer called himself Zodiac for the first time. Another letter arrived at the *Chronicle* on October 13, three days after Stine's murder. Until then, San Francisco police had thought the cabdriver's death was a robbery. But that wasn't the case. To prove his involvement, Zodiac included a bloody scrap of Stine's shirt.

The next day, the *Chronicle* received another letter, accompanied with another piece of Stine's blood-soaked shirt. This letter contained a threat. Zodiac said he was planning to kill schoolchildren on a school bus. A card with another cryptogram—the 340 Cipher—was mailed on November 8, 1969. The next day brought a long letter stating that two San Francisco police officers had spoken with him shortly after he killed Stine. On December 20, 1969, another letter was mailed to San Francisco attorney Melvin Belli, claiming that Zodiac wanted the lawyer to help him. Someone purporting to be Zodiac also called Belli's house. And two more cryptograms had been received, both short, which made decoding difficult.

Other letters arrived sporadically, into the 1970s, with gaps measured in years. Over the ensuing decades, several cases of murder and missing persons had been laid at Zodiac's door, some in the early 1960s, another in Southern California in 1966, others taking place in the early 1970s. Depending on which account you were reading, the evidence backing up such claims was minimal or unproven.

The list of suspects was long and varied. Graysmith's first book on Zodiac described a likely suspect but gave the man a pseudonym since he was still alive. After the man died in 1992, Graysmith wrote another book that named Arthur Leigh Allen as a probable Zodiac. The detectives investigating the case in San Francisco and Vallejo had zeroed in on Allen. But they had never been able to obtain conclusive evidence against him.

The most recent news items concerned the Zodiac ciphers. Two of them had been decoded. In August 1969, a Salinas couple had cracked the 408 Cipher. It took another 51 years, until 2020, before the 340 Cipher was decoded by a team of mathematicians. Neither of the ciphers contained a name. Instead, the messages rambled as the killer wrote that he enjoyed killing. The other cryptograms had not yet been decoded.

I opened a separate browser tab and did a search on Ann Lombardi and Edward Baldwin, adding Zodiac to the search terms. High up on the list of hits were links to several *San Francisco Chronicle* articles. I clicked into these, reading each in turn, coming up with a summation of the facts.

Ann Lombardi was 20 years old in 1969, living at home in Alameda with her parents and two younger siblings. Her boyfriend, called Eddie Baldwin in the article, was 22. He was an aviation structural mechanic at the Naval Air Station in Alameda, living in barracks on the base.

I paused, looking at the notes I'd made earlier. AM, aviation structural mechanic, the same Navy rating that Gary had mentioned, interpreting the letters marred by the scratches on the footlocker. Coincidence? Possible. The air station was a big base, especially during the Vietnam era, and a lot of sailors had been stationed there through the years.

Ann and Eddie had been dating for about six months, according to Ann's family. On Saturday, October 4, they planned to go out for dinner, then to a movie. Eddie drove a green 1965 Pontiac Bonneville with plates from Colorado, his home state. At 5:30 PM, Eddie had called for Ann at the Lombardi home. She wasn't quite ready to leave, so he waited in the living room, talking with her mother and younger sister Tessa. Ann's father and younger brother Ronny were out. Ann told her mother she'd be home by midnight. She wasn't. Her parents, increasingly worried, called the police in the early hours of October 5. The Alameda Police Department checked with the Navy authorities and determined that Baldwin hadn't come back to his barracks either. His Pontiac was nowhere to be found.

An official missing persons report was filed after the customary 24 hours. Investigators turned up witnesses who'd seen the young couple sharing a meal at a Chinese restaurant on Park Street in downtown Alameda. Other witnesses had seen them in line at the box office of the South Shore Twin, the movie theater located at the island city's shopping mall. One man told police he was sure he'd seen the young couple outside the nearby bowling alley.

After that, nothing.

The police speculated that Ann and Eddie may have gone out for coffee after the movie, since the bowling alley had a coffee shop, but none of the employees there had recalled seeing them. The investigation turned up no other sightings of the couple. A sailor stationed aboard a ship docked at the air station told police he'd seen a Pontiac Bonneville driving on one of the base streets in the early hours of the morning, but none of the guards at the entrances to the base recalled seeing the car, which never turned up.

Ann and Eddie had vanished on October 4, one week after the September 27 attack that resulted in Shepard's death and one week before the October 11 murder of Paul Stine. That led to lots of theories that the young couple were victims of the Zodiac killer.

Several of the Zodiac's victims had been young couples. And the attacks on the seven confirmed victims had occurred near water. The movie theater and the bowling alley were both on Shoreline Drive, which ran along the beach on San Francisco Bay. Proximity to water was a fit for the Zodiac pattern.

But Zodiac usually left victims for others to find, even calling the police to claim credit for the murders. Though the long letter Zodiac sent to the *Chronicle* on November 7, 1969 threatened to change the pattern by not announcing his kills and making them look like routine crimes.

As I examined the website links, I encountered two later articles. In October 1979, on the tenth anniversary of the disappearance, *Chronicle* reporter Maggie Constable had done a feature on the couple and the unsolved case. She had written another story in 1994, when the pair had been missing for twenty-five years.

Was Maggie Constable still around? If she'd worked at the newspaper in the 1970s, she could be retired, or dead. And she might have moved out of the area.

As it turned out, she was very much alive. She was semi-retired, writing the occasional article for the *Chronicle* as well as other publications. Over the past few years, she'd been teaching at the Graduate School of Journalism at the University of California in Berkeley. I sent an email explaining who I was and asking if we could set up a time to talk. A short time later, I got a response. She wanted to talk with me, but she was out of town. She would contact me when she returned, to set up an appointment.

# Twelve

---

It was time to find Graham Costa, the former tenant of the large upstairs apartment in Gloria's house. I'd obtained his phone number from the rental records and had left several messages for him, but he wasn't returning my calls.

I was harder to ignore in person.

On Friday morning, I left my office and walked down Broadway, to the 19th Street BART station, to catch the next train to San Francisco. The first stop in the city was Embarcadero. I emerged onto Market Street near the Ferry Building and headed into the district known as SOMA, shorthand for South of Market Street.

This area close to the bay had once been Rincon Hill, one of the original seven hills that made up San Francisco. The neighborhood had beautiful views and a sunny climate, and soon was full of fashionable homes. That didn't last. In 1869, the Second Street cut sliced through the hill to give access to the south waterfront and its surrounding industrial areas. The canyon resulting from the cut was a hundred feet deep, cleaving Rincon Hill, destabilizing the homes that remained. The neighborhood deteriorated. The fashionable section of San Francisco moved to the north of Market Street, where elegant mansions rose on Nob Hill. The 1906 earthquake leveled what remained of the Rincon Hill neighborhood. The San Francisco anchorage of the Bay Bridge, constructed in the 1930s, stands atop what's left, as did the old Embarcadero Freeway.

Then came another earthquake, called Loma Prieta, in 1989. The freeway was irreparably damaged by the quake. After much debate, it was torn down. The developers swarmed in with lots of money and a new name for the neighborhood, the East Cut, eager to exploit the potential of a neighborhood that was walking distance to downtown and close to all sorts of public transit. Now there were sleek high rises going up all over the South of Market district, all sharp angles and glass windows.

Costa worked at a tech company with offices in one of those high rises, on Fremont Street between Market and Mission. Peggy Slocum had described him, so I had an idea of how he looked. Under six feet, she'd said, with hazel eyes and brownish blond hair, worn long and slicked back from his face. A casual dresser, like many of the people I saw on the street, but one with a penchant for colorful tropical print shirts. That would help, but I hoped for a clearer identification.

I located Costa's office building. I'd called earlier to find out if he was in the office that day, since many of the techies worked from home, at least part of the time. He was in the building, I learned, and conveniently for me, in a meeting and couldn't be disturbed. Was he in the habit of going to lunch rather than camping out at his desk? Some forty minutes later, I found out.

The flamingos caught my eye, a vibrant eye-popping pink against dark green leaves on a short-sleeved shirt worn over faded jeans and a pair of gray running shoes. That had to be Costa. He had barely left the building when I got confirmation. A man who hurried past me called, "Yo, Graham."

Costa stopped and turned, focusing on the man who had now caught up with him. I hung back and watched. The two spoke briefly, then the other man gave Costa a friendly slap on the shoulder and entered the building. Costa headed up First Street, stopping at a deli near the corner. He emerged a few minutes later, carrying a sack and a can of Coke. A block later, he turned and crossed the street. He was headed for the transit terminal.

The old Transbay Terminal, where busses from all over the Bay Area had converged on San Francisco, wasn't there anymore. The old building had been designed by architect Timothy Pflueger, who'd also designed two of the East Bay's opulent Art Deco movie palaces, the Alameda Theatre and Oakland's Paramount. The 1939 building was rundown by the time it was damaged in the 1989 Loma Prieta earthquake. It was demolished and a shiny new transit center rose to replace it. Right now it contained an aboveground bus terminal and empty subterranean tunnels that were supposed to house tracks for CalTrain, the commuter rail that ran down the Peninsula, and the high speed rail line that was being built to link the Bay Area with Los Angeles. It seemed the latter option was far in the future, but the terminal was here and now.

One of the transit center's best features was a 5.4 acre rooftop park, located five stories above the street. It had a walking trail, a play area for kids, and a small amphitheater for events. The landscaping featured a desert garden at the western end and a wetlands garden at the east. There were bird walks, garden tours, and regular activities for children. Then there was the bus fountain, where sensors built into the bus deck below triggered 247 geysers, an innovative work of public art. No wonder the park was so popular with residents and workers alike.

Costa took the elevator up. He waited for a woman pushing a stroller to enter the car, then he stepped in. I followed, safe for the moment since he didn't know who I was. As I suspected, he was headed for the garden to eat his lunch. At the top, we waited for the woman with the stroller to exit, then he let me get off before he did. I paused for a moment, looking around, as he strode down the path, moving quickly past a couple of women with a brace of toddlers. I followed. He sat down on a vacant bench, opened his Coke, and took a wrapped sandwich out of the bag. I felt a hunger pang as he took a big bite of what looked like roast beef on a baguette. The thick sandwich, oozing mustard and mayo, looked delicious. Costa ate his way through his lunch, checking his phone and texting all the while. He deposited the remains of his lunch in the bag, balled it up and sat for a while longer, sipping the Coke and soaking up sunshine.

I walked up and stood over him. "Graham Costa."

He looked up, startled.

"You haven't returned any of my calls."

"Calls?" Now he looked perplexed. I handed over one of my business cards. "Private investigator? What is this about?"

"I'm interested in why you moved out of the apartment in Alameda."

He frowned. "What? Why?"

"All three of the tenants moved out around the same time. I'm wondering if there was a reason."

He smiled but it didn't quite reach his eyes. "You mean Peggy moved out? I find that hard to believe. I thought she'd be there till the next millennium."

"She left about a month after you did."

"Why would she do that?" Then he answered his own question. "Is the place being sold?"

"Yes, as it happens. Gloria has moved into a senior apartment building."

"That doesn't surprise me," he said quickly. "She talked about it. Said the maintenance on the house was too much for her. She's in her seventies, after all." He made it sound like Gloria was as old as a stegosaurus.

I wasn't letting him divert me with talk about Gloria's age and infirmities. "Why did you move?"

"What in the world does that have to do with anything?" he countered.

"Someone suggested that the tenants were encouraged to move."

"What? That's crazy." He was getting restless, eager to leave.

"Maybe it is. If you'll just answer the question, I'll let you go back to work."

His face closed up for a second. Then his lips moved into a tight approximation of a smile. "I decided the commute from Alameda to the city was getting old. Got a line on an apartment in a building close to my office. So I gave notice and moved. Nothing strange and unusual about that. Happens all the time."

Something was setting off my bullshit detector. I didn't believe him. Maybe I just didn't like the guy. Maybe his answer was too pat and he was too slick. I gave him a nod, as though I accepted his answer. He escaped, tossing his lunchtime trash into a nearby can and walking briskly back down the path.

Gloria's rental records showed that Costa had given her a forwarding address. It wasn't the same as his work address, so it must be his new apartment. It was indeed close to the building where he worked, just a couple of blocks away. Earlier, I'd looked it up on the Internet. The building where Costa now lived had a name—the Odalisque. I left the rooftop garden and took the elevator down to street level.

I walked toward Costa's new address. There was a small market on the corner, selling groceries and other necessities for people in the neighborhood. The woman walking a few paces ahead of me veered into the market, picked up a red basket from a rack near the check stand and moved to the display of fruits and vegetables. She selected several apples and dropped them into the basket, then stood contemplating the tomatoes.

Next was a coffee shop. It was mid-afternoon and it looked like the place was getting ready to close. Chairs had been set on top of the tables and one of the employees ran a mop over the floor while another wiped down the counter. Up ahead I saw shallow steps and double doors, recessed a couple of feet from the sidewalk. ODALISQUE was spelled out in shiny steel letters affixed to the side of the building, just above the entrance.

The building looked brand new, its exterior clad in a sleek silvery metal, with views of the San Francisco waterfront and the Bay Bridge, tiny balconies perched above the street. It wasn't as tall as its neighbors. I leaned back and counted twelve floors, the top of the building pointing toward the blue October sky. I wouldn't want to live in a high rise, I thought. Earthquakes and all that. With limited space in San Francisco, going up was the way to increase housing capacity. But still.

Farther to the left of the building entrance were two gates, a larger one for cars and a smaller for people, leading into the building's parking garage. I walked over to the gates and peered inside, seeing vehicles parked in numbered spaces. One door beyond had a sign that read TRASH AND RECYCLING. Next to this was another door, marked MAINTENANCE.

According to the website, the Odalisque had lots of amenities to lure potential tenants. A clubroom and a fitness center, a pool and hot tub on the rooftop terrace. I'd called the number on the website, posing as a prospective tenant interested in moving into the building. The monthly rent at this place was a lot higher than the rent Costa had been paying for the apartment in Gloria's house. What had prompted the move to such a fancy place? Had he gotten a raise? Or was there something more to it?

I turned from the garage gates and headed back to the lobby doors. I walked up the steps and looked at the electronic panel on the right side, containing a keypad and an intercom. The door in front of me had a pad as well, for tenants to swipe a key card. No way was I getting in without a card, or without someone buzzing me in as a visitor.

I peered inside, seeing a couple of elevators and a bank of mailboxes, all with locks. A counter near this held two packages that had been delivered. Beyond the counter was a door. I guessed that it led out to the parking garage.

As I considered my options, one of the elevator doors opened. A dark-haired man stepped off, dressed in slate blue coveralls, with something embroidered in red on his left breast pocket. There was a utility belt around his waist and he carried a gray metal toolbox in his left hand. He paused for a moment and took a cell phone from his hip pocket, putting it to his ear. He talked for a few seconds, then ended the call and shoved the phone back into his pocket. He pushed through a door at the back of the lobby, the one that I'd guessed led to the parking garage.

I retraced my steps to the gate at the driveway and looked inside. Sure enough, the man in the blue coveralls was unlocking the door marked MAINTENANCE. He went inside. A moment later, he came out again, minus the utility belt and toolbox. Now he carried a black and red backpack bearing the logo of the San Francisco 49ers. He slung it over one shoulder and walked toward the gates, exiting the garage to the sidewalk.

I was close enough to see what was embroidered on his pocket, the name SAL. He set off at a brisk pace, walking in the direction of Market Street. I followed. When he reached the corner market, the light turned red and he stopped near the crosswalk.

I stepped up next to him. "Excuse me, you work at the Odalisque?"

He turned and looked me over. He was in his forties, I guessed, with olive skin, brown eyes and curly brown hair receding from a high forehead. "Yeah, what's it to you?"

"I'm interested in a tenant who recently moved into the building."

"Who wants to know? And why?"

"I'm doing a background check on the guy. His name is Graham Costa. He moved in last July."

He looked me in the eye. "I'm not supposed to talk about the tenants."

"I understand. But—" I handed over a business card, with a folded bill wrapped around it.

The light changed and the walk signal flashed, but Sal didn't move. Instead, he took the money and put it in his pocket, then scanned my card. "Private eye, huh? Must be important if you're handing out cash. Thing is, I don't know names. I know apartment numbers. What does this guy look like?"

"I have a picture." I took out my phone and pressed the photo icon, calling up the picture of Costa that I'd snapped earlier in the afternoon, before I'd approached him at the rooftop garden a few blocks away.

Sal peered at the photo and his mouth tightened. His next words were drenched with scorn, "Oh, him."

"What about him?"

"That's the guy who lives in twelve-B. He's a pain in the ass."

"How so?"

"One of those arrogant, entitled types who gives the techies a bad name."

I nodded. It had become common over the past few years to blame many of the city's ills on the tech industry, whose highly paid employees were accused of doing everything from driving up rents to increasing traffic. "Give me an example."

"He's got a fancy new sports car. Why he needs a car, I don't know. The guy walks to work, I see him leaving in the morning. He has a hissy fit if anyone looks at the damn car. Not long after he got the car, it turned up with a little scratch and he accused me of doing that, because I was doing some work in the garage at the time. It wasn't me scratched his damn car and I sure as hell didn't like him accusing me of it."

"He sounds like one of those annoying people who straddles two parking places because he doesn't want anyone scratching his car." Costa annoyed me because he'd dodged my questions.

"You got that right." Sal shook his head. "I guess he can afford a new car, because he's not paying rent."

I swiveled my head and stared at him. "No rent? Where did you hear that?"

"One of the rental agents told me. This guy's got a large one-bedroom on the top floor with a major view. Normally that goes for megabucks, but he's got that place rent free for a whole year. In this market? Really? Who do you have to kill to get a deal like that?"

What do you have to do, I thought, to get a deal like that? Graham Costa had given notice that he was moving out of Gloria's house about the same time that his fellow tenant Peggy Slocum got a visit from the unidentified man who told her the place was being sold and she had to move out. Peggy had been adamant from the start that she didn't want to leave and that's when the threats and vandalism started. Perhaps Costa had used leverage and negotiation to parlay his move into a whole year of paying no rent. I looked at the brand new South of Market high rise, with all the bells and whistles and amenities. Who owned the building? Who could make a decision to offer that kind of sweetener to a prospective tenant?

"Do you know who owns the building?" I asked.

He shrugged. "Not really. I get paid through a property management outfit called CLB Properties. They provide all kinds of stuff for apartments and condos, including maintenance people. I've been with them for a few years now. Before this, I worked at another building, over on Folsom Street. This building is fairly new, just opened in the past couple of years."

The name CLB Properties didn't tell me much, but I could do the research online once I got back to my office.

"Look, I gotta go," Sal said. The light had changed several times as we'd been talking. It was still red, but he stepped closer to the street, ready to be on his way.

"Thanks for the information. I appreciate it."

He waved at me as the light flashed green again and set off. I followed at a slower pace. When he reached Mission Street he crossed as the light turned amber. I waited on this side of the street and watched him head for a bus stop. A moment later, an articulated bus in silver and orange braked to a stop. He got on it, along with several other people. The bus pulled out into traffic.

I continued on to Market Street, where I headed for the nearest BART station and took the stairs down to the platform. I had research to do when I got back to my office. I wanted to know just who owned the Odalisque and who had given Graham Costa an expensive apartment, rent-free for a year.

# Thirteen

I EXITED THE BART station at 19th Street in Oakland and walked up Broadway, stopping at a sandwich shop to buy lunch. Back in my office, I ate at my desk while I checked messages. Then I fired up the computer.

The Odalisque was managed by CLB Properties. The company's website listed an office on Folsom Street near Second, the same South of Market area as the apartment building. The firm managed business and residential properties in California. But it didn't give me any names or ownership information.

I turned to another website, that of the California Secretary of State. Here I could search for a company's business name. The search result would tell me whether the company was active, had been suspended, dissolved, or merged. It provided the name of the agent for service of process. In California, the agent is a person or a corporation that's designated for the purpose of receiving official legal documents, such as lawsuit papers and subpoenas. Finding out who the agent was might give me a lead.

I clicked on the CLB Properties name under the heading ENTITY NAME, which got me to a web page listing the company's physical and mailing addresses. It also gave me links to download PDFs of the company's statement of information, a document that had to be filed every year and which contained the names of the company's chief executive officer and secretary.

I downloaded the documents for CLB Properties and opened them. Carol Bertram was the CEO and secretary of the company. She was also the agent for service of process. Bertram's name didn't sound familiar. But it was a place to start. I amassed a few details about her, enough to know that she was in her fifties and that she had been affiliated with several companies, including one called Bertcor. I wondered if that was a variation on her first and last names. I looked up that company on the Secretary of State database. It was a real estate development company. Carol Bertram was also listed as agent for Bertcor.

More digging was needed. But my phone had just pinged with a reminder. I had a meeting with a client whose office was in the Kaiser Center, a few blocks away. If didn't get going, I would be late.

Later that afternoon I returned to my office, where I began another foray to the Internet. Antoine was looking for Monk Guidry in Louisiana. I went looking for him in 1960s San Francisco.

According to Gloria, Monk's band was called the Mad Monks. As I searched the web, I discovered that a number of rock bands over the years had used the name Mad Monks, including one in New Jersey. I refined my search, using different keywords, finally locating the band that had played in San Francisco in the sixties. I scrolled through a website that had information and images of concert posters from that era, places like the Fillmore, Winterland, and the Avalon Ballroom, venues that hosted bands like Big Brother and the Holding Company, Jefferson Airplane, and the Grateful Dead. A few posters mentioned the Mad Monks. I found a trove of short newspaper clips. Most were announcements of one sort or another, listing bands that would be playing at a particular venue on a certain date.

Then I found a clipping from one of the many underground newspapers that had sprouted like weeds in the San Francisco of the 1960s. The short article said that the up-and-coming band the Mad Monks would be playing a gig with the Grateful Dead.

The clipping contained a blurry black-and-white photo of the band. I saved a copy onto my computer and enlarged it, printing it out. I also peered at the screen, looking for details. The photo had been snapped in a club called the Beldame, on Haight Street. I'd never heard of it, but in those days, clubs appeared and went out of business just as quickly. In the photo, people crowded in on all sides. On the bandstand, harsh lighting overhead, were four young men—three with guitars and a fourth behind the drums. They wore loose-fitting Cossack-style shirts, light in color, with dark-colored strips of embroidery at the necks and on the left side over the heart.

The photo caption listed the names. Monk Guidry, the lead guitarist, had curly dark hair, a long mustache, and a devil-may-care smile. Next to him, holding another guitar, was a tall, lanky man with a prominent nose and light-colored hair tied back in a ponytail. He was identified as Liam Ebbets, rhythm guitar. The bass player, Richie Wayne, looked like a blond. As for the drummer, Gene Prager, he had dark hair but a cymbal blocked part of his face. I leaned forward, trying to make out his features in the blurry photo on my screen.

There was a hand on his shoulder. It belonged to a woman, her face just visible to one side. Could that be Gloria Rossiter? Yes, it was, I was sure of it. Gloria, in a patchwork jacket and tight jeans, long hair framing her face. I looked for a date on the article and found it—February 1969. Gloria had told me that she and Monk broke up in the spring of 1969, so this photo had been taken in the twilight of their relationship.

Where were those other band members now?

Richie Wayne was the easiest to locate. I found his obituary. He'd been living in Santa Monica with a wife and two children when he was killed in a car accident in 1987. Gene Prager had also moved to the Los Angeles area, living in a variety of places, from Hollywood to Studio City to Burbank. He had played with several bands over the next thirty years. And he'd been married twice, with children by both spouses. Eight years ago he'd left LA and moved to Billings, Montana. He owned a club and still played in a band.

Liam Ebbets, too, had continued playing music. And he'd stayed in Northern California. I found his name listed on a number of playbills and announcements for clubs in the area north of San Francisco. He also owned a woodworking business in the Sonoma County city of Petaluma. Research on the company showed that it had been founded in the late 1940s. Now there were three people named Ebbets on the company's roster. A family business, one that went back decades.

Petaluma was about 45 miles northwest of Oakland. I picked up the phone. A young woman answered. She told me Ebbets wasn't available. I left a message with my contact information.

It was late in the day and I had another appointment, this one in North Oakland, near my house. I'd meet with that client and then head home. I was getting ready to leave the office when my phone rang. I answered, and heard a man's voice.

"This is Liam Ebbets. I got a message that you called."

"I did. Thanks for getting back to me, Mr. Ebbets."

"If it's carpentry work or wanting some custom cabinets, my son handles most of that."

"No, it's you I want to talk with. I'm a private investigator."

"Okay," he said, slowly drawing out the word. "What's this about?"

"Monk Guidry."

There was silence on the other end of the phone. Then he said, "There's a name I haven't heard in a long time."

"I'd like to find out more about him. And what happened to him."

"You and me both."

"Look, Mr. Ebbets, my office is in Oakland. I'd like to talk with you in person. Can we set up a meeting? You pick whatever time and place works for you."

"I'm not available this weekend," he said. "But I can meet with you on Monday. How about you come over to the shop? We open at nine."

I glanced down at my calendar. I didn't have much on it for Monday. "That works for me."

# Fourteen

I spent Saturday at home. It was good to have time to focus on something besides cases. I put on faded jeans and a T-shirt and spent the afternoon in the garden, deadheading roses and transplanting a pot-bound perennial. I picked the last of the tomatoes and summer squash, keeping an eye on the acorn squash I'd planted, as well as a vine that was about to reward me with several bright orange pumpkins. I wondered how long this warm, sunny October weather would last. We needed rain, of course, and usually late October or early November brought the first big storm of the season. But drought had became a pervasive reminder of climate change. So had the wildfires, and there was another one tearing through a remote area in the Sierra.

Sunday morning, Dan and I drove to Castro Valley, meeting my father for brunch. Returning home later that afternoon, we relaxed and read, sipping wine on the patio.

On Monday, it was back to the routine. I got an early start, contending with stop-and-go traffic as I went over the Richmond-San Rafael bridge, the northernmost of the four bridges that spanned San Francisco Bay. It was a sparkling morning, with blue skies above, San Quentin and Mount Tamalpais in the distance, and the bay below, its dark blue water roiled here and there with whitecaps.

On the other side of the bridge, I drove past the exit for the prison, continuing on to San Rafael. Traffic knotted at the usual spot, the interchange where Interstate 580 merged into Highway 101, with cars and trucks jockeying for the downtown exit. The congestion thinned out a bit as I headed north past the Marin County Courthouse. I drove through the next big town, Novato, and crossed the line into Sonoma County. The undulating hills were golden brown. Amid dark-green stands of pine, valley oaks blazed with red and gold leaves.

A high bridge spanned the Petaluma River. A few miles to the north, I exited the freeway at Washington Street, heading west to downtown, where the main boulevard was lined with picturesque, iron-fronted Victorian buildings. Ebbets Woodworking was a few blocks further, on Western Avenue. I pulled into the small parking lot, shaded at one end by a huge oak tree, leaves russet against the blue sky.

Inside the building, I saw an array of cabinets, tables, bookcases and entertainment centers. I stood for a moment, admiring a small oak cabinet with shelves and drawers, wondering if it would fit in my living room—and my budget. Excellent work, with a price tag to match.

A young woman behind the central counter said, "If I can help you with anything, please let me know."

I turned from the cabinet and walked toward her. "My name's Jeri Howard. Liam Ebbets is expecting me."

She nodded and picked up the phone, pressing an intercom button. She spoke in a low voice, then hung up the phone and pointed toward a doorway in the back wall. "Go through there to the workroom."

I thanked her and headed for the door. The workroom I entered was redolent with the smells of freshly sawed wood, linseed oil, varnish, and furniture polish. Off to my right, a woman in coveralls, her hair pinned up on top of her head and protective goggles on her face, was operating a table saw, the whine of the blade against wood nearly drowning out the music coming from a CD player on a long counter against the back wall.

A man walked toward me. He was tall, in his late seventies. His faded jeans and green T-shirt were stained with oil and who knows what else. The ponytail in the 1969 photo had been replaced by a tonsure of white hair surrounding a bald pate. His face was long and lean, with lines deeply carved on either side of a hawk nose. Brown eyes regarded me from behind a pair of horn-rimmed glasses.

"You must be Jeri. I'm Liam." He stuck out his right hand, the hand of a man who'd done carpentry most of his adult life. The calluses on the tips of his fingers told me he still played guitar. "Would you like some coffee?"

"I'm always up for coffee."

He led the way to the counter. As we got closer, the table saw stopped. Now I could hear the song coming from the CD player, Jimi Hendrix and "All Along the Watchtower." I smiled. Yes, I figured a guitar player would like that.

Next to the small wooden crate holding CDs was a coffeemaker, the carafe half-full. There was a selection of mismatched mugs and plates arranged on a plastic tray. A square metal baking pan held what looked like homemade coffee cake. Several pieces had been removed with the spatula that was propped on the edge of the pan.

"How about some coffee cake?" he asked. "Yogurt pecan. My wife made it fresh this morning."

"It looks wonderful. Thanks, I will." He reached for the spatula at the side of the dish and cut a couple of squares, transferring them to plates. Forks protruded from a glass mug and I took one. Liam poured coffee into a couple of mugs. He led the way to a small table with several wooden chairs, to the right of the counter. I took a bite of the coffee cake, topped with a generous pecan streusel and moist from the yogurt. I tasted cinnamon, nutmeg and ginger. "This is delicious."

"Yeah, it's a favorite of mine." He smiled. "Of course, I like everything my wife bakes."

"Family business?" I asked, after I'd chased a mouthful of cake with a sip of coffee.

"Yeah. My dad started it, when he got home from World War Two. He wanted me to take over from him, but I had to go sow my wild oats first. Did that for a few years and then came home. I ran the company for a long time. These days my son and nephew are in charge, along with my granddaughters." He gestured toward the woman operating the saw. "That's one of my grandkids, and the other you met in the front office." He paused for a sip of coffee. "I'm what you call semi-retired. I make a few pieces of furniture now and again, just to keep my hand in."

"Still play guitar?"

He grinned. "Guitar players never retire. They just get arthritis in their hands." As he spoke, he flexed his fingers. His expression turned serious. "You said on the phone you want to talk about Monk. Is this about those bones in the house in Alameda?"

"Yes, it is." I scooped up a pecan with the tines of my fork.

"I thought so. It's Gloria's house, right? I was there once, years ago. I don't remember the address, but when they showed it on TV, I recognized the house. Does Gloria still live there?"

"She recently moved to a senior apartment complex in Alameda."

He nodded. "Not surprised. She's the same age as Monk and me, give or take a few years. And upkeep on that house, well, upkeep on any house. What's your interest in all this?"

"I'm the one who found the bones. Gloria's great-nephew and his wife are friends. We were inventorying the contents. Gloria already has a buyer for the house."

"The way real estate is these days, yeah, I'm sure she could get a good price." He took another sip of coffee.

"What can you tell me about Gloria and Monk?"

He took his time answering, choosing his words carefully. "Gloria. Well . . . That woman always had a touch of the crazies. I'm not the only one to think that. I knew her because she was with Monk. When I say with Monk, you can interpret that loosely. They were together when I met Monk, living together for most of that time, but she was always looking, checking out the guys to see if she could move on. Hell, she tried it on with me once. But I shut her down. I was with a woman named Anita then and I didn't need any trouble. And I wouldn't have done that to Monk. He was my friend." He sighed. "To this day, I wonder what happened to him."

I tilted my head to one side. "According to Gloria, someone told her that Monk went back to Louisiana."

Liam shook his head. "That's what she told me, when I went over to her house that one time, after he disappeared. That's bullshit. I didn't buy it then. I still don't."

"When did Monk disappear?" I asked.

"September of nineteen sixty-nine," he said. "He dropped off the radar. I couldn't find him. I called Gloria's number, several times. Either she didn't answer, or when she did, she always had some excuse why she couldn't talk with me right then. And she never called me back. So one day I drove over to Alameda and knocked on her door. I figured I'd be harder to ignore if I showed up on her doorstep. She gave me the rough edge of her tongue, like she couldn't be bothered to give me the time of day. Too busy with her new boyfriend. He was in her living room when we were standing there at her front door, her acting like she wanted to slam it in my face. Finally she tells me she heard that Monk went back to Louisiana."

"But you didn't believe her?"

"No way. He never said anything to me about heading for Louisiana." He drank coffee, a pensive look on his face. "I could see him going for a short visit. He did that at Christmas a couple of years before. But for him to leave and not come back? That didn't make any sense. We were supposed to cut a record in October. A record deal, for God's sake, with a big label. Three years we'd been playing together, gig after gig, trying to get noticed. Finally we did. We hit the Holy Grail. We were going places, the big time, everything we'd been hoping for. Why would Monk leave and not come back?"

"Good question."

"I told Gloria I didn't believe her," Liam said. "I wanted to know where she got that story about Monk heading back to Louisiana. And I wanted to know where I could contact him. She told me she had no idea. I knew Monk was from Lake Charles, Louisiana. But he'd never been all that forthcoming about his family. I didn't know how to get in touch."

He frowned. "Damn it, I should have made more effort. But I was pissed off. So were the other guys in the band. Our big opportunity to cut a record, down the tubes. How could Monk do that to us, when we'd worked so hard to get to that point? And to me, his friend? Then I started to wonder why he didn't tell me he was going, why he never called. But I didn't go looking for him. Those were the days before the Internet, of course. I did a search, a few years back, on the web. Do you know how many people there are in Louisiana named Guidry? A bunch." He hesitated, as though he was about to say something else and thought better of it. Instead, he picked up his fork and cut off another bite of coffee cake.

I backtracked. "How long had you known him?"

Liam set down his fork. "I met him in 'sixty-six. He'd just come to San Francisco from Louisiana. He and I met one night at the Avalon. We went looking for a drummer and found Gene. He introduced us to Richie, the bass player. So, we were the Mad Monks, lining up gigs wherever we could." He laughed. "Wearing those crazy Russian shirts. Anita made those for us."

"I found a photo of the band." I took the printout from my bag and unfolded it, handing it to Liam.

He grinned. "Hey, I don't remember that picture. What a bunch of good-looking guys we were. So young. When was this taken?"

"February nineteen sixty-nine, according to the publication date. You were doing a gig at a club called the Beldame."

"The Beldame. Yeah, I remember that place. It was on Haight Street. We played there several times. The place was a dive. Really bad acoustics. But hey, as far as we were concerned, it was a paying gig, and that was all good."

I reached for the photo and pointed at the woman standing near the drummer. "Is this Gloria?"

Liam squinted behind his glasses. "Yeah, I think it is. Trying to put the moves on Gene."

"She told me she sang with the band."

Liam shrugged. "Yeah, off and on. So did Anita. Then Monk and Gloria broke up. Anita sang with us for a while. Then it was this girl Monk was dating." He shook his head. "Damned if I can remember her name."

"When did Monk and Gloria break up? And why?"

"They broke up sometime during that spring. As for why, who knows? They hadn't been getting along for a while, fighting, shouting matches. And the fallout was messy. They'd been living in a flat on Ashbury Street and Monk left. That's when Gloria moved to Alameda."

"You said when you went over to see her, she had a new boyfriend. Tell me about him."

He thought for a moment. "The guy was tall. About my height, and I'm six one. Well, used to be six one. This guy was maybe six feet, blond. Short hair. I thought, that's one for the books, Gloria took up with a sailor."

"How did you know he was a sailor?"

"I don't know for sure that he was," Liam said. "I just assumed. That house is a few blocks from the Navy base there in Alameda. I figured a lot of Gloria's tenants must be sailors. He had that look. The short haircut, I guess it was, at a time when most guys his age had long hair. And he was young, younger than her by a few years. I figured him for early twenties, but maybe he just had a baby face."

"Did you get a name?"

He shook his head. "No, didn't even hear him speak. He was just in the background when she answered the door, giving me the eye, like he was warning me to stay away from her."

"What happened to Monk after he and Gloria broke up and she moved out?"

"He crashed at my place for a while, but I was living with Anita at the time, and three's a crowd. Monk moved into a studio flat near the Panhandle. That was about the time he took up with his new girlfriend and she started singing with the band. I don't know where he met her, but Monk told us she had a great voice and we should give her a try. Turned out she was pretty good." He set his plate on the counter. "Monk and the new singer seemed happy. Then he was gone, and she was too. Didn't see her around and wondered if she'd moved on. Like I said, I don't recall her name. As for what she looked like, all I remember is long hair. She was like so many of the girls hanging around the Haight back then. Pretty little waifs."

"With flowers in their hair," I said, echoing the lyrics of a song from that era.

"Yeah, right." Judging from his expression, Liam wasn't hearing the same echo I was.

"What happened to the band after Monk disappeared?"

"We broke up, went our separate ways. Richie joined another band. Gene went down to LA, worked there for years, playing in other bands and as a studio musician. Richie's dead. Car accident back in the eighties. He was living in Santa Monica with his wife and two kids. Gene called to tell me and I drove down there for the funeral. I used to see Gene from time to time, but he moved to Montana."

"What about you? What did you do when the band broke up?"

"Anita and I decided it was time to move on from San Francisco. Things had really deteriorated," he added. I recalled Gloria's comment that after the Summer of Love ended, things went bad over in the Haight. Liam's next words underscored that. "Crime, drugs, a lot of stoned people squatting in buildings and OD'ing on the sidewalks. Now, I admit I smoked my share of weed back in the day. I'm not gonna cop to anything else." He smiled. "These days, I'm a respectable businessman, with a wife, kids and grandkids. Anita and I went up to Mendocino for a while. Played gigs, did some carpentry and woodworking. Then I decided I was done sowing the wild oats. By that time I'd met my wife, when I came home to visit my folks. Right here in Petaluma. We got married and here I am, fifty-plus years later."

A smile played at my lips. "But old guitarists never die."

"Of course not. I played guitar at a local bar on weekends. Still do, when the opportunity presents itself."

"Do you have any photos of Monk?" I asked.

"Probably. In a box somewhere at the top of a closet. I'd have to dig them out. I'll see what I can find, scan a few and email them to you. Anita's got pictures, too. She kept stuff like that." He paused. "Do you think those bones belong to Monk?"

"Too early to tell."

He took another swallow of coffee, a perplexed look on his face. "This is going to sound weird."

"Try me."

"When Monk disappeared, Anita was totally convinced he was dead."

"Who did she think was responsible?" I asked, wondering if I'd hear Gloria's name.

Liam grimaced. "The Zodiac."

That rocked me back on my heels. This was the second time the Zodiac Killer had come up. First time was last week, when I'd been doing research on the missing persons database and found out that Ann Lombardi and Eddie Baldwin had vanished on October 4, 1969. And now Monk Guidry, who had disappeared around the same time.

"Anita thought Monk was killed by the Zodiac?"

Liam nodded. "Still does. Me, I'm not sure. But there's got to be a reason he disappeared. After a while, I figured he was dead. Now, with those bones you found in the house . . . " His voice trailed off. "That doesn't make sense. Gloria is flaky, for sure. But not that flaky."

"I'd really like to talk with Anita."

"You're in luck. She's just down the road in Point Reyes Station."

"That works. It's about twenty miles over there. Would she be willing to talk with me?"

"Probably. Let me call her."

"Just tell her I want to talk about Monk. Don't bring up the Zodiac just yet. I want to ease my way into that one."

"Fair enough." He got up and pulled out his cell phone, walking toward the back door of the workroom that led out to a yard where lumber was stacked. I heard him talking on the phone. Then he turned and walked toward me, holding out the phone. He'd put it on speaker. "Here she is," Liam said.

"Hi, Jeri," Anita said. "Sure, I'll talk with you. Come on over."

# Fifteen

D Street ran southwest out of Petaluma, a two-lane road leading from Sonoma County to western Marin County, where it became the Point Reyes Petaluma Road. It meandered through rolling hills, sere and brown as they always were in the fall. Nicasio Reservoir, on the south side of the road, was low at this time of year. White-plumed great egrets waded in the shallows, searching for fish to eat. Past the reservoir, the road wound into the forested coastal hills, with green pines and oak trees blazing gold and bronze. I reached the junction where Platform Bridge spanned Nicasio Creek and took a right, crossing the bridge. A few miles on, the twisting road ended at Highway One.

The Point Reyes National Seashore is one of my favorite places to visit, great for hiking, birding, watching elephant seals at Chimney Rock or Drake's Beach, looking for migrating whales from the lighthouse. The Pacific Ocean forms the western boundary, while the east side of the point is long, narrow Tomales Bay, where the San Andreas fault runs into the ocean.

The small, unincorporated town of Point Reyes Station is here, above the marshes of Tomales Bay. Highway One, the Pacific Coast Highway, runs through it. At the junction, I turned left onto the highway and followed it into town, where another left turn took me into the heart of the small business district. The Bovine Bakery sign triggered a strong desire for one of the bakery's delectable morning buns. Though I suspected that in the middle of the day, all the morning buns would be gone.

Anita Ryker lived in a cottage near the corner of Third and B Streets. She'd told me I could find her in the detached garage that served as her workroom. There was no lawn; the area in front of the house was full of succulents and native grasses. The front porch held a comfortable-looking rocking chair, angled next to a trellis climbed by bright, flame-colored nasturtiums. Terra cotta pots held chrysanthemums in white, yellow and bronze. The porch railings were decorated with sea shells and strings of beads. A beautiful hummingbird feeder made of clear glass and decorated with red beads hung from the eaves.

I walked up the driveway to the workroom, where a woman sat on a wooden armchair with a cushioned seat. It was pulled up to a rectangular oak table, its surface scarred with years of use. Her attention was on the table, but as I approached, she looked up and smiled. "Hi, I'm Anita. Are you Jeri?"

"I am." I set one of my business cards on the table.

"Have a seat." She gestured toward an armchair in the corner, its floral upholstery faded and torn. I pulled over the chair, sat down and glanced at the workroom. Shelves lined the walls. To my right was a counter with a sink, a stainless steel electric kettle and a wooden box containing two mugs and several boxes of herbal tea. Next to the basket was a shallow ceramic bowl filled with fragrant, ripe apples. A wooden stand held three more hummingbird feeders similar to the one I'd seen hanging on the front porch. Each was slightly different in shape, the color of the glass and beads. I wanted one.

At the end of the counter was a small CD player. Music poured from it, filling the air with a familiar tune. "Joni Mitchell, *Court and Spark*. That's one of my favorites."

"Mine, too." Anita smiled. "Back when I had the LP, I played it over and over. The record is fine but the album jacket is held together with tape." She pointed at the large ceramic mug on the work table. "Can I offer you some tea? I drink it all day long."

"No, thanks."

Anita appeared to be in her late seventies. Her hair had once been brown. Now it was mostly silver, long and curly, a good six inches past her shoulders, somewhat tamed by oval silver barrettes at each temple. She wore a roomy pair of faded jeans and a pale blue pullover with three-quarter sleeves. Silver hoops threaded with crystal beads swung from her earlobes. She wore no makeup on her round face, just plenty of laugh lines around her wide mouth and blue eyes.

Liam had told me that Anita made jewelry. The table held three glass bowls filled with an assortment of beads, roughly sorted by size. They were all colors and shapes—bold reds, yellows and oranges, blues ranging from dark navy to pale sky, mossy greens and bright lime. Some were cloisonne, others were made of metal such as silver, pewter and brass. A square pottery dish held polished and faceted stones. I identified some of them—citron and rose quartz, green malachite, dark gray hematite, and black obsidian. The table also held a large rectangular wooden box. The handle on one side told me it had once been a drawer. Now it looked like a pirate's treasure box, half-filled with old jewelry. I saw bracelets and brooches with missing stones, bracelets with broken clasps and necklaces with damaged chains.

The reason for this cache of discards became clear as Anita reached into a large tool box on the right site of the table. It was divided into compartments, some of them hinged for easy access to the bottom of the box. The contents included all sorts of fittings and fasteners, as well as wire, and three different kinds of pliers. The tool that she picked up now was a wire cutter. She had a light blue cloth spread out on the table, holding a bracelet that was missing a clasp. The bracelet appeared to be gold, set with eight small green squares.

I gestured at the drawer filled with jewelry. "I gather that's the reason for the treasure box. Is that jade?"

She chuckled. "Treasure box indeed. Yes, this is jade, nephrite. And the setting is pure gold. I found it in a bin at a thrift store. You'd be surprised what I find at thrift stores. And antique stores. Estate sales are great for this stuff. A lot of costume jewelry of course, sometimes some real finds. This was definitely a find."

Wire cutters in hand, Anita dismembered the bracelet, carefully cutting apart the pieces. She set the gold filigree setting to one side and lined up the jade squares. "I'm going to make a necklace and matching earrings," she explained. "Two sets, which will take six squares. As for the other two, I haven't decided. Maybe earrings. I like to take old things, tarnished and broken, and use them to create something new. Here's a piece I made yesterday."

She reached into a small wooden box and pulled out an oval pendant, with a dark purple amethyst set in gold. She handed it to me. I turned it over in my hands and saw that it was signed, the initials AR engraved on the back, small but still readable. I handed it back to her. "It's beautiful."

"Thanks." She put the pendant in the box and leaned back in her chair. "Liam said you wanted to talk about Monk. And this has something to do with those bones that were found in the house in Alameda. Gloria's house. I heard about that on the news."

"Yes, the bones. Quite a sensation, for a few days. The news cycle has moved on, which is just as well." I settled back in my chair. "I want more information on Monk. I'd also like to get a better sense of Gloria, and her relationship with Monk."

Anita gave me a wry smile. "You've talked with Gloria?"

"I have. I got the impression I wasn't getting the full story."

"I doubt anyone knows the full story. Especially Gloria. She's one for selective memory. I suppose we all are, come right down to it. Let's just say I remember things differently than she does."

"Tell me what you remember."

"Sure." She set down the tool she was holding and leaned over, reaching under the table. She pulled out a box covered in purple fabric and straightened, setting it on the table. "I grabbed this from the closet after Liam called. Photos from the old days. I keep telling myself I should have this stuff digitized, but I haven't yet. It was a long time ago. A lot of these snapshots are so faded you can barely see who's in them."

She removed the lid and took out several smaller envelopes that held photos and negatives, the kind you'd receive when you had a roll of film developed, back before the digital age.

I peered at a snapshot showing a young woman with strands of beads twined in her long brown hair. "Is that you?"

Anita laughed. "That is indeed me. Fifty plus years ago, a few pounds lighter, and no gray in my hair. Though I still have beads." Her face took on a faraway look as she sifted through the faded snapshots, pulling out one after another. She held up one that showed a young couple, the man dressed in tight jeans and the woman in a tie-dye tunic over plum velvet pants. It was a street scene and in the background I saw a vertical marquee reading AVALON.

She looked at the back of the photo, where a date and had been scribbled. "This is Liam and me, outside the Avalon. It was taken in May of nineteen sixty-six. And this one—" She reached for another photo. "This one is inside the Avalon, near the stage. If you really squint at the background, you'll see Janis Joplin." She pointed at a dim figure with wild hair. I couldn't tell it was Joplin, but I'd take her word for it.

I took out the photo I'd printed from the article. "Here's a picture I found online."

She took it from me, examining the grainy, blurred shot. "Where was this? Wait, let me think. The Beldame, on Haight Street."

I nodded. "Liam said it was a dive."

Anita laughed. "Oh, yes, it was. A lot of those places were." Her finger tapped a figure just visible on the left side on the photo. "That's me."

I indicated the woman on the right, her hand on the drummer's shoulder. "And that's Gloria."

"So it is." Anita's voice was lukewarm. It was clear she didn't much care for Gloria, not then and not now. "Looks like she's putting the moves on Gene, the drummer. Which doesn't surprise me in the least."

"Liam said the same thing."

"She was always doing that," Anita said. "Flirting with the men. Even Liam, and she knew we were together." She sounded irritated by this, even after all these years. She sifted through the pile of photos in the box and handed it to me. "Here's a picture of Monk. This is a better likeness."

"It is." Faded as it was, the snapshot was clear enough that I could see more details, the curly dark hair brushing Monk's shoulders and a square face dominated by a luxuriant handlebar mustache. Was his complexion sallow, or was it the quality of the old picture? I couldn't tell. He was dressed in the obligatory tight jeans, wearing a red shirt with blousy sleeves, decorated with gold embroidery on the neck and cuffs. It looked like a traditional Russian tunic, in keeping with the band's name.

"I made the shirts for the band members," Anita said. "Russian Cossack shirts. In several colors. I really liked that one, with the red and gold." She sorted through the photos and came up with another one, handing it to me. This one showed Monk in jeans and a shirt. The woman with him was Gloria, a smile on her face, her hair light brown, long and parted in the middle. She wore a bronze velvet vest and a long swirly green skirt.

"Gloria again," I said. "I understand she sang with the band."

"So did I." Anita tossed her head, setting her beaded earrings in motion. "I had a pretty good voice back then. Better than hers, believe me." She spread three more photos on the table surface. "This is the band. That's Richie, the bass player, on the left and Gene Prager on drums. Monk's there. And that's Liam."

I examined the photos, seeing the band members in different colored shirts this time, blue and green as well as red.

"It was a crazy time," she said. "Exhilarating, exasperating, wonderfully creative. With a dark side, of course. That's why we left, the dark side won out over the light. The band had a deal to cut a record. I'm sure Liam told you that. When Monk disappeared, the deal fell through and the band broke up. Liam and I left the Bay Area after that. There was no point in staying. The scene in San Francisco had changed, a lot. The whole hippie-counterculture thing had been going downhill for a couple of years by then. Then came the Zodiac. People were spooked."

She paused for a sip of tea. "We decided it was time to leave. We packed up our stuff and headed for Mendocino. That was November of 'sixty-nine. I remember we spent Thanksgiving with friends who had a cabin on the Big River." She smiled. "I loved Mendocino, still do. There's a big arts community up there. I felt right at home. We had a little cottage and I had a studio at the art center. But in the end, Mendocino was too remote for Liam. We split up. He came back to the Bay Area. Well, Sonoma County. Joined the family carpentry business in Petaluma, got married, had kids. He's a grandfather now. And I'm a grandmother, too. Hard to believe." She shook her head.

"You got married, too?"

"Not married. Just had a baby." She smiled. "A daughter. With another guy, not Liam. She's all grown up and has two kids of her own. Anyway, I stayed in Mendocino for another twelve years."

"What brought you back?" I asked.

"Elderly parents. We've all been there, right? Mine were in Novato. After my dad had a heart attack, I decided I needed to be closer. That's when I moved to Point Reyes Station. After all those years in Mendocino, I have to be near the ocean. And at my age, access to good medical care is important. My parents are gone now, but my daughter and grandkids are up in Santa Rosa. So this is a good location for me."

"Back to Monk. When did you meet him?"

"Summer of 'sixty-six." She paused in her beading and reached for the mug, taking a sip of tea. "Monk and Liam had already started the band, the Mad Monks. The other guys were Richie and Gene." She set down the mug and tapped one of the band photos with a finger. "I'm sure Liam told you that. The band was playing gigs in the city. I went with some friends to a place in the Fillmore and they were on the bill. I was attracted to Liam right away. Monk wasn't my type, but he seemed really nice. He was with Gloria then. She was singing with the band. She had aspirations of being the next Janis Joplin." Anita pulled a face that told me what she thought of that.

"I take it you didn't like Gloria."

Anita paused, her fingers moving over the jade pieces. Then she looked down at the snapshot that showed Monk and Gloria. She sighed. "Well, I thought she was okay, at first. Pushy, full of herself." She sipped tea. "But later, she showed her true colors. She turned out to be a greedy, selfish bitch. And she had a roving eye. She was always looking at other guys, flirting, fooling around. And yet, when Monk broke up with her, she really went off the rails. Petty vindictive stuff. Monk moved out and what he didn't take with him, she threw into the street, screaming like a harpy, from all accounts. He stayed with us, temporarily, then he got a place of his own."

"When did Monk and Gloria break up?" I asked.

She thought for a moment. "It was in the spring, April, I think. Next thing I heard was that she moved to Alameda and bought that house. Which surprised me. I mean, why Alameda, of all places? And where in the world did she get money to buy a house? She wasn't working, not to my knowledge. She must have gotten a loan from her family."

But Glenda, Gloria's sister, said that wasn't the case.

"And she certainly didn't get it from Monk. They were on the outs by then. Besides, he was a musician." She laughed. "Where would a broke-ass guitar player get money for the down payment on a house? If Monk had come into any money, he would have used it to buy another guitar. Or an amplifier. Or even a new car, since he was driving a ratty-ass old Chevy Impala that he drove out here from Louisiana. That's the thing about guitar players, you know, they're never satisfied with having just one guitar."

I smiled. "Liam said much the same thing."

"Hah! Liam's a guitar player. He should know. When we were together, he never went anywhere without at least two guitars. He told me it's because each different guitar has its own unique sound, so it depends on what kind of music the guitarist is playing. It really is a condition peculiar to guitar players." She peered at her cup. "I need a warm up."

She got up from the chair and dumped the remains of her tea onto a plant, then poured water from the electric kettle over a new teabag. Then she sat down again.

"When I talked with Gloria," I said, "she mentioned going to a rock festival in May of nineteen sixty-nine and implied she went with Monk. It was in San Jose and Jimi Hendrix was one of the performers. But she broke up with Monk in April, before she bought the house. So the festival would would have been a month later."

"That festival she's talking about was at the Santa Clara County Fairgrounds, late May, and yes, it was after Monk and Gloria broke up. Monk, Liam and I were there, and so was Monk's new girlfriend, the one who'd started singing with the band. We did run into Gloria. She was with someone else, a new guy. He looked younger than her. Tall, blond, really short hair. I wondered if he was one of the sailors from the base who rented a flat at the house. He had that look about him."

I nodded. This was similar to what Liam had told me, about going to the Alameda house to ask Gloria about Monk. There had been a man with her, possibly a tenant, in her living room. Liam had assumed he was a sailor because of his short haircut and the house's proximity to the Navy base.

"Did Gloria introduce the guy?" I asked.

Anita shook her head. "No. We said hello. She gave us a look and cut us dead. She was being a bitch. She didn't like seeing Monk with his new girl. As for the guy, she definitely didn't introduce him. But—" She hesitated. "They were walking away from us and she said something to him. I thought it was his name. What was it?" She shook her head. "Sorry, I can't remember. Maybe it will come to me."

"You have my card. If you remember, call me. Monk's new girlfriend—what was her name?"

"She called herself Sunflower."

I smiled. "Now that's a sixties hippie name if I ever heard one."

She laughed. "I know, I know. It was the thing back then. I can't tell you what her real name was. If I ever knew it. She said to call her Sunflower, so we did. Later it was just Sunny. Gloria didn't take it well. She was really possessive, the whole time she was with Monk. Remember, this was the sixties. Drugs, sex, rock 'n roll, and all that. People moved in and out of relationships all the time. Liam and I were together for about five years, off and on. We both had flings with other people. But we kept getting back together."

"Gloria told me that she and Monk split up because, as she put it, they had both moved on."

Anita shook her head. "Hah! That may be what she's saying now, but back then, Gloria was royally pissed off at Monk. She thought they were going to stay together. At some point during the relationship, Monk gave Gloria a ring. It was a present, not a commitment. It wasn't a diamond, but a deep blue sapphire in an old-style white gold setting. It was a beautiful ring. I think Monk found it in an antique store. Art Deco, as I recall. But Gloria didn't like it. She made fun of it, called it a tacky old thing with a tiny stone. So Monk said, fine, give it back. She wouldn't. Typical Gloria. That woman is defined by her peccadilloes and oddities."

"Did Monk ever get the ring?"

She shook her head. "I doubt it. I'll bet Gloria still has that ring, the one she didn't even like. She kept it, just to prove a point or make Monk mad, take your pick. She blamed Sunny for the breakup, but that's not true. Monk and Gloria split up before Monk met Sunny."

"Tell me more about Sunny. What was she like? How did they meet? And when?"

Anita thought for a moment, a slight smile curving her lips as she remembered. "She was sweet. A really bright, good-natured kid. I say she was a kid. She told us she was in her twenties, but I think she was younger. There was just something about her, fresh and a bit naive. And she was obviously quite smitten with Monk. It was sometime in the spring of 'sixty-nine. As for how they met, I'm not sure. My guess is she was hanging around the clubs and the bands, looking for an opportunity to sing. Monk brought her to a rehearsal one day and suggested that the band try her out, let her sing with them for a set. She gave it a go, the band liked her, and so it went."

"She had a good voice. That's what Liam told me."

Anita nodded. "Better than good. More Laura Nyro than Janis Joplin. I was a better singer than Gloria, that's for sure. Sunny had the potential." Anita's laugh was rueful. "Oh, to be that young again. Sunny was green around the edges. And starstruck, thrilled to be over in the city where everything was happening. Singing with the band and going to gigs. We were a bit jaded by it all at that point. But to Sunny, it was new and wonderful. She enjoyed every minute of it."

She sighed, hands wrapped around the mug. "Roads not taken. I'll always wonder. If, if, if— The Mad Monks were good. If Monk hadn't disappeared, if the band had been able to follow through on that recording contract, well, I'll always wonder what might have happened. But that's pointless, isn't it? It didn't happen. The band broke up and we all moved on. Except Monk and Sunny. She dropped off the radar the same time he did. I have this image of them, frozen in time way back then. I suppose that's why I think they're both dead. Something happened to them. I'd certainly like to know what it was."

"So would I. Did Sunny ever say anything about her past, her family?"

Anita tilted her head to one side. "She said she'd been out on her own for a while. I had my doubts about that, but on the other hand, but maybe she had." She paused. "Come to think of it, she once told me she was a Navy brat, traveling all over the country with her family."

That brought me up short. "A Navy brat? Do you have any pictures of her?"

"I think so." Anita set down her mug and reached for the box that held the photos. She sifted through the packets until she found what she was looking for. She held up two faded snapshots. One showed a young woman with straight blond hair tumbling down her shoulders. The other showed Monk and Sunny together, his arm around her shoulder, dark hair touching light. He wore a flowered shirt open and the collar and she had on a gauzy lilac tunic.

"I made those pendants they're wearing," Anita said, pointing at the photo of Monk and Sunny together. "I found this cool bracelet in a second-hand store. It had oval onyx pieces set in gold, with small gold fleur-de-lis glued onto the onyx. Monk really loved it because of the fleur-de-lis, the Louisiana connection. I took the bracelet apart and made the pendants, one for each of them. I engraved their initials on the back and he gave that pendant to Sunny."

I took the photos from Anita. "Do you have a magnifier?"

"I certainly do. I use it in my work all the time." Anita reached into her box of tools and utensils and pulled out a folding magnifier with a base and a light. She unfolded it and set it on the table.

I used the magnifier to examine the snapshots, noting the onyx pendants. But it was the faces that interested me most. I set down the photos and reached into my bag, pulling out a folded sheet of paper, the printout of a page from a website. Without a word, I unfolded it.

She took the paper and stared at it. Her eyes widened. "Oh, my God."

I took the snapshot and the printout from Anita, holding them side by side for comparison. It was the same woman, no doubt about it.

"Her name was Martha Post," I said. "She was eighteen. She graduated from high school earlier that year. Her family reported her missing in June nineteen sixty-nine. They told the police she had a habit of running away and hanging out in the Haight. They, and the police, assumed that Martha had run away, again."

"Holy crap," Anita said, her voice subdued. "And Monk disappeared in September. That's the last time I saw Sunny. She wasn't around and I heard a rumor she'd gone to LA, singing with another band."

"Is it possible they went away together?"

Anita shook her head, frowning. "I don't think they went away. I think they were murdered, both of them. It had to be the Zodiac."

I sat back in the chair. Now we were getting to it. Liam had told me Anita was convinced that the infamous serial killer was involved. "Zodiac left bodies for other people to find," I pointed out. "And he usually claimed credit for the murders."

"Not always," she said. "There was that letter he wrote in the fall, where he said he was going to make his murders look like routine crimes or accidents."

True enough. The letter Anita referred to had been received on November 7, nearly a month after the Paul Stine murder in San Francisco. But I wasn't as convinced as she was that the disappearance of Monk Guidry and his girlfriend Sunny could be laid at the elusive feet of the Zodiac.

"Tell me about Monk's disappearance. What happened?"

"Monk disappeared in September," she said. "Look at the timing. There was a Zodiac attack on the Fourth of July and the next one that we know about, that he claimed credit for, happened in late September. And Monk just disappeared. None of the band members knew where he went. Liam kept calling Gloria and he finally went over to the house. That's when she told him Monk went to Louisiana. But I'm not buying that, then or now. If Monk had done that, he would have told Liam, not Gloria." She shook her head, frowning. "What happened to them? And why? Even though it's been more than fifty years, I wonder. And I'd like to know."

I nodded. "So would I."

# Sixteen

I BOUGHT ONE OF Anita's beautiful glass and bead hummingbird feeders before I left. After stashing my purchase in my car, I walked over to the Bovine Bakery and snagged the last morning bun in the display case. I sat on the bench outside, enjoying my pastry with a cup of coffee. When I finished, I wiped the sticky residue from my hands and deposited the napkin in a nearby trash can.

Then I took out my phone and called the Alameda Police Department. Bradley Chen was in his office. "I'd like to get an update on your investigation. Any chance I can stop by later?"

"Sure," he said. "I'm free now. But I have a meeting in about forty minutes."

"I'm in west Marin. It's nearly one. Depending on traffic, I could be in Alameda in a couple of hours. Three or after?"

"Let me see." He paused, checking his schedule. "Three-thirty would work for me."

"Okay. See you then."

Back in my car, I got on the road again, retracing my route as far as the reservoir. This time I turned and drove southeast through the little town of Nicasio, then onto Lucas Valley Road. The two-lane road wound through the tall coastal redwoods and over the undulating hills, heading toward Highway 101 and San Rafael.

As I drove, I considered what I'd learned. Monk had disappeared in September 1969, at an inopportune time, blowing the band's record deal. Liam certainly didn't think Monk had gone back to Louisiana, no matter what Gloria told him. And Anita's explanation for the guitarist's sudden disappearance was that he'd fallen prey to the Zodiac killer. I wasn't sure I bought that. But there was the timing. Monk vanished in the middle of the Zodiac's 1969 killing spree—it might have some validity.

Then there was Martha Post. The teenager reported as a probable runaway turned out to be Sunny, Monk's new girlfriend. She had dropped out of sight for good about the same time Monk did.

Lucas Valley Road widened as I reached the outskirts of San Rafael. At Highway 101, I took the southbound on ramp. This was where the traffic usually clogged and today was no exception. Finally I made my way over the Richmond-San Rafael Bridge to the East Bay. It was a quarter past three when I reached Alameda.

The Alameda Police Department stood at the corner of Oak Street and Lincoln Avenue, across from the new library. New, in that the building was constructed and opened in the twenty-first century. Before that, the library was housed in a small but beautiful old building dating to 1903, built with a grant from the Andrew Carnegie Foundation. The old library still stood at the corner of Oak and Santa Clara. I hoped that someday it would be repurposed, perhaps turned into a museum.

I parked on Oak and fed the meter, then walked back to the red brick APD building and went up the front steps. I rang the buzzer at a window near the front door. An officer appeared at the window. I held up one of my business cards. "Lieutenant Chen is expecting me."

Ten minutes later, I was in Chen's office, taking a seat in a chair opposite his cluttered desk. It was the first time I'd seen the lieutenant since that Saturday when I'd found the bones.

"Noel Benjamin and Lakshmi Srinivasan have hired me to look into this matter," I said. "Of course, I'll take care not to get in your way."

Chen leaned back in his chair. "I have no objection to you conducting your own investigation. I figured you would, given that you found the bones. I'll share information with you, up to a point, as long as it doesn't interfere. I just hope that if you find out any information, you'll share it."

"I will." In fact, I was going to tell him about Martha Post, aka Sunny. But I wanted to get his update first. "Have you found out anything about the bones?"

He tapped a finger on a nearby file folder. "I heard from the medical examiner. We have two sets of bones mingled together in that footlocker. One male, one female."

"Any idea how old the bones are? They looked as though they'd been buried for a while."

"No determination as to age. Just that they were in the ground for a long time, which accounts for the discoloration. Then at some point they were dug up and transferred to the footlocker."

"What about the feathers that were mixed in with the bones? I took photos of those and sent them to my dad. He's a birder. I've since talked with him. He identified the larger feather as that of a California gull. The smaller feather is from a least tern. An endangered species. And there's a colony on the old air station, between two of the runways."

Chen nodded. "You're right about the feathers, on both counts. In addition to the feathers, dirt, rocks and plant detritus were mixed in with the bones. And a couple of other things."

A look flashed briefly on his face and I wondered just what those other things were. Something that could identify the bodies? Such as the metal disk I'd glimpsed at the bottom of the footlocker?

He went on. "We're looking at the possibility that the original burial site was at the Navy base, near the least tern colony."

"The bodies could have been buried while the base was open," I said, "and the feathers mixed in when the bodies were dug up. Though burying a couple of bodies would have been difficult back when the base was open. There were people around, all the time. It would have been easier once the base closed. What about identification of the remains?"

"We hope to get some DNA samples, though the coroner's bureau tells me if the bones have been in the ground for a long time, the chances of DNA are slim. We can use dental records, of course. Once we get an idea of whose remains they are."

"My guess is that you're looking at people who've been reported missing from Alameda or the East Bay. Though it could be farther. People who bury bodies have been known to transport them to other locations. But two bodies. That would be difficult to move without attracting attention. So, I'm thinking closer to Alameda. In fact, I searched the California Department of Justice missing persons database, looking for missing persons cases reported by the Alameda Police Department."

"And you found Ann Lombardi and Eddie Baldwin," Chen said. "Reported missing in October nineteen sixty-nine."

"I found a lot of articles speculating that they were victims of the Zodiac killer."

"The timing certainly makes me wonder. I pulled the files out of storage." He pointed at a stack of bankers boxes on the floor next to his desk.

"Give me the short version." I knew the details from the articles I'd read, but I wanted to get his perspective.

Chen laced his hands together and leaned back in his chair. "Ann Lombardi was a local girl, twenty years old. Her boyfriend was a sailor named Eddie Baldwin. He was twenty-two, stationed at the base. They had been dating for several months. On Saturday, October fourth, they went to a movie. And vanished. That was the last time anyone saw them. The stories tying their disappearance in with the Zodiac started right away. Young couple out on a date, plus it had been just a week since those two people were attacked at Lake Berryessa."

"And a week later, the cabdriver was killed in San Francisco," I said.

The Zodiac killer had targeted young couples, at least among his known victims. The cabdriver was the anomaly, a lone man who had picked up a fare who then shot him. I could see how the disappearance of Ann Lombardi and Eddie Baldwin fit the pattern. They were a young couple out on a date like several of the other victims.

But — "Zodiac's victims were shot or stabbed."

"The couple in Benicia were shot," he said. "So were the couple in Vallejo and the guy in San Francisco. The two people at Lake Berryessa were stabbed."

"One of the skulls in the footlocker had a crack. That made me think the victim was bludgeoned."

"The other skull also showed signs of blunt force trauma," Chen said. "There was other damage to the bones as well. Did it happen at the time of death? Or were the bones damaged later? I'm waiting for the medical examiner to answer those questions."

"You mentioned a couple of other things mixed in with the bones. There was something metal at the bottom of the footlocker. I took a photos of it. There was a hole at one end, as though it had been on a necklace or a charm bracelet, and some engraving I couldn't make out."

Chen hesitated. "The metal item found with the bones might be something we can use to identify the remains. Right now we're focusing on Ann and Eddie. We're in the process of getting dental records."

I nodded. "Thanks for the information. Now, I'm going to tell you something that might rain on that parade. I've learned about two other people who disappeared in the same time frame. One of them was a man named Louis Guidry, known as Monk. He was a musician, had a rock band called the Mad Monks. At one time he was involved with Gloria Rossiter, the woman who owns the house where I found the bones. He supposedly left town in September nineteen sixty-nine to visit his home state of Louisiana, but I'm not sure he did. None of his California friends heard from him again. In fact, they were upset about his disappearance. Liam Ebbets, a former band member, told me the Mad Monks had a recording contract. They were set to cut an album that October, but the deal fell through because Monk disappeared."

I paused, then went on. "I've contacted an investigator I know in New Orleans, to see if he can track down any information on Monk. I have a feeling Gloria is not particularly reliable, based on my one conversation with her. She's good at spinning tales. Also good at avoiding questions she doesn't want to answer."

"Who's the other person who went missing?"

"When Monk split up with Gloria, he took up with another young woman who also sang with the band. She called herself Sunflower, Sunny for short. But her real name was Martha Post. She was reported missing in June nineteen sixty-nine."

Chen sat up in his chair. "I came across the name when I was looking at old missing persons cases. Eighteen-year-old, father an officer at the Naval Air Station. She was reported as a possible runaway."

"I believe she ran away, to San Francisco. She was in the Haight, living with Monk and singing in the band. According to Anita Ryker, another of Monk's friends, Sunny disappeared about the same time Monk did. Maybe she went away with him, if he did indeed go to Louisiana. Or maybe something else happened. Anita heard rumors that Sunny had gone to LA."

I reached into my bag and pulled out the printout of the missing persons listing, and the photo that I'd gotten from Anita. "This is Sunny."

Chen examined both, then looked up, with a wry smile. "Thanks, you just made my job a lot more interesting. Let me make copies of these. Then I'll dig out that file on Martha Post."

---

I HEADED BACK TO my office. Since I had been out most of the day, I had plenty to do before I called it a day. Despite the legwork and the interviews, there's always paperwork, though these days much of it was computerized.

Before I got started, though, I called and left a message for Lloyd Humphrey, the former NCIS agent. He called back half an hour later.

"I'm still working on that information you sent to me," he said. "I'll be in touch when I have something."

"Thanks. I have a name for you, one that could be related to this investigation. Edward Baldwin." After my conversation with Lieutenant Chen, the details were fresh in my mind. "Baldwin was a sailor stationed at the Alameda Naval Air Station. He was reported missing in October nineteen sixty-nine."

"How does he figure into this?" Humphrey asked.

"That might be him in the footlocker. Or not. Suddenly I have a lot of candidates for that role." I gave Lloyd the details.

"That's quite a story," he said. "Baldwin would have been reported AWOL, absent without leave. There would have been an investigation on the Navy side. I'll look for that."

Paperwork, I thought, after ending the call. I had lots to do.

I spent the next hour or so working on other matters of business. I finally got to a stopping place. I was ready to wrap things up and go home.

Instead, I was drawn back to the Internet and those missing persons reports.

The information available on Martha Post's June disappearance was minimal when compared with the news coverage about Ann Lombardi and Eddie Baldwin in October. The speculation that the Zodiac killer had murdered the young couple was a potent brew guaranteed to generate lots of headlines.

Martha, on the other hand, was a possible runaway. When her parents reported her missing, they told the police that she had done it before. Several times in the past, Martha had left home and stayed away, turning up days later at the home of a relative or a friend. And in the six months before she disappeared, she had been leaving home for few days at a time, hanging out in the Haight with the other hippies.

Then Martha left, and she stayed missing. Her family never heard from her again.

She was eighteen when she disappeared. And it was the sixties. I could guess what the official reaction had been. Another lost flower child, a hippie, taking to the road as so many kids had back then. Since she was female, I could imagine the dismissive comments about the girl shacked up somewhere with her boyfriend. I'd heard those comments and assumptions before, more recently than 1969.

Did Martha's family, or the police, know she had a boyfriend? If they did, did they know he was a rock musician named Monk Guidry? Would they have tried to contact Monk in San Francisco? I didn't have answers, and wouldn't unless I searched for them. Lieutenant Chen planned on digging out the original file on Martha's missing persons case and said he'd share information with me, if he could.

Was Monk dead? Or alive and living somewhere in his home state of Louisiana? I hoped Antoine Lasalle, my contact in New Orleans, would be able to find some Guidry family members willing to talk with me.

During our conversation in Point Reyes Station, Anita Ryker told me she thought the Zodiac had killed Monk Guidry and his girlfriend Sunny, who turned out to be Martha. I wasn't convinced, despite the timing.

Henry Post was a lieutenant commander in the Navy when his oldest child Martha went missing. I located an obituary that told me he had retired as a captain from a command at North Island Naval Air Station, near San Diego, and he'd stayed in the area. Not surprising, as that gave him access to the Balboa Naval Medical Center as well as other amenities available to military retirees. He was survived by his wife Esther and three children, Frank, Sarah and George. No mention of Martha. By the time Henry died, 30-plus years had passed since Martha's disappearance. Given the grim statistics about missing persons, it was likely that she was dead.

I went looking for Esther's obituary and found it. She had remained in the family home after her husband's death. Her younger children lived in other states, but Frank was in Southern California at the time, having followed his father into a Navy career. At the time his mother died, he was stationed at Miramar Naval Air Station.

Frank, too, had retired as a captain, according to the article I found. He'd stayed in the San Diego area, He was active in a number of organizations, including the Rotary Club and the Friends of the San Diego Public Library. With some digging, I tracked down an address and phone number in the Mission Hills neighborhood. A recording invited me to leave a message and I did, identifying myself as a private investigator, adding that I had questions about his sister Martha.

I glanced at the clock. It was time to go home. I called Dan. "I'm ready to leave the office. Any thoughts about dinner?"

"Pizza from Zachary's?"

"Sounds good to me. Call in the order and I'll swing by there on my way home."

I left the office, heading out the back door to my car. As I slid into the driver's seat, my phone rang. I pulled it out and looked at the caller ID. I didn't recognize the number, but I recognized the area code—San Diego.

I answered and identified myself.

The man's voice was gruff. "This is Frank Post. I'm returning your call. What's this about? My sister went missing over fifty years ago."

How much should I tell him? At this point I had no way of knowing whether the bones I'd found were those of his sister. It could be that he wasn't interested in the past and would find my questions intrusive.

"I'm working on a case in the Bay Area," I said. "Human bones were found in a house in Alameda."

His voice was at once resigned and hopeful. "Is it Martha?"

"The bones haven't been identified yet. The person in charge of the investigation is Lieutenant Bradley Chen of the Alameda Police Department. He's looking into missing persons cases in Alameda and I'm sure he'd like to talk with you. So would I."

After a brief silence, he spoke again. "You and Lieutenant Chen are in luck. My wife and I are flying to the Bay Area tomorrow. We're visiting our daughter and her family. They live in Fremont. I can meet the following day. And arrange to talk with Lieutenant Chen in person."

"That would be great, Mr. Post. Let me give you his number at the Alameda PD." I recited the number and he repeated it back to me. That done, I said, "As for meeting with me, Fremont's a big city. If you'll tell me your daughter's neighborhood, I can suggest a location."

"Call me Frank," he said. "My daughter lives in Niles, near the Alameda Creek Trail and an old railroad that runs on weekends and during the holidays. They used to make movies there."

"I know it well. There's a coffee shop on Niles Boulevard, across from the old depot. Day after tomorrow, then. Would 10 AM work for you?"

"It would."

"Great." I gave him the name of the place. "By the way, if you have photos of Martha and the family, I'd really like to see those."

"I have pictures," he said. "Lots of them. I'll bring them with me."

"Thanks. I'll see you then."

I ended the call and then checked my email.

Maggie Constable, the *San Francisco Chronicle* reporter who'd written about the disappearance of Ann Lombardi and Eddie Baldwin, was back in town. Could I meet her tomorrow? Yes, I definitely could.

# Seventeen

UC Berkeley's North Gate, marked by two tall pillars, wasn't as busy as South Gate, which opened onto Sproul Plaza. That site was in front of the administration building and had been the scene of so many gatherings through the years, all the way back to the Free Speech Movement and antiwar demonstrations of the 1960s.

Southside was busy, with Telegraph Avenue and the surrounding streets. Here on the northside, Euclid Avenue dead-ended at Hearst. Both streets were lined with cafes and coffee shops catering to the campus population. As I watched, a university shuttle bus pulled up to the stop just below the intersection and disgorged people, students mostly, some staff and professors added to the mix. Some headed into campus, down the slope that led to Memorial Glade and the library. Others headed across Hearst to Euclid, where they bought coffee and pastries to see them through the morning.

I turned from the street and walked toward the steps leading up to the west entrance of North Gate Hall. The brown-shingled building, dating to the early part of the twentieth century, was a Berkeley landmark. I'd found a photo of Maggie Constable on the Graduate School of Journalism's website, so I recognized the woman who walked through the front door a few minutes before ten. She headed down the steps toward me. She was short, an inch or so over five feet tall, with a compact, stocky body dressed in dark gray slacks and a lightweight gray jacket over a slate blue shirt. Her curly brown hair brushed her shoulders. As she drew closer I could see lots of gray mixed with the brown.

"Jeri Howard?" She tilted her head up, her eyes hazel behind a pair of wire-rimmed glasses.

"Yes," I said, handing her a business card. "And you're Maggie Constable."

"Call me Maggie."

"Thanks for taking the time to talk with me."

"I was intrigued by your email. It's been a long time since anyone asked me about Ann Lombardi and Eddie Baldwin." She gestured toward the street. "Let's get some coffee."

We joined a group of students waiting for the light to change. Euclid Avenue sloped upward, heading into the northside neighborhood. We dodged other pedestrians as we made our way up the street, passing a Mexican restaurant and a sandwich shop. Maggie led the way into a coffee shop, where I inhaled the aroma of fresh ground coffee.

"On me," I said. "What will you have? Coffee and a mid-morning nosh?"

"Thanks, I'll take a latte. And a mid-morning nosh would be great. I'm partial to the cranberry scones."

Maggie grabbed a small corner table as I queued up at the counter. A few minutes later, I returned to the table, bearing coffees and scones—cranberry for her, lemon for me. We settled in for a talk.

"I've read about you," Maggie said. "You were instrumental in solving that murder over on the waterfront. And those arson fires in Oakland."

"I've read about you, too." I'd looked her up once I found her articles. "You started working for the *San Francisco Chronicle* in nineteen seventy-four. It must have been fascinating, at the *Chron* in the seventies. The Hearst kidnapping, the Symbionese Liberation Army, and everything that happened afterward. Plus the Milk-Moscone murders, the Peoples Temple, and Jonestown."

Was it my imagination, or had a flicker passed over her face? Perhaps the mention of those times called forth memories that she'd rather stayed in the past.

She nodded. "Puts me in mind of that phrase, 'may you live in interesting times.' I have at that."

"You went to school at the University of Colorado."

"That's right. Bachelor's degree in news-editorial journalism. It was the School of Journalism back then." She rolled her eyes. "The powers-that-be downgraded it to a department a few years back. That really pissed me off. I can tell you, the practice of journalism has changed drastically, what with the Internet. I remember the first job I ever had, right out of J school. It was a small-town daily in Colorado and I was typing copy on a Smith-Corona manual. That newspaper isn't there anymore. Newspapers keep disappearing. The *Rocky Mountain News* in Denver went out of business after a hundred and fifty years in print. Anyway, I moved on, to San Francisco." She smiled. "Small-town reporter hits the big city. I got the job at the *Chron*. I was there for a long time. Still have my hand in, writing articles now and then."

She took another bite of her scone and chased it with a sip of coffee. "So, what's your interest in a couple of articles I wrote about a missing persons case from the sixties?"

"Something that's been in the news the past few days. A story about some bones found in an old house in Alameda. I'm the one who found them."

She set her cup on the table. "Yes, I did see the story. Intriguing. Why were you there? An investigation?"

"I wasn't there in an official capacity, not at the time, anyway. My fiancé and I were helping friends inventory the contents of the house, which is owned by a family member who has moved to a senior apartment complex. I found the bones in a footlocker that had been stashed in a storeroom."

"Are you in an official capacity now?"

I nodded. "Looking into it, as a favor for the friends."

"Tell me about the bones. Any theories?"

"I got a good look at the contents of that footlocker. I also took photos. In addition to bones, there were pebbles, clods of dirt, feathers from seagulls and one from a least tern. I also saw a bit of metal, round, about the size of a quarter. There was dirt stuck to it, but it was engraved. Here are the pictures." I pulled out my phone and clicked into the photos, finding the shots. "Some of them are a bit blurry. As for that piece of metal, that engraving looks like a Navy anchor."

I handed the phone to Maggie. She used her fingers to scroll through the photos, enlarging the one with the metal disk. "Yes, I think you're right. That could be an anchor. So, possibly a connection with the Navy base. What do the police say?" She handed back the phone and I set it on the table.

"Lieutenant Chen at the Alameda Police Department says the remains have not been identified. He did say he would share information."

"I'd take that with a grain of salt," Maggie said. "But hey, that's an old newspaper reporter talking. So, do you think those are the remains of Ann Lombardi and Eddie Baldwin? That's why you contacted me, because I wrote those follow-up stories on the anniversary of their disappearance."

"When I found Ann and Eddie on the California Department of Justice missing persons database, I did a search on their names. And found—"

"The Zodiac Killer," Maggie finished.

"A lot of speculation. I will say that the timing of their disappearance does raise a red flag."

"A week after the Lake Berryessa attack, and a week before the cabdriver was killed in San Francisco. I know all the details, of course. I wasn't working on the Zodiac story, though. In 'sixty-nine, I was still in J school. I started working for the *Chron* just in time for the whole Patty Hearst circus." She took another sip of her coffee. "Ann and Eddie vanished while all the Zodiac frenzy was going on. So people thought the Zodiac might be responsible. I never did, for a lot of reasons I outlined in my articles. Yes, there were patterns. Young couple out on a date, though the cabdriver's murder didn't fit. And the murders took place near water. Okay, so Alameda's an island. But the Zodiac liked publicity. Look at the way he was drawing attention to the murders. If he'd killed Ann and Eddie, I think he would have taken credit for it."

"Then he taunted police by saying he wasn't going to announce his killings."

"Point taken. Anyway, I don't think the Zodiac killed Ann and Eddie. And now we have your footlocker full of bones. So maybe it's them."

"Or maybe not," I said.

She tilted her head, eyes narrowing. "You have other candidates?"

"I do. When I searched the database, I found another person who disappeared from Alameda, in June of that year. Her name was Martha Post. She was the daughter of an officer stationed at the Naval base."

Interest sparked in Maggie's eyes. "You're right. Martha's name came up when I was researching my article. Her parents thought she ran away. So did the cops."

"That was the easy answer," I said. "Teenaged girl who liked to hang out in the city. It was convenient for people to think that she ran away again."

"At the time she went missing, a cop was overheard by a colleague of mine, expressing the opinion that Martha was just another hippie slut who was probably over in the Haight, taking drugs and screwing her brains out." Maggie's mouth twisted. "Those were the days. Not that I think attitudes have changed that much. My take—Martha wasn't considered a good girl and Ann was. To hear her family talk, Ann was a paragon. And I don't have any reason to believe she wasn't. She lived at home, went to Mass every Sunday, worked at the family deli in town. She was not the kind of girl who would run away from home."

"As I've discovered, Martha did run away. She had an alter ego. She called herself Sunflower, Sunny for short. She was in San Francisco, singing with a rock band called the Mad Monks."

"Well, I'll be damned," Maggie said. "And you figured this out how?"

"Sunny had a boyfriend named Monk Guidry, lead guitarist and founder of the band. I talked with a former band member and his girlfriend. When she mentioned that Sunny was a Navy brat, I showed her the picture of Martha Post from the database."

"Why were you talking to these folks? Is Monk Guidry part of this whole situation?"

"Maybe. Monk was the former boyfriend of a woman named Gloria Rossiter, who also sang with the band. They had an acrimonious breakup in the spring of nineteen sixty-nine and after that Gloria bought the house in Alameda."

"The house where the bones were found." Maggie cocked an eyebrow at me. "So, where is Monk Guidry now?"

"He disappeared in September of that year. So did Sunny, it appears."

She shook her head. "Oh, that's way too many coincidences."

"Gloria says Monk went back to Louisiana, his home state. According to his bandmate, the Mad Monks had a deal to cut a record album in October and he never would have let that break slip through his fingers. I contacted an investigator friend in New Orleans who's looking to see if he can find a trail for Monk, or any family members."

"What does Gloria say?"

"Not much. She likes to tell stories and sometimes they don't always jibe with the stories she's already told. When it comes to Monk and the house, she really doesn't want to talk about those two subjects at all."

"So, the Alameda PD has skeletal remains for two people and you have four people missing. This is quite a tangle to unravel." She paused. "You should talk with Tessa Lombardi, Ann's sister."

"How do I contact her?"

"She still lives in Alameda, works at the family business. I'll call her," Maggie added. "We've kept in touch."

I swallowed the last of my coffee. "What do you think happened to Ann and Eddie?"

"Hell, I don't know. Maybe they went somewhere for a cup of coffee after the movie let out. Or a walk along the beach, which was near that movie theater. One rumor was that they eloped. But why? The Lombardis liked Eddie. They wouldn't have had any objection to those two getting married, other than Ann was so young. I suppose Eddie could have gone AWOL. But again, why? His enlistment period was coming to an end. I figure they were murdered. But at the time and ever since, there was no evidence, no clues. If those bones you found in Alameda are Ann and Eddie, somebody sure as hell went to a lot of trouble to hide the crime. If they were buried somewhere, why dig them up?"

"I have my own theory about that."

"Don't keep it to yourself."

"What if the bodies were buried on the air station? Once the Navy closed the base, they handed it over to the city of Alameda. There's a lot of development going on and more projects in the works. What if the killer thought the bones would be found and decided to move them?"

She nodded. "Good theory. I like it. If this really does turn out to be connected with Zodiac, I want the story. Oh, hell, I want the story anyway. I still write for the *Chron*."

# Eighteen

I LEFT MAGGIE AND walked down Hearst Avenue toward Oxford Street, where I'd left my car in a metered space. My phone rang. Lakshmi, according to the readout. I stepped into the shade of a nearby tree and answered the call.

"Hi, Lakshmi. What's up?"

"Can you stop by the office?" she asked. "We really need to talk about Gloria."

Ah, Gloria. What now? I didn't have to see Lakshmi's face. I guessed her mood from the tone of her voice. She was annoyed by her husband's aunt on a good day and it sounded like this was a bad day.

"I have a meeting with a client in Lafayette. That should take about an hour. I could be at your office maybe half an hour after that, depending on traffic."

"Thanks, we'd really appreciate it."

I ended the call and walked to my car. Parking was always difficult near campus and downtown Berkeley. A hopeful driver slowed and put on his blinkers as I unlocked my Toyota. When I pulled out of the space, he quickly pounced.

I drove through Berkeley and got on the freeway, heading east through the Caldecott Tunnel that went beneath the East Bay hills. The client in downtown Lafayette was an attorney who wanted me to investigate an insurance matter. The meeting went well and I was out of there in forty minutes. I got on the freeway and headed west, toward Alameda. I arrived at the publishing company office on Clement Street earlier than expected. I pushed the intercom to let Lakshmi know I was there. A moment later, the door opened and she admitted me to the building.

"Thanks for stopping by," she said as she let me in.

"What's going on?" I asked.

She rolled her eyes. "I'll let Noel explain." I followed her back to Noel's office. He was at his desk, looking perturbed as he fiddled with a letter opener.

I sat down. "Has something happened?"

Lakshmi took the chair next to me and looked expectantly at her husband.

"It's Gloria," Noel said, his voice and face glum. "She's upset that we hired you. She's insisting that we fire you."

I had been fired from cases before. That didn't stop me from investigating further, if I was so motivated. In this case, I was. Having found the bones, I was determined to find out who put them there, and why.

It was a delicate situation, though. Dan had a working relationship with Noel and Lakshmi. They published his books. They'd been his friends for a number of years. Me, I'd known them just for the past few months.

I chose my words carefully. "The cat is out of the bag. I doubt it can be crammed back in. I've already uncovered a number of details and I've shared them with Lieutenant Chen at the Alameda Police Department. That was the deal. He'll be open with me if I cooperate with him."

Lakshmi nodded. "And those things can't be unsaid."

"Have you made up your mind that this is what you want to do?"

"I haven't," Noel said. "But I want to be mindful of Gloria's feelings."

Lakshmi slammed her fist on Noel's desk, startling him—and me. "Gloria's feelings be damned. For God's sake, we've got two skeletons in a trunk at her house and the police are involved. If you think this is going away, you're crazy. We need to get to the bottom of this. What if your aunt knows more than she's saying?"

My thoughts exactly.

Noel looked dismayed. "You never did like her."

"Let's just say I'm not as fond of her as you are." Lakshmi sighed. "Look, this is murder. Those people didn't just crawl into that trunk and die. Someone put them there. If Gloria is involved in this, we need to know."

The look on Noel's face told me he had considered this. And he didn't like it one bit. "You think my aunt is an accessory to murder?"

I couldn't tell if he was asking the question or trying to convince himself that she wasn't.

"At this point we don't have enough information to make a determination," I said. Which was true. We didn't. "Did your aunt know those bones were in her house? I need to answer that question."

"Which is why you should keep investigating," Lakshmi said.

I turned to Noel. "You said Gloria told you she didn't want the house listed for sale with a realtor, that she already has a buyer. Could be she's afraid the publicity surrounding the discovery of the bones will somehow scare off the buyer."

Noel nodded. "Yeah, that might be where she's coming from. I don't know what to do about this. Gloria was so insistent when she called. Let sleeping dogs lie, that's what she kept saying."

"Sleeping dogs can wake up and bite you," I said.

"Yes, they can. I guess Gloria's concern is that what we're doing might wake up the dogs." He paused, considering his options. "I'll admit, I'm curious enough to want to get to the bottom of this, regardless of what Gloria says." He sighed. "Can we just sleep on it and revisit it later? We only wanted you to come over so we could talk about it in person instead of on the phone."

"Sure," I said. "We'll talk again, soon."

I knew that I'd keep digging, no matter what Gloria—or Noel—wanted. I wanted to know what happened, and why.

"I'll walk you out," Lakshmi said.

I guessed that she wanted to talk further, and I was right. As soon as we were out the front door and on the sidewalk, she turned to me. "I want you to keep investigating, no matter what Gloria says. I have a feeling about this and it's not just because I'm annoyed with her. She knows more than she's saying about those bones. What if she knows who they are or even how they wound up in the trunk?"

She was voicing what I'd already thought, that Gloria Rossiter might have played a part in the whole thing. It could be she wanted me to stop investigating because she was guilty of something and she was afraid I'd find out.

"Let me know what you decide," I said.

"I've already decided. Keep at it. Go back over to Gloria's place and rattle her cage. I'll handle Noel." She waved at me as I drove off.

Late morning, and I still had paperwork waiting for me at my office. But I didn't have any appointments until the afternoon. And Lakshmi's words about rattling Gloria's cage stuck with me. Another visit, I thought. I'd drop in on her unannounced and see how she reacted. The more I put the woman off-kilter, could be she would reveal something important.

Instead of going back to the office, I drove to the senior residence where Gloria now lived. I parked in the lot and walked toward the building. Inside the lobby, I glanced out the window that looked out on the large square courtyard in back.

Gloria was there, sitting at a round cafe table on the far side of the patio, under a blue and white striped umbrella. She wore faded jeans and another oversized floral shirt, long earrings tangled in her unruly gray curls. A book lay discarded on the table, next to a mug.

She wasn't alone. A man sat in the chair to her left, his head angled toward her. He was about her age, in his seventies, with a well-preserved face with a prominent nose, topped with a head of neatly trimmed silver hair. Dressed more formally than she was, he wore a gray suit and a blue shirt with a tie.

I found a set of doors leading out to the patio. It was a courtyard, really, perhaps forty feet square and surrounded on three sides by the building and a tall hedge on the fourth. There was a fountain in the middle, with tables and chairs scattered throughout the space. Large ceramic pots held an assortment of flowers, chrysanthemums and geraniums.

There were others on the patio, enjoying the October sunshine. At one table, a man and two women played a game of Scrabble, while two women sat at another table, talking and drinking glasses of iced tea. I saw a gray haired man on a bench, a book on his lap and a walker parked next to him. To my right, an elderly woman entertained visitors, a woman my age and two small children, one of whom had climbed onto a wooden bench and looked as though he was about to fall. His mother grabbed him by the arms and lifted him down to the grass.

The spot where Gloria and her visitor sat was more secluded, in the far left corner, where a large terra cotta pot of succulents served as a divider. I hung back for a moment, observing them as they talked. Well, no. It didn't look like a conversation. The man talked and Gloria listened, a frown on her face.

I recalled what Noel had said that Saturday when we met at the house. Gloria had enough money to pay for a year at this upscale facility. But she needed to sell the house in order to stay here long-term. That explained why she was eager to go through with a sale.

Gloria insisted she didn't need to put the house on the market because she had a buyer. Was this man the buyer?

Or were they friends? The more I looked at them, the more I wondered about that. I couldn't hear what they were saying, so I focused on their body language. It looked to me like these two people knew each other, and had for a long time. There was familiarity in their interaction.

I thought back to my conversation with Peggy Slocum, the former tenant. When I'd asked about Gloria's regular visitors, she'd told me that she had seen a distinguished-looking man, tall and silver-haired, who drove an expensive car. And Lakshmi had given me a similar description of the man she'd seen Gloria with over in the city, outside a restaurant. A tall man, well-dressed, with silver hair.

This man fit the bill, though he was sitting and I couldn't tell how tall he was. He shifted in the chair, then he leaned toward Gloria, mouth moving as he spoke. She leaned back, a reflexive action, as though she didn't like what he was saying.

That was my cue. I walked up to them. "Hi, Gloria."

She looked up at me, startled. Then her eyes widened as she realized who I was.

I turned to the man. "I don't think we've met. I'm Jeri Howard."

I saw a flicker in the man's pale blue eyes, as though he had recognized my name. It was quickly masked. He didn't bother to smile. Nor did he introduce himself. Instead he checked the expensive-looking gold watch on his wrist. Then he stood. Yes, he was tall.

Gloria gave him a tight smile. "Remember what I said, Lee."

An angry look flashed across his face, disappearing so quickly that I wouldn't have seen it, if I hadn't been looking directly at him. Why? Was he upset with her for using his name? Probably. With even a first name, I could find out more about him. And I planned to do so. I was betting Gloria had told him about me, the private investigator who was nosing around.

"I'll be in touch," he said.

He turned and headed for the door leading into the lobby. I sat down in the chair he had just vacated. Then I remembered something. The other day, when I'd talked with Gloria upstairs in her apartment, she'd gotten a call on her cell phone. I'd seen the screen readout, with the name Lee.

"Is Lee an old friend?" I asked. "Or is he the buyer you have in mind for the house? From his body language, I'd say he's getting impatient. Too bad everything is on hold because of those bones."

Gloria narrowed her eyes and hissed at me. "What are you doing here? I told Noel to fire you. I don't need you messing in my business."

"It's too late for that. I did speak with Noel and Lakshmi earlier, by the way."

"Lakshmi. That meddling bitch." So, Gloria didn't like her nephew's wife any more than Lakshmi liked Gloria. "This was her idea. She leads Noel around by the nose." She glared at me. "And you need to butt the hell out and leave this alone."

I smiled. "I'll tell you what I told them. The cat's out of the bag and you're not going to put it back in. Sooner or later Lieutenant Chen is going to identify those bones. What do you know about them?"

"I don't know anything about them." Gloria's voice raised in a shout, earning us looks from the three people playing Scrabble at a nearby table. She stared back at them. They returned to their game. She lowered her voice. "I don't know anything. How could I? Someone left a footlocker in my house, so what? It could have happened years ago, left there by anyone. How would I know about that? I've had hundreds of tenants over the years. As long as they paid their rents on time, that's all I was interested in. So fine, let the police do their thing. Why the hell should you be involved?"

"Because I found the bones."

Her mouth twisted in a semblance of a smile. "So you feel all warm and tender for a box of bones? You don't have enough real work to occupy you, so you have to butt into this?"

"Curious, I suppose, as to why anyone would leave a couple of skeletons in your house. By the way, I spoke with a couple of old friends of yours. Liam Ebbets and Anita Ryker."

"Friends?" She picked up the coffee mug and took a sip, then grimaced and set it down again. "I haven't seen either of them in fifty years. Haven't wanted to."

"When I spoke with you earlier," I said," you told me that someone told you that the band broke up and Monk went back to Louisiana."

"That's what I heard."

"From whom?"

"How am I supposed to remember that?" she snapped. "It was a lifetime ago."

"Liam says he tried to get you on the phone several times, to ask you about Monk. But you never would talk with him. So he came over to Alameda to confront you. The band hadn't broken up at that point, despite what you told me. When Liam showed up at the house, you told him that Monk went back to Louisiana. He didn't believe you. Still doesn't."

"And he's still harping on it?" Gloria shot back. "After all this time? I only told him what I'd heard. So Monk didn't go to Louisiana. I have no idea where he went. Musicians come and go. Besides, we broke up. Why would I keep up with Monk and his whereabouts?"

"Did you and Monk break up because of Sunny?"

That touched a nerve.

"That little bitch," Gloria spat. This earned her another stare from the Scrabble players. She gave them a withering glare and again lowered her voice. "I saw girls like her all the time, hanging around the clubs, spreading their legs for the guys in the band. That's what Sunny was doing. She came along and waved her tail at Monk. He caught a whiff and followed."

I was taking anything Gloria told me with a large grain of salt. She was spewing bile and I could tell she was still upset about the breakup with Monk that had occurred more than fifty years ago. I had known people to hold grudges that long, and it appeared Gloria was one of them.

There was something else, though. Fear. Gloria was afraid of something. Was it me finding out more about the bones? About the past? Or did it have something to do with Lee's visit? He appeared to be a friend but I'd picked up on an undercurrent from seeing the two of them together.

"I understand Sunny disappeared around the same time Monk did," I said. "Do you think—"

She didn't let me finish. "I don't have time for this bullshit," she said. She stood up and strode away from the table. As she swept toward the building, the Scrabble players looked at her, and then leaned toward each other. I could almost hear the buzz of gossip.

Well, then.

Lee, a first name, probably. Someone who'd had dinner with Gloria in San Francisco and who'd visited her at the house and her new building. So they were friends, old friends. How long had they known each other? And who was he?

I stopped on the way to my office to pick up a sandwich for lunch. I ate at my desk as I responded to phone calls and emails, then I wrote client reports and did some online research for an investigation. In the middle of the afternoon, the phone rang. The number on the phone's caller ID had a 707 area code. Lloyd Humphrey, I guessed, hoping that the retired Navy investigator was calling me with information.

He was. "I have some intel for you. I'd rather talk in person."

"So would I. Where are you located?"

"Solano County, up by Vacaville. We could meet somewhere in the middle. How about Benicia?"

"That works for me. Meet for coffee? I run on the stuff."

He chuckled. "So did I, when I was working. Still do, if truth be told. But a cafe, no. I'd rather talk in a place where we won't be overheard."

"Understood. How about eleven o'clock? Name the place. I'll pick up coffee. Do you like your caffeine plain or fancy?"

He chuckled. "Plain and black. And high test. No decaf or steamed milk for me. Head all the way to the end of First Street, just before the circle and the road that leads out to the pier. Last palm tree on the right. I'll be on the bench."

That sounded very cloak-and-dagger, I thought, ending the call. Maybe it was because of Humphrey's years as an investigator with NCIS. I felt sure I could find the palm tree in question.

# Nineteen

WEDNESDAY MORNING, I DROVE northeast out of Oakland, through Contra Costa County and onto the toll bridge that crossed the Carquinez Strait. It was named for the Karkin people, part of the Ohlone group that had lived on both sides of the water, part of the tidal estuary where the Sacramento and San Joaquin meandered through the delta, waters comingling in Suisun Bay as they flowed toward San Francisco Bay. Benicia was tucked into the rolling hills of southern Solano County. I took the freeway exit into town and eventually turned left onto First Street, the small city's downtown area.

Benicia, too, had a story. The town was named after Benicia Vallejo, a member of an old Californio family and the wife of General Mariano Vallejo, one of the town's founders. It had been the California State capitol for a year before the capitol was moved to Sacramento. Now a state park, the restored building on West G Street was full of period furnishings and exhibits.

First Street was a good place to spend time on a sunny day, lined with cafes and restaurants, as well as shops selling everything from clothing to crafts to antiques. I stopped at one of the many coffee shops along the way.

Back in my car, I drove toward the end of the street, where the traffic circle and the road extended to the pier, with parking and a shorter fishing pier. As I approached the circle, I spotted the last palm tree on the right. Under it, a man sat on the bench. A car had just pulled out of a parking space and I grabbed it and got out of my Toyota.

"Lloyd Humphrey? I'm Jeri Howard."

He stood, a man in his early sixties, with buzz cut iron-gray hair. He was about my height, dressed casually in faded jeans and a checked shirt. "Yep, that's me."

"Thanks for doing this. I really appreciate it." I waved a hand at the pasteboard box I'd set on the bench. "That one is a large regular coffee, black. Same as Gary drinks. Must be a Navy thing."

"Could be. I never cared for all those fancy drinks with foam and flavors."

We settled on the bench. I sipped my latte and pointed. "That bag contains cookies. Chocolate chip."

He grinned. "Is there any other kind?"

We each took a cookie. A seagull landed on a nearby railing and stared at us with beady, covetous eyes. I heard a train whistle and looked past the pier, across the choppy blue-green waters of the Carquinez Strait to the other side, where an Amtrak train moved around a curve on the tracks that bordered the shoreline, its silver cars bright against the autumn brown hills beyond.

Humphrey set his coffee on the bench. "Okay, I may have found the guy who belongs to the footlocker. He was at the Alameda Naval Air Station in the late sixties. And he was an AM, an aviation structural mechanic, so that accounts for the initials on the footlocker. As for those numbers you sent me? I made out six of them and they match with six of the numbers in this guy's social security number."

"Sounds good," I said. "Name? And do you have a photo?"

"Kelvin Delbert Ward."

"That's a mouthful."

"Yeah." Humphrey sipped his coffee. "A handle like that brings to minds all sorts of nicknames. As for a photo, there's the one from his Navy ID card, which was issued when he joined up. And a high school yearbook picture, nothing else. I'm still looking. There must be another picture of him out there somewhere. Though it's possible that he—or someone else—has made a diligent effort to get rid of all those images. I brought a copy of the ID card, front and back."

He pulled a folded sheet of paper from his pocket and opened it. The ID was red, with a heading that read ARMED FORCES OF THE UNITED STATES. In the center of the card was a black and white photo of Kelvin Delbert Ward, with an unsmiling face above a ID board that listed his last name, first name and his service number. The back of the card had two fingerprints and Ward's date of birth. It also told me he was six feet one inches tall and, with blond hair and blue eyes, blood type O. I looked at the photo of Ward again, his hair barely visible in the buzz cut.

"And where was this high school?" I asked.

"Bellingham, Washington. Ward was born there. It's a town located about twenty-five miles from the Canadian border. He had a low draft number and got called up in nineteen sixty-six. He joined the Navy instead of going to the Army. He had some experience working with planes at the local airport, during and after high school. When he enlisted, he went to boot camp and A school, which is what they call apprenticeship training. He was assigned to a unit at the Naval Air Station Alameda in nineteen sixty-eight and he went AWOL in October the following year."

"Absent without leave—so he deserted. Why did he do a runner? Was it Vietnam?"

"Not in the way you think. Ward didn't go AWOL to avoid service in Vietnam. He was being investigated by the Naval Investigative Service, which was a precursor to NCIS. They got an anonymous tip that summer, saying Ward was smuggling and distributing drugs. He was put under surveillance while they worked to build a case against him and find out who else was involved."

"How was he doing it?"

Humphrey paused for another sip of coffee. "At first they thought he might be hiding it on the planes. He worked on all sorts of aircraft and systems. But aircraft is checked thoroughly before flights. Though it's possible something could be hidden in a wheel well at the last minute before takeoff. But that wasn't how he was doing it. One of the investigators finally tumbled to it. Simple, really. Someone on the Vietnam end would give the pilot or a member of the crew a box of candy to take home to his girlfriend. Who's gonna think twice about doing a favor for a buddy?"

"But it wasn't candy."

"Right," Humphrey said. "Uncut heroin masquerading as a box of chocolates. A three-pound box of that kind of candy would have been worth a quarter of a million bucks back then."

"That's a lot of cash. Did they figure out how the drugs were distributed?"

"The investigators weren't quite sure about that. Ward may have used several methods once the stuff got to Alameda. The investigators were watching him, hoping to figure out how Ward was moving the drugs off base, and who else was involved. But something, or someone, tipped him off. Ward vanished, into the wind. One morning, he didn't show up for work. He was reported AWOL. Since he grew up so close to Canada, the most popular theory at the time was that he'd gone across the border."

"Did they ever find the guy?"

"Not a trace," he said. "If Ward went to Canada, he hid his tracks very well. Believe me, there are people who keep an eye on that sort of thing.

No sign that he ever crossed the border. No sign he went back to his home town. No sign of him anywhere."

"Maybe he's dead."

"Possible. It's over fifty years since he went missing. He could have died right after he disappeared or he could have died last week. If he's still alive and out there, he's done a bang-up job of hiding himself. Changed his name and he was careful. Or he had help. Or he went to some other country instead of Canada."

I thought about it for a moment. "I don't think he's dead. Call it a hunch. He may have some connection to those bones in the footlocker."

He shrugged. "Could be."

"Where was Ward living at the time he disappeared?"

"Officially, in the barracks on base," Humphrey said. "Unofficially, he had a place out in town. Back in those days, sailors didn't make that much money. And they were expected to live in the barracks. But Ward had money, so he could pay the rent on an apartment. He had a fancy car, a Mustang Fastback. People were noticing that he had a lot of cash, and wondering where it came from. He was spending his money on several girlfriends. There was something in the file indicating he might have been living with someone, possibly a woman."

"Ward's girlfriends," I said. "Maybe they were involved in the smuggling scheme, picking up those boxes of candy on the base and delivering them on the other end."

He nodded. "The investigators had the same thought. The boxes were picked up by several women. However, one of them was pulled over on base, ostensibly for running a stop sign. When they checked the candy box, they found chocolate. Ward made the switch at some point after taking possession of the box."

"Who were the girlfriends?" I asked.

"I'll have to check. My contact who looked over the notes from the investigation didn't mention a list of names."

Was Gloria one of those girlfriends? But maybe I was reaching, looking for things that weren't there.

I had another question. "Where was the apartment he was supposedly renting?"

"His official address was on base and he was receiving mail at the unit where he worked. And if he was living with someone rather than renting a place on his own, then his name might not be on file anywhere."

True enough. Though I was contemplating another look through Gloria's rental records, to see if Ward's name cropped up. And if that was his footlocker, what was it doing in her house? Had it been there since he went AWOL in 1969?

"That other name you gave me," Humphrey said. "Edward Baldwin, reported missing in October, along with his girlfriend Ann Lombardi. They went out for a date and were never seen again. There's a big file on that one, as you can imagine."

"A big one at the Alameda Police department, too. And lots of press coverage."

"Yeah, all that speculation about the Zodiac Killer. Well, you're going to like this. Baldwin and Ward were both aviation structural mechanics. And they worked in the same unit."

I sat back on the bench. "Is it possible—" I stopped.

"I'm on the same wavelength," Humphrey said. "Wondering if it was Eddie Baldwin that tipped off the authorities that Ward was running drugs."

"Where did Ward and Baldwin work?"

"One of the squadrons at the air station. The commanding officer had just been transferred and the executive officer was the acting CO for several months before he left, too. He had orders to San Diego and he's now deceased. His name was Lieutenant Commander Henry Post."

I stared at him. "Henry Post? You're kidding?"

"I'm not. Why?"

"Henry Post had a daughter, Martha, eighteen years old. She was reported missing in June of that years Her family thought she ran away. She'd done it before, according to her brother. He's a retired Navy officer from San Diego. I spoke with him on the phone and I'm planning to meet with him. He'll be in town for a few days, visiting family."

"I've got to hand it to you, Jeri. You've got a strange case."

"It gets stranger by the minute. Martha did run away, to San Francisco. She had been hanging out in the Haight, calling herself Sunny. She took up with a musician named Monk Guidry and sang with his band. Then Monk disappeared, in September. Supposedly he went back to his home state, Louisiana. I'm working on that, to find out if he did. And nobody knows what happened to Sunny. When I spoke with her brother on the phone, he told me the family never heard from her again."

"Four people missing in a short time span in the same year," he said. "That's too many to be a coincidence. You find out who those skeletons are, let me know."

# Twenty

BACK IN MY OFFICE, I immersed myself in the photocopies of Gloria's rental records. It was a good thing I'd put them in chronological order earlier, when I removed them from the boxes at the publishing company office. Given what Lloyd Humphrey told me, I focused on 1969, looking for any mention of Kelvin Delbert Ward. I didn't find anything.

I set aside the folder and took a break. I had other cases to deal with, and one of them required a trip over to the Alameda County Courthouse to look up some records.

I had just returned to the office when I got a call. Antoine Lasalle's name flashed on the screen.

"Monk Guidry," he said when I answered the phone. "His real name is Louis Robert Guidry. He was born in nineteen forty-two, in Lake Charles, Louisiana, the oldest of five children. Parents Robert and Leanne Guidry, both dead. I found the other siblings, two brothers still living in the Lake Charles area, and two sisters, one up in Shreveport and another in Mandeville. Also various cousins scattered all over Louisiana."

"Thanks, Antoine. I'd like to talk with a family member, preferably one of the siblings."

"Charlene Hebert, Monk's sister, definitely wants to talk with you. In fact, she wants to do a video call, as soon as possible."

"Tell me about her."

"She's a retired schoolteacher, lives in Mandeville. She told me Monk went to California in 'sixty-six. He wrote the occasional letter and postcard, called the family from time to time. He came home for Christmas in 'sixty-seven, stayed a week. The last they heard from him was a phone call in the summer of 'sixty-nine, when one of the brothers had a birthday. After that, they never heard from him again. The family figures he's dead."

"I've got a feeling he never left the Bay Area. I don't have any evidence to back it up. Not yet."

"Charlene says if her brother was still alive, he would have gotten in touch with the family."

"There's another angle to consider," I said, reflecting on my recent phone call with Frank Post. "Monk had a girlfriend named Martha Post. He and his friends called her Sunny and she sang with his band. Her family reported her missing in June. They figured she was a runaway, because she'd done it before. In this case, she wound up in San Francisco. Earlier that year, she had been hanging out in the Haight and at some point, she and Monk became a couple, and she started singing with the band. They were together through the summer, but she dropped out of sight around the time that Monk disappeared."

"So, you're wondering if Monk and Sunny have been holed up in Louisiana all these years?"

"Sounds thin, I'll admit. But I'm running into dead ends everywhere I turn."

"I hear that. Been there. It's a real longshot, since it's been over fifty years, but what the hell. It's worth checking out. I'll see if I get a flutter on Martha Post, aka Sunny," Antoine said. "In the meantime, what about that video call with Charlene?"

"The sooner the better. Today?"

"Great. I'll call her and see when she's available."

Antoine called me back a few minutes later to tell me today was fine with Charlene. She'd suggested a time that worked for me. He gave me her email address. I set up the call and sent the invitation.

I grabbed my wallet and phone and left the office. At a deli down the street, I got a pastrami on rye and a container of potato salad. Back in my office, I ate at my desk, then cleared away the remains of my lunch. Then I turned to my computer and initiated the call. For a minute or so I was the only person in the virtual room. Then another face appeared on the screen.

Charlene Guidry Hebert was a woman in her seventies, with strong features. She looked a lot like her brother Monk, fifty years on. Her dark hair was streaked with gray.

She brushed back an errant strand of hair and maneuvered her laptop for a better angle. A large gray and black tabby cat jumped onto the back of the armchair where Charlene sat, in the comfortably cluttered living room of her home in Mandeville, Louisiana. The city was on the north shore of Lake Ponchartrain, some thirty-five miles over the causeway from New Orleans, and a good two hundred miles from Lake Charles in western Louisiana, where she'd grown up.

"That's Matilda." She smiled and stroked the cat with one hand. "She loves video calls, has to be the center of attention." Matilda flicked her tail and butted her head against Charlene's ear.

"Thanks for agreeing to talk with me," I said.

Her smiled dimmed. "I would truly like to know what happened to my brother. So would the rest of the family. We haven't seen him since Christmas of 'sixty-seven. When that investigator from New Orleans told me that Monk supposedly came back to Louisiana in 'sixty-nine, well, all I can say is he never got here."

"I'd like to know more about Louis Robert Guidry."

She laughed, a warm easy chuckle. "Well, for one thing, we never called him anything but Monk. If Mama or Daddy called him Louis, he knew he was in trouble."

"Where did the nickname come from?" I asked.

"My grandmére. She said he looked like a little monkey when he was a baby, with dark hair and a scrunched-up face. So she started calling him monkey and then it was Monk. The nickname stuck, that's for sure."

"So, he was the oldest?"

Charlene nodded. "He was. I was in the middle, with a brother between me and Monk, and a sister and brother younger than me. When he left home, I was in my senior year of high school. After Monk graduated from high school, he went to work at an oil refinery in Lake Charles. But music was his first love. He played guitar from the time he was a kid."

Matilda demanded attention, getting between Charlene and the computer. She paused and moved the cat, scratching it behind the ears. "Monk was in a band. They played gigs at local clubs. It wasn't the old traditional music. It was rock 'n roll, all the way. In this part of the county, you can imagine we had a steady diet of Fats Domino, Little Richard, and Jerry Lee Lewis. He got caught up in the British invasion bands, too. The Beatles, the Rolling Stones, the Animals. That's what people were listening to back then. But he never lost sight of his roots. He used to sit in with the local bands as well, like the one Daddy was in. Cajun music, well, it's a family tradition. My grandpére was in a band and so was Daddy, years later."

"Did Monk ever have any money?"

She chuckled. "Other than a month's rent and the price of a tank of gas? I doubt it. If he had, he would have bought another guitar," she added, echoing what Anita Ryker said earlier. "My family never had much money and my brother continued that tradition. Why do you ask?"

"I just wondered. His former girlfriend, Gloria, bought a house around the time she and Monk split up, which was April of nineteen sixty-nine. I'm not sure where she got the cash for a down payment."

"She certainly didn't get it from my brother. This woman Gloria, she's the one who told Monk's friend that my brother went back to Louisiana in the fall, right?"

"Yes, she did."

"Well, she's lying." Charlene's eyes flashed. "Or maybe I should give her the benefit of the doubt and say she's mistaken."

"Did Monk have a girlfriend when he left home?" I asked.

Charlene nodded. "He did. A girl he went to high school with. She was hoping they would get married, but Monk was determined to head for California. He wasn't that great about keeping in touch. He'd call from time to time and I did have a phone number for him in San Francisco. He moved in the spring. I guess that was when he broke up with this Gloria. Later he called and said he had a new place and he gave me that phone number. He wrote the occasional letter. And sent postcards. That was it mostly. The last correspondence I have from him is a postcard." She glanced at a small covered box on the side table. "I kept them all."

"What did he say in that postcard?"

She lifted the lid from the box and reached inside, pulling out a postcard with a view of San Francisco's Coit Tower. She held it up to the screen and I read the words scrawled there. He had a new girlfriend, he wrote, named Sunny, adding that Charlene would like her. He also said the band was doing well and maybe had a record deal in the works.

"So, he did stay in touch," Charlene said, returning the postcard to the box.

"Sunny went missing, around the same time Monk did," I said.

She looked troubled. "Then I'm convinced that something bad happened to Monk. And probably this girl Sunny. I think my brother was murdered." She paused. "I've talked this over with my brothers and my sister. I want to hire you to find out what happened to Monk. We're all willing to contribute to the cause."

"I already have a client for this case," I told her. "But if I find out anything about Monk and Sunny, I will definitely let you know."

Charlene and I ended the call. I sat for a moment, mulling over the conversation. Then I looked at the emails that had arrived while I was talking with Monk's sister. One was a message I'd been expecting from

Maggie. She had smoothed the way for me to talk with Ann Lombardi's sister, Tessa.

Lombardi's Delicatessen, on Park Street near Central Avenue, had been a fixture in downtown Alameda for years. When I was growing up in the island city, I used to go over to the deli for my favorite sandwich, pastrami on rye. And their cannoli was delicious.

I clicked into my web browser and did a search for the deli. The website told me that Lombardi's now had two locations—the original and another outlet at Alameda Point. I made a call to the phone number Maggie had sent in her email.

A woman answered. "Lombardi's, Alameda Point."

"Tessa Lombardi?"

"That's me."

"Ms. Lombardi, my name is Jeri Howard. I'm a private investigator in Oakland. I got your phone number from Maggie Constable and I'd like to talk with you in person."

She sighed. "Yes, I talked with Maggie this morning. I've been expecting your call. We're on Monarch Street, near the old runways. Do you need directions?"

"No, I'll find you. I'm in downtown Oakland. It won't take me long to get there."

# Twenty-One

I DROVE DOWN WEBSTER Street, with the usual slow traffic in Chinatown, where cars double-parked, blocking lanes of traffic, and pedestrians crowded the sidewalks as they moved from shops to bakeries to restaurants and spilled over to the street, in and out of crosswalks. Once past the intersection of Seventh and Webster, the street fed into the dark confines of the Tube, heading under the estuary. Emerging into the sunshine on the Alameda side, I passed the College of Alameda, then turned right onto Atlantic Avenue, which led straight to the old Navy base.

This site on Alameda's west end had once been wetlands, filled in 1927 to create an airport. In 1936, the city ceded the land to the federal government. Construction of the Naval Air Station began in 1940. In 1941 came Pearl Harbor and the American entry into World War II. Fleet Air Wing 8 began scouting and patrol missions here, and in 1942, the aircraft carrier USS Hornet loaded up the planes that would be used in the Doolittle raid on Tokyo. NAS Alameda was a bustling presence in the Bay Area, all through World War II, the Korean War and into the Vietnam era and beyond. At one time, five aircraft carriers were anchored here. In addition to the huge military population, thousands of civilian employees worked here as well, doing everything from overhauling aircraft to staffing administrative positions to running the cash registers at the Navy Exchange and the commissary.

At the end of the Cold War, the Base Realignment and Closure (BARC) commission added the air station to the list of more than 300 military bases that would be closed. Eventually the land was turned over to the city of Alameda and the site was named Alameda Point. Redevelopment was in the works, with plenty of fits and starts. Sometimes proposals went nowhere and in other cases, the land and the buildings had been given over to new uses.

At the intersection of Atlantic Avenue and Main Street, a road led into the former base, where I could see buildings under construction, surrounded by workers and equipment. A billboard told me this was destined to be apartments. I didn't go that route. Instead, I turned right on Main Street, which took me past the old commissary, where military personnel and their families had shopped for groceries. The building, long empty, looked as though it was falling apart. Weeds had pried their way through cracks in the asphalt, threatening to take over the entire parking lot.

Nearby, the Alameda Point Collaborative had turned former Navy duplexes into supportive housing for people who needed help.

On the other side of the street were new homes and apartments built during the last decade or so. Main Street gradually curved and I passed Ploughshares Nursery, on the left side of the road, where residents of the collaborative trained and worked, selling everything from plants to garden goods. Farther on, I caught a glimpse of the back side of the old officers' club, which was now available to rent as an event space.

To the right was the Bay Ship and Yacht Company, with its dry dock and repair facilities, and a marine supply store. Nearby was the terminal for the San Francisco Bay Ferry. I saw a white catamaran decorated with blue and green stripes. It was pulling away from the dock, heading across to the Jack London Square pier in Oakland. From there it would chug up the estuary and into the bay, docking again at San Francisco's Ferry Building.

Main Street dead-ended at Navy Way, the location of the air station's main gate. In years past, when this was an active Navy base, the gate would have been staffed with Marines, checking IDs and passes before permitting drivers to enter. Now the gatehouse was empty, a relic of those days.

The parking lot outside the gate was the site of an antiques and collectibles fair held on the first Sunday of each month, crowded with vendors and shoppers. Beyond the parking lot was a section of 600-plus acres that had been turned over to the federal government. Plans were in the works for a Veterans Administration outpatient clinic to be built here, along with a national cemetery, a fitting use for a place that had been a military base for decades.

I drove into the air station, past a monument decorated with an aircraft, a Douglas A-4 Skyhawk according to the sign. I was on Lexington Street, which led to the administration building, once the bailiwick of the commanding officer and the rest of the staff running the base's day-to-day business. It had been turned into a branch location for Alameda's City Hall and Public Works Department.

Up ahead was the old seaplane lagoon and beyond that, the piers where ships had been moored. The only ship tied up there now was the USS Hornet. The old aircraft carrier had been turned into a museum. It was rumored to be haunted. Over the years, crew members and visitors had reported such manifestations as objects moving around on their own, people being pushed by unseen hands, and apparitions in military garb. Every year around Halloween there was a fundraiser called the Monster Bash, with bands and dancing, food, dance and costume contests, and tours of what the organizers called the "spooky spaces."

A block past the admin building, I turned right onto Midway Avenue and drove past a row of derelict barracks, heading for Monarch Street, which looked out on the old runways. This area contained several businesses, including a sports and fitness center, breweries, and wineries. I turned left on Monarch and a block farther, pulled into a parking area. When I got out of my car, I stood for a moment, listening to the seagulls cry as they circled overhead. I imagined the sounds I would have heard back in the days when the air station was home to ships and squadrons, with the blasts of ship horns and the scream of jet engines, the thrum of rotating propellers and clanking of anchor chains.

One sign pointed to a winery tasting room. A smaller sign indicated the way to Lombardi's Deli, on the other side of a wide patio with planter boxes full of succulents and round tables shaded by blue and white striped umbrellas. Several of the tables were occupied, by people tasting wine as well as those having meals. The deli was open for breakfast and lunch, closing at three. It was past the lunch hour, but there were plenty of customers. Just outside the front door, a man sat on a bench, polishing off the second half of a Reuben sandwich, washing it down with swigs from a bottle of root beer. Two young women sat at a nearby bistro table, sharing a salad.

The front door opened and two men in hard hats walked out, carrying paper sacks and soft drink cans. I went inside. A cooler near the front door held a variety of beverages, including soft drinks and beer. I saw a pitcher of iced tea and another full of lemonade. At the end of the L-shaped counter, a glass case held an assortment of desserts—big cookies of several flavors, cheesecake, pie and my favorite, cannoli, with those crisp pastry tubes stuffed with a creamy sweet ricotta filling studded with chocolate chips.

A young couple stood near the cash register, waiting for their order. I stepped past them and looked at the contents of the long counter, where deli meats such as pastrami, salami and prosciutto vied for space next to cheeses and metal tubs containing salads. Behind the counter, a short woman with an athletic build and curly brown hair was constructing a salami sandwich. Next to her, a young man in his late teens scooped potato salad into a container.

The woman cut the sandwich in half and wrapped it in white butcher paper. She set the sandwich and potato salad on the counter in front of the young couple, who'd already chosen soft drinks from the cooler. She rang up the purchase and the customers headed out the front door.

The woman turned to me. "Hi, what can I get you?"

"Tessa Lombardi? I'm Jeri Howard."

She looked me over, then nodded. "We can go outside to talk. Want something to drink? Or eat?"

I smiled. "I live in Oakland now, but I grew up in Alameda. I used to go to Lombardi's on Park Street for the cannoli."

"Okay. Cannoli it is." She walked to the case, took out one of the pastries, and placed it on a couple of paper napkins. I took it from her as she turned and spoke to the young man. "Cory, take over for a while. I need to talk with this lady."

He looked up. "Sure thing, Gran."

Tessa reached for a stainless steel bottle, filled it with ice, and poured in lemonade from a pitcher in the cooler.

She beckoned me toward the door and we went outside. "Cory is my oldest grandson. He's taking classes at College of Alameda, helps out at the deli part-time." She shook her head. "Can't believe I'm old enough to have grandkids."

She led the way to one of the round tables shaded by an umbrella. This strip of Monarch Street overlooked the air station's old runways, with views out to the bay. In the distance, the Bay Bridge and San Francisco shimmered in the early afternoon sunlight. I looked out at the abandoned runways and wondered where the least tern colony was.

We sat in silence for a moment, me making short work of my cannoli, Tessa sipping lemonade. Then she sighed. "I used to work here on the base, back in the day. I was a cashier at the Navy Exchange. Now I'm here again, running my old man's deli."

"Tell me about Ann," I said.

"Ann." She took another sip. "She was twenty. I was sixteen. She graduated from high school a couple of years before she disappeared."

"Did you and your sister get along?"

Tessa shrugged. "We got along okay. I mean, two teenaged girls in the same house, battling for the bathroom. Plus we shared a bedroom and that was a pain in the butt. That summer, she was talking about getting her own place, an apartment somewhere in town. Which did not go down well with my dad. He was an old-fashioned Italian-American papa. As far as he was concerned, she was supposed to live at home till she got married."

"How did she and Eddie meet?"

"Ann worked at the deli on Park Street, after she graduated from high school. All us kids did that at some point. She wasn't interested in going to college, at least not then. That was the only deli, back then. My dad and grandpa started that business after World War Two. Eddie came in one day and ordered a sandwich. She flirted with him and he wound up asking her out."

"When was this?" I asked.

"March, I think. Just after her birthday. They'd been dating about six months when they disappeared. They went out almost every weekend. Movies, dinner, walks on the beach. Once he took her to a softball game on the base. She really enjoyed that, except—" She paused.

"Did something happen at the softball game?"

"Ann was dating another sailor before she met Eddie. I don't recall his name, but he worked at the same command as Eddie. Something happened and she broke up with that guy. She told me about it at the time. He asked her to do something she didn't want to do. When she told me that, I thought she meant he was pressuring her to have sex. But she said no, that wasn't it. Something dicey, she said, and she didn't want to do it."

"Something illegal?" I asked.

Tessa shrugged. "Could be. Maybe he wanted her to smoke pot. I'm sure she experimented with that. I did. But if Dad had found out— Anyway, this other sailor was at the game and he said something to Ann. He made a nasty remark, that's how she described it. Though she never told me exactly what he said. Whatever he said, it upset her. Sounds like she was well rid of the guy. Eddie was much nicer, a real gentleman." Tessa paused. "Ann dated a Marine before that. Remember, at that time, with the base open and the Vietnam War going strong, this town was full of sailors and Marines. Me working at the exchange, I dated a bunch of those guys, too. Nearly married one of them, but came to my senses before I made that mistake," she added with a wry smile.

"Dating every weekend—sounds like they were serious."

She thought about it for a moment. "I think Eddie was more serious than she was. When they disappeared, one theory was that she and Eddie had run off to get married. But Ann wouldn't have eloped. If and when it was time for a wedding, she wanted the whole production, with the white dress and the church. I couldn't see Eddie going for an elopement either. Or AWOL, for that matter. He was conscientious, as straight-arrow as they come. Nice guy, really polite, looked so handsome in his sailor suit. He'd been in the Navy four years, had Good Conduct medals. Besides, he was the kind of guy who would have checked with my dad to see if it was okay to propose to Ann."

"So, Ann wasn't interested in getting married, at least not then."

Tessa shook her head. "Nope. She wanted to be on her own for a while. It was the sixties, after all. Peace, love and hippies. I remember Dad getting really upset with Ann for taking the bus over to the city to hang out in the Haight. With all those freaks, as he called them. He hated the clothes, he hated the music. Which just made it all the more attractive to Ann." She laughed. "And me. Truth be told, I went over to the Haight myself. It was quite the thing to do. Anyway, Dad was afraid Ann would take up with one of those hippies. Instead, she took up with Eddie, the nice normal guy from— Where was he from? Colorado, I think."

She paused. We both looked out beyond the runways, at San Francisco in the distance, with the Bay Bridge rising high above the bay. A lot had changed in the five decades since Ann and her sister had taken the bus over to the Haight to hang out with the hippies. Those high rises in the Financial District weren't there back then. The Embarcadero Freeway—now demolished—would have been visible near the Ferry Building. And the hippies were long gone.

I finished the cannoli and wiped my hands on the napkin. "Tell me about the night Ann and Eddie disappeared."

"They usually went out on Saturday nights. That night, they were going to grab a bite to eat and go to a movie at that theater down at South Shore Center, the one that got torn down a few years ago. The South Shore Twin. It had just opened the year before, the second weekend in November. We went there that Saturday it first opened, Ann and me. It was a double feature. Sidney Poitier in 'For Love of Ivy' and 'With Six You Get Eggroll' starring Doris Day." She laughed. "Why in the world I would remember that? I don't know. Maybe it's because it was me, out with my big sister."

She paused and sipped her lemonade. "Anyway, that night they disappeared, Eddie came by the house to pick her up. We lived over by Franklin Park. Ann wasn't ready, so we waited in the living room, Mom, me, and Eddie. Dad wasn't home. He and my little brother had gone to a ball game. After about ten minutes, Ann came out. She was wearing a pair of brown slacks and a plaid blouse, with a cardigan. It was a pleasant night. I remember her saying she might need the sweater later."

I recalled my conversation with Sergeant Chen. He hadn't come right out to say it, but he'd implied that something had been found mixed in with the bones, the dirt and rocks and the feathers, something that might help with identification. Jewelry?

I asked the question. "Was Ann wearing any jewelry that night?"

Tessa frowned and then she nodded, touching her left hand to her throat. "Yes, she was. She had a gold chain with a little heart, an aquamarine. That was her birthstone. And she had this charm bracelet she always wore. Grandma Lombardi gave it to her a few years earlier and Ann started collecting charms for it. You know the kind. Little trinkets that you get when you travel and go places. Come to think of it, Eddie gave her a charm. I don't remember what it was, but I remember Ann really liked it. She was wearing the charm bracelet that night."

The bit of metal I'd glimpsed at the bottom of the footlocker, I thought. Could that be a charm from Ann's bracelet?

But the bones hadn't been identified yet. "What else can you remember?"

Tessa took another sip from the bottle. "They left the house and walked down the front walk to Eddie's car. He opened the door and held it for her while she got in. He walked around the car and got behind the wheel. Then they drove off." She sighed. "That's the last time I saw my sister."

"What happened when she didn't come home?"

"Ann was supposed to be home by midnight. When she wasn't, Dad started fuming. He was ready to get in his car and drive around town looking for her. I suppose he thought Ann and Eddie were parked somewhere, necking or doing worse. But they weren't. They were just gone. Vanished. Into thin air."

Her hands tightened on the bottle she held. "Everyone was baffled. At first there were all sorts of—I guess you'd call them sightings. Witnesses claiming to have seen them that night. Two people said they saw Ann and Eddie having dinner at a Chinese restaurant on Park Street. Two other people swore they'd been at Jim's, that diner at the corner of Park and Lincoln. Someone told the cops they were in front of the old library at Oak and Santa Clara. Others saw them in line at the theater box office. And later in the lobby, buying popcorn. But the person selling movie tickets didn't remember them at all. I assume they did go to the movie, though. And something happened after."

"Where would they have gone after the movie?" I asked. "Out for coffee?"

"Not coffee," Tessa said. "That wasn't really a thing back then, like it is now, with all these coffee places. They might have stopped for a Coke. Or ice cream, maybe. There was a coffee shop called Carl's at South Shore. Loard's Ice Cream was there back then, at least I think so. Mel's Bowl had a restaurant called Alameda Joe's. If they'd gone downtown, on Park Street, there was Ole's or Jim's. And Tucker's Ice Cream, of course. It's been around since the forties."

"What about Webster Street? That's closer to the Navy base."

"Webster was where all the sailors hung out, either causing trouble or getting into trouble. My dad didn't like us going there. I remember a bar called Frankie's. Queen's pool hall. Tillie's Diner. And the Doggie Diner," she added with a smile. "With that revolving dachshund head for a sign. Long gone. It's true, though, if kids were looking for fun they'd walk Webster." She shook her head. "But I don't think Ann and Eddie would have gone to Webster Street. They were already at the movie theater there at South Shore, probably, since that's where they were planning to go. I could see them going over to Alameda Joe's for a Coke. And then maybe a walk on the beach. But who knows. Nobody saw them. They disappeared. It was like they dropped off the planet. After that, lots of leads that didn't go anywhere"

"Then came all the rumors about the Zodiac Killer."

Tessa grimaced. "God, yes. As soon as the news people found out about the disappearance. Everyone was talking about the Zodiac. It was the end of September when that young couple was attacked at Lake Berryessa, and the second week in October when the cab driver was murdered in San Francisco. So when Ann and Eddie disappeared, there was all this stuff in the papers and on the news wondering if they had been killed by the Zodiac. It was everywhere and it just broke my parents. They couldn't listen to the news or open a newspaper."

"What do you think?"

"It wasn't the Zodiac." She shook her head. "I mean, I've read about that case. The people he killed and the people he was supposed to have killed. He liked to publicize his murders. Ann and Eddie disappeared during his big spree, when he was writing those letters to the newspapers. If he'd killed them, he would have been advertising that all over the place."

I had to agree, and so had Maggie Constable when I talked with her.

"If those skeletons are really Ann and Eddie." She stopped. "We'll know, I guess, when they finish checking the dental records and the

DNA. You know, they talk about closure and I don't see how that happens. I said goodbye to Ann a long time ago. After she'd been missing for a while I figured she wasn't coming home. Finding her body now, well, it doesn't make the loss go away. She's just as dead now as she was fifty years ago, in my mind anyway. Mom and Dad died a few years back. My brother and I are still here, along with some cousins. I guess if those are her bones, we can put them in an urn and have a memorial service. Strange to think that might happen, after all this time."

# Twenty-Two

I WENT BACK TO my office in Oakland. I didn't have any more appointments, but I did have paperwork. I was working on a client report when the phone rang.

It was Anita Ryker. "I remembered something. I told you about seeing Gloria at that music festival at the Santa Clara County Fairgrounds in May of 'sixty-nine."

"Right. You said Gloria ignored you because Monk was with Sunny."

"Yeah. And she was with a guy. I figured he was her latest."

"You thought he was a sailor because he had short hair." Presumably the same man Liam had seen in Gloria's living room when he went over to the Alameda house, looking for information on Monk. Liam too had mentioned the short hair and speculated that the man was stationed at the nearby Navy base.

"Yes, he did look like a sailor," Anita said. "Anyway, Gloria said something to him as they walked away. I couldn't recall it when you were over here the other day, but I remember it now. It was a name. She called him Scotty."

Anita and I talked a moment longer, but that was the only detail that she recalled. We ended the call and I sat staring at my computer screen.

It wasn't much to go on. Just a name, Scotty, possibly the name of the man Gloria had been involved with after she broke up with Monk. Scotty, for Scott. Which could be a last name, first name, middle name—or just a nickname. Or it could be nothing, just another wisp of information that might lead nowhere.

A name. And a hunch.

But still, I had a feeling it was important.

I got out the folders containing the copies of Gloria's rental records and pulled out those from 1969. As was the case with Ward, I didn't find anyone named Scott.

I closed the file and sat for a moment, feeling frustrated. Then my phone rang.

Emma, the real estate agent, was at the other end of the line.

"Sorry for the delay in getting back to you," she said. "It's been nearly a week since you called. Work has just been crazy. Plus, I had to do some digging and make a bunch of phone calls. But paydirt! I have some information for you, about who is buying up all those old houses in that West Alameda neighborhood."

"All of them? That's at least four houses. I only saw 'Sale Pending' signs on two of them."

"Well, the other two that had 'For Sale' signs now have offers. And they're all from the same entity."

"Entity rather than person," I said.

"That's right. It's a company called Bertcor. A real estate development outfit."

Bertcor. I'd made some notes during an earlier Internet search and now I reached for that lined yellow pad. Yes, Bertcor. The chief executive officer was Carol Bertram, who was also CEO of CLB Properties, which managed the Odalisque apartment building in San Francisco, the one where Graham Costa lived now.

"What do you know about Bertcor?" I asked. "The people behind it, I mean."

"The CEO is Carol Bertram. She's been in the Bay Area real estate game for years. She's done partnerships with companies who are building all those high rises south of Market in San Francisco. And she invests in other real estate projects."

"Why is Bertcor buying houses in Alameda, a town that has a lot of restrictions on what kind of housing can be built there?"

"The real estate agent grapevine," Emma said. "I get a lot of good scoop that way. Rumor has it that those houses are going to be turned into upmarket, very expensive condos. The project is jumping through various hoops at the Alameda planning department, but it hasn't been approved yet."

"What happens to the tenants? Assuming the house is already a rental property?"

"Someone at the planning department could answer that question better than I could. Or you can look it up on the city's website. But the short version is you have to give the tenants plenty of notice and there's lots of paperwork involved."

I was thinking out loud. "But if all the tenants have moved out and the building is empty, then—"

"Right. No tenants to deal with, less paperwork."

I doodled on one corner of the pad, thinking of Gloria's tenants. Andrew Vogel had left on his own. Graham Costa had been offered a year's free rent in a building managed by a company with ties to Bertcor. And Peggy Slocum had been threatened.

I pictured the man who had paid a visit to Gloria. "This is a longshot question. Do you know of a real estate developer named Lee. Not sure if that's a first name or a last name, but it's the name I heard. I've been searching on the Internet but I haven't found anything concrete. At least not yet."

"Longshot indeed." Emma laughed. "Lee is a fairly common name. Have you actually laid eyes on this person?"

"I have. A man. He's tall, silver hair. In his seventies, I'd guess, but takes good care of himself. Pale blue eyes, practically ice."

She was quiet for a moment. "Wow. The eyes. That sounds familiar. I wonder if you mean Lee Corland."

"Spell that last name. I'll do a search on him."

She reeled off the letters. "He tries to keep a low profile. But every now and then he does something cutthroat that lands him in the news. I've heard people describe his eyes as chips of ice."

Even as she spoke, my fingers moved over the keyboard, typing his name into the search bar. "Lot of hits. But no pictures."

"He's camera shy. But these days, there's probably a picture out there somewhere."

I scrolled through the list. "It seems Corland has a reputation. Not always good."

"I have another rumor for you," Emma said. "Nothing verified, the accusations didn't stick. But in the past, Corland has been accused of bribing people in various planning departments."

"Does the rumor include what cities?"

"Three that I heard of. Menlo Park, Novato, and Santa Rosa. Hey, I have another call and I need to take it."

"Thanks for the information."

I turned back to my computer and stared at the monitor, thinking. Surely there was a photo of Lee Corland, somewhere, even if the developer was publicity-shy. It took some digging through the Internet but I finally found one.

Lee Corland was the man I'd seen visiting Gloria Rossiter. My guess was that Corland was also part of the Bertcor project that was purchasing houses in the neighborhood in order to turn them into condos. Bertcor—was the company name a combination of both last names? Were Bertram and Corland operating as one business entity? Was he Gloria's mysterious buyer?

I went back to the list of news articles about Corland and began reading. As Emma had said, the man had a reputation as a cutthroat businessman who would cut corners as well. His company, called LC Plus, was based in San Francisco. It had been in the news a couple of months ago, the subject of an unfavorable article in the *San Francisco Chronicle*.

Corland had purchased a multi-unit apartment building in a rapidly-gentrifying Oakland neighborhood, planning to remodel the building. This included cutting existing two-bedroom units in half, making them one-bedroom units or studios, in order to cram in more apartments. And his usual pattern after a big remodeling job was to raise the rent into the stratosphere, making sure that only people with lots of money could afford to live there. He had done it several times over the past few years, in cities all over the Bay Area, mostly notably San Francisco, Oakland, and Berkeley.

Oakland was a "just cause" city, meaning a landlord must have just cause to evict a tenant. According to the news report, Corland got around this by pressuring tenants to leave, as had many landlords and developers before him. Corland employed a repertoire of nasty tactics, such as making sure the building was increasingly uninhabitable. Former tenants described dirty conditions, plumbing that constantly backed up, elevators that didn't work, coin-operated laundry equipment that was always out of order.

In this instance, and in others, Corland had also strong-armed tenants, encouraging them to leave. Threats from thugs—that sounded very much like the story Peggy Slocum told me, about the young man who showed up at her apartment strongly suggesting that she move. When she refused, her garden had been vandalized. Then the man showed up again, making threats.

The newspaper article had uncovered other instances, in other buildings and other cities. Failure to repair an elevator in a building in San Francisco's Mission District, forcing tenants to use the stairs. Refusal to deal with insect or rodent infestations, all in the hope that tenants would "self-evict" and leave the properties uninhabited so Corland could move ahead with his projects. The article also mentioned the allegations that he had bribed a city official in Santa Rosa and colluded with a San Jose city council member, in both cases to issue permits and look the other way concerning violations.

Corland had denied any wrongdoing, of course.

My uncle Neal had been a city planner in Santa Rosa, for thirty-plus years. He was retired now, and had been for several years. But he would know if anything down and dirty had happened.

Neal liked to play tennis. Which was fine with Aunt Caro, my father's younger sister. She was a writer who'd authored a number of historical novels and she wrote better without her husband underfoot. At least that's what she told me.

"You're in luck," Caro said when she answered the phone. "He just got home from a tennis game. He's in the shower but I think I heard the water stop running."

We chatted for several minutes, catching up on family news, then I heard her call to my uncle. He picked up the extension. "Business or pleasure?" he asked in his usual brisk manner.

"Business," I said. "What can you tell me about Lee Corland?"

"Oh, he's a piece of work. A real asshole. Don't tell me he's come up in one of your cases."

"Yes, he has. I don't like the look of him. Or what I'm reading about him online."

"You're not the only one. Let me tell you about this stunt he pulled up here in Santa Rosa."

I knew I could get the unvarnished details from Neal, and he didn't stint. The incident occurred some four years earlier, when Corland was trying to build condos on the west side of Santa Rosa. He was having some difficulty getting the necessary permits, my uncle said, so he offered money to one of the officials. She promptly reported it. An investigation ensued, with Corland denying the whole thing and the city official standing by her story.

"It was a standoff," Neal added. "A he-said, she-said situation, and it went nowhere. I know the woman and I think she was telling the truth. She had no agenda. But Corland made it sound like she was out to get him."

"Did he ever build his condos?"

"Eventually. But he had to change his plans before he could get his permits. He was not happy about that."

"Thanks for the information. What do you know about him? Other than he's an asshole."

He thought for a moment. "Not much. He's been in business for thirty years or more. I first started hearing about him and his company, LC Plus, in the late eighties. Keeps to himself, doesn't have any family, that's what I've heard."

"Have you heard of a company called Bertcor? It's a real estate development firm and a woman named Carol Bertram. She's also the CEO of CLB Properties, which manages apartment buildings in the area."

"I have," Neal said. "Bertram and Corland do business together. I think he's the 'cor' in Bertcor. But like I said, he's good at staying in the background, hiding his involvement with various companies upon companies."

"I suspected as much."

"What's this all about?" Neal asked.

I outlined what I'd discovered, that Bertcor was in the process of buying old houses on Alameda's West End, with plans to convert them into condos.

"That sounds above-board," he said. "You can look up planning and building applications on the Alameda planning department's website. And I do know someone there. Might be worth a phone call."

I wrote down the name and phone number he gave me. "Thanks for the information."

"You're welcome. Come up for dinner one of these days. We haven't seen you in a while."

When I went back to my computer I continued to dig for information. I found out Carol Bertram was in her fifties and had come to the Bay Area from Los Angeles. She had a track record going back three decades. So did Lee Corland, which was unusual because I guessed that he was in his seventies, around Gloria's age, and twenty years older than Bertram. His trail should have gone back farther, but it didn't. Try as I might, I couldn't find anything about the developer that was earlier than the 1980s, when he first appeared on the scene working with another real estate developer in San Francisco. He would have been in his thirties then. What was he doing before then? I couldn't find anything that told me where he was born, where he came from, or how he wound up working as a developer. It was as though Corland, and LC Plus, had sprung to life, full grown and fully developed.

That raised a red flag for me. People had pasts, and sometimes they tried, with varying degrees of success, to hide their pasts. Was that what Corland had done? If that was the case, why?

And why was Corland visiting Gloria Rossiter?

If he was involved with Bertcor, then he must be involved in their project to buy up old houses on Alameda's West End and convert them to condos. A business relationship, surely. But there was something in the interaction I'd witnessed between Gloria and Corland that told me it was more than that. They knew each other, and had for a while.

I followed up on Neal's suggestion, heading for the Alameda planning department's website, where I looked up the planning and building applications for the condo conversion project. It looked as though Bertcor intended to gut the old houses, leaving the exteriors and some of the internal architectural flourishes. I reached for the slip of paper on which I'd written the name and number of Neal's contact in the planning department. He was in his office. During our conversation, he assured me that all the requirements for the condo conversion had, or would be, met. After I hung up, I went back to my earlier question. Why was Lee Corland visiting Gloria? What was going on between those two?

Money. It was at the root of many a plot. Time to do a deep dig into Lee Corland. And Gloria's finances.

Earlier I had done research on CLB Properties and Bertcor. Now I turned my attention to Lee Corland and LC Plus. As I went through websites and databases, I learned that Corland had formed a number of companies over the years. I jotted down the names as I found them. Soon I had eleven companies on a list. As I looked into each one, it appeared that most of them were shell companies, existing only on paper, with no physical office or employees. Just a name or two for the principals, and the name and address of an agent for service of process. Which in several cases was the same company used by CLB Properties and Bertcor, though the companies used different law firms.

I found a company formed twenty years ago by Lee Corland and Carol Bertram, with a third party, Richard Chandler. That company had been dissolved. Chandler's name appeared again, on another company formed by Bertram. My research on Chandler turned up the information that he had died five years ago. I found his obituary in a Sacramento newspaper and learned that Chandler was Bertram's brother. Keeping it all the family, I thought.

I stood up and stretched, then made a pot of coffee. After my break and a fresh jolt of caffeine, I retrieved the tenant records from the filing cabinet and carried the accordion folders to my desk. Earlier, when I'd been looking for information, I focused on the most recent tenants. Now I went all the way back to 1969. Inside the folder holding the earliest tenant records, I found a deposit slip from the Bank of America in downtown Alameda, attached to a rental receipt with a rusting paper clip. The ink on the slip was so faded I couldn't read the account number. I went through the rest of this folder and the next, finding another deposit slip that gave me a partial account number.

I reached for the next folder. When I picked it up, the folder ripped and the contents tumbled to the floor. I knelt to gather up the papers. My fingers encountered something I wasn't expecting.

It was a bound notebook measuring about four-by-six inches, with a moss green cover. Gloria's handwriting filled the ruled pages. Most of the notes were written in ink, black and sometimes blue. Here and there I saw penciled notes, some of them in red and green.

It was some sort of financial record. Of what?

When I'd grabbed the folders from one of the bankers boxes, to hold the copied tenant records, I thought they were all empty. But this one wasn't. It held the notebook. And what else?

I sorted through the papers, setting the tenant records to one side. The papers that remained included several bank statements, a bank book for a savings account, and three canceled checks. The statements and bank book were from Bank of America.

The checks, all dating from the 1990s, had been deposited to the Bank of America account. They were drawn on an account at Wells Fargo, a branch located in downtown San Francisco's Financial District. The account holder was Casement Co. I reached for the notes I'd made, listing the companies formed by Lee Corland over the years. Yes, one of them was Casement Co. I saw three other variations incorporating the word "case"—Balfour-Case, Case Hamilton Ltd., CaseCor. A pattern, I thought. Casement was one of Corland's shell companies. It had been formed in 1983 and dissolved in 1987. In most states, including California, it was possible to reuse the name of a corporation if it had been dissolved, sometimes after waiting for a period of time. Sure enough, Corland had resurrected the name—twice. He'd formed a company called Casement that existed from 1992 to 1999, and used the name again in 2014. The most recent version of Casement was still active.

I reached for the green notebook again and carried it to my copier, where I copied each page. I set the sheaf of copied pages on my desk and went through the pages slowly, a yellow highlighter in hand. I looked at the notations for deposits into Gloria's savings account and I saw it over and over—the word "case." It looked like Lee Corland had been providing money to Gloria Rossiter for decades, through his various companies.

Why?

This was more than Gloria deciding to sell her house to Corland. His fingerprints were everywhere.

I returned to the tenant files and went through them again, looking for any papers that might have been mixed in with them. Anything I may have missed when I was looking for contact information on the last three tenants. Anything that Gloria might have misplaced.

Then I found it. A business card from the senior apartment building where Gloria was now living. There was a note written on the back, with a date in August of this year and the words, "Ck recd Case 1 yr."

I turned the card over in my hands, thinking what the words might mean. It looked to me like Gloria had received a check from "Case" on that date. But there wasn't a matching notation in the green notebook. Then who had received the check? Suddenly it came to me.

Lee Corland was paying Gloria's rent in the fancy new senior living digs. For one year. Why? To get her out of the house?

# Twenty-Three

I WAS MEETING FRANK Post on Thursday morning in Niles. It had once been a small rural township, founded in the 1850s, a farming community as well as a railroad town. In 1956, it had joined four other towns—Mission San Jose, Warm Springs, Irvington, and Centerville—incorporating as Fremont, which was now one of the largest cities in the Bay Area.

The town, located at the mouth of a twisting canyon carved by Alameda Creek, had been the site of the western branch of Essanay Studios. Silent movie star Broncho Billy Anderson and his partner George Spoor made movies here, from 1912 through 1916. In addition to acting, the prolific Anderson wrote, directed, and produced the films, from a studio located on what was then Front Street, now Niles Boulevard. Charlie Chaplin's *The Tramp* was filmed in nearby Niles Canyon, one of over 300 movies filmed here. Despite the passage of time, the celluloid flickers lingered on at the Niles Essanay Silent Film Museum, housed in the old Edison Theater.

The old railroad depot was also a museum, highlighting the town's railroad past. The historic train Frank Post had mentioned was the Niles Canyon Railway. Using steam and diesel engines, the railway carried weekend passengers through Niles Canyon to the small town of Sunol. From Thanksgiving through the Christmas holidays, the railway ran its enormously popular Train of Lights. Volunteers decorated vintage railcars with lights and decorations. One year I'd booked seats in the parlor car, where coffee and hot chocolate were provided—with or without alcohol—by volunteers dressed in holiday finery. It was a lot of fun and tickets sold out quickly. Dan and I were doing it again. I'd been ready on the day tickets went on sale earlier this month, and we had a parlor car reservation for early December.

I found a parking spot on Niles Boulevard, across the street from the depot and the wide green plaza that fronted it. The coffee shop was in a narrow storefront tucked between two of the many antique stores in town. There were round bistro tables on the sidewalk as well as inside, and it was decorated with posters from silent films.

An older man sat at a round table against the wall to my left, just this side of the long counter and under a framed poster from the silent film *Broncho Billy's Conscience*. The man was leafing through a copy of the *San Francisco Chronicle*. On the table was a large brown expanding folder, its flap held shut by an elastic band.

Frank Post, I guessed, mentally comparing his face with the photographs I had seen of his sister, from the snapshots that Anita had shown me, as well as the missing persons listing that I'd printed out from the database. She was frozen in time at eighteen, the age she had been when she disappeared. More than fifty years had gone by and the man in front of me showed his age in the lines on his face and the iron gray hair cut short and receding from a high forehead. There was definitely a resemblance, though.

As I walked toward the table, he set aside the newspaper and stood up. He was a few inches taller than me, trim and fit, and he wore a neatly pressed pair of khaki slacks and a short-sleeved shirt in a muted plaid.

"Jeri? I'm Frank." We shook hands.

"Yes. Thanks for meeting with me. What can I get you? Coffee, pastry?"

"Nothing to eat, thanks. But I'll take a cappuccino."

I set down the envelope I'd brought with me, stepped up to the counter and ordered a cappuccino and a latte for myself, ignoring the urge to get a cheese danish. After all, I'd had breakfast just a few hours ago. I carried the coffees back to the table and sat down.

Frank took a sip. "I called Lieutenant Chen, right after I spoke with you. I have an appointment with him at the Alameda Police Department later today. I'm really hoping he can help me find out what happened to my sister. I'd like to take a look at whatever files he has." He paused. "How did you get involved in this?"

"I found the bones." I wrapped my hands around my coffee cup, feeling the warmth. "They were in a footlocker in the storage room of a house on the West End of Alameda. It's owned by an older woman who recently moved to a senior apartment. Her nephew and his wife were doing an inventory of the contents, furniture and so forth, so things could be put in storage and the house sold. They're friends, so my fiancé and I were helping them. When I opened that footlocker, the bones were inside, jumbled up. We called the police."

"You're a private investigator," he said. "Doing this on your own?"

"Looking into it, at the request of the nephew and his wife, and with Lieutenant Chen's knowledge." I paused and drank coffee. "I did a search on missing persons cases in the state database, looking for people reported missing in Alameda. I found a listing, and a photo, for Martha, with a note indicating that she may have run away."

"That's what my parents thought at the time. The local cops, too." He sighed and a shadow passed over his face. "Even if she did run away, I always thought if she was alive, she would have gotten in touch with us, just to let us know she was all right. But she never did." He was silent for a moment. "We were a year apart in age. Close when we were growing up, but when the teenage years hit—" His smile was rueful.

"I didn't find that many news articles from the time of her disappearance, and they didn't mention her siblings. I found your name when I did a search on your father's name."

"No, there wasn't much news coverage. I'm sure it was because they called her a runaway." He sipped his coffee. "So, do you think those bones might be Martha?"

"It's possible. Just so you know, there were two sets of bones in that footlocker. And two other people who were reported missing in the same time frame. At this point, no one is sure how long those bones have been there. There were pebbles, dirt and bird feathers mixed in with the bones."

He shook his head. "Why the hell would anyone do that? Bury somebody and then dig them up? Well, covering tracks, I suppose."

"Martha ran away before," I said. "That's what the missing persons report said."

He took his time answering. "Several times. That's why my parents told the police they thought she had taken off again. The first time she ran away was—" He thought for a moment. "She must have been fourteen, so that would be nineteen sixty-five, before we came to Alameda. You see, Dad was career Navy. Every couple of years, he'd get orders to another duty station. We would pack up and move to another base. Martha hated that. She'd just get settled in a place, make friends, and we'd leave. That first time when she ran away, we had been living in Pensacola, Florida, where Dad was stationed. He got orders to Corpus Christi, Texas. So, off Martha went. She turned up a few days later at my aunt's house in Louisiana."

"You have family in Louisiana?" That made me wonder. If Monk in fact went back to Louisiana, had Martha gone with him? But I had no evidence that Monk returned to his home state.

Frank nodded and fingered his coffee cup. "My mother's family was from Shreveport. My aunt, my mother's younger sister, lived in Baton Rouge. Why do you ask?"

"Just curious as to where Martha would go. Where did she go the next time she ran away? Was that when your father transferred from Texas?"

"No. We went from Corpus Christi to Alameda in nineteen sixty-seven. When Dad got those orders, Martha was really excited about going to California. It was the sixties, of course. She was all about getting to San Francisco to check out the Summer of Love. She had just turned sixteen, really into the music and all that hippie scene." He smiled. "Me, I was more into *Star Trek*. The original series. It was on TV at the time and I was on team *Enterprise*. Anyway, we moved into officers' quarters at the base in Alameda. It was easy for her to walk to Webster Street and catch the bus over to San Francisco. Off she'd go to the Haight. She wanted to be a flower child and sing in a band."

I sipped my latte. "How did that go over with your family?"

He shook his head. "Not very well, as you can imagine. My dad was Navy all the way, a military man, had no use for long hair or people protesting the Vietnam War or that rock 'n roll music. As for my straitlaced Southern mom, she had ideas about how a teenage girl should act and Martha wasn't going with the program. She was always staying out late and talking back to my folks. My sister marched to a different drummer, that's for sure. I recall some heated arguments. They tried to rein Martha in, but she wasn't having any of it, determined to go her own way."

"Which meant running away?" I asked.

"Yes, twice when we were in Alameda. Once, when she was just starting her senior year in high school. I was a junior. That was the fall of nineteen sixty-eight. She had a fight with Mom and Dad. I don't remember what it was about. I just remember a lot of yelling and tears, from Martha and Mom. Martha stormed out of the house and didn't come home for a couple of days. Which really had my parents in a state. Mom was crying and Dad was upset, snapping at the rest of us. Turns out Martha was staying with a high school friend there in Alameda. The friend's mother said, enough, and called my parents."

He sighed. "So, Martha came home. The second time was in the spring of nineteen sixty-nine. A similar situation. She had a fight with our parents, packed a bag and left. Mom and Dad called the high school friend and talked with her mother. But Martha wasn't there. The friend finally told my parents Martha was in San Francisco, staying with some hippies she'd met on one of her jaunts over there, camping out with those other kids in a rundown rooming house in the Haight. Dad tracked her down and persuaded her to come home. But she kept going over to the city, staying out late, coming home early hours of the morning. Now that I look back on it, I can see why my parents thought she'd run away again."

She had, of course. Those frequent trips to the Haight must have been when she'd met Monk, I thought. Singing in the band, with gigs that went on till midnight or later. Monk was living in San Francisco, first with Gloria and after they parted, staying with Anita and Liam before moving into a place of his own.

Frank looked troubled. "I said she never got in touch with us. But something happened that makes me wonder to this day. It was later that summer, the first part of August. The phone rang. I was in the living room and I picked it up and said hello. I heard a woman's voice say, 'Frank? Is that you?' Then my mother picked up the extension in the kitchen. Whoever was on the other end of the call hung up. I've always wondered if that was Martha. If it was, she didn't call again."

Maybe it had been Martha, willing to talk with her brother but not her mother. We'd never know for sure.

"I understand she called herself Sunny."

Frank nodded. "That's right. She hated the name Martha. Wanted everyone to call her Sunny. Sunny for Sunflower. How did you know that?"

"I talked with someone who knew her back then, knew her as Sunny rather than Martha."

"How did she know Martha?"

I leaned back in my chair. "Back in the sixties there was a local band, called the Mad Monks. The leader was nicknamed Monk. He played guitar. The bass guitarist was a man named Liam and his girlfriend at the time, Anita, sang with the band. I spoke with Anita a few days ago. She identified Martha as the young woman who called herself Sunflower, Sunny for short. She was Monk's girlfriend. And she also sang with the band."

"She did?" Post's grin was unexpected. "She really did get to sing in a band? That's great. She had such a good voice. She loved Janis Joplin and Grace Slick. When she was younger, she'd sing in the church choir. Or we'd have sing-alongs in the car when we were driving. That's how we traveled from base to base when we transferred. We'd pack up the station wagon and drive across country. Singing and playing games. You know the kind, where we'd see how many license plates we could spot from different states."

I smiled at the picture he was creating of his family's long-ago travels. "She was singing with the band before she left home. Did she ever mention it?"

He shook his head. "Not a word. That would explain her going over to San Francisco every chance she got, staying out late. But she wouldn't have told me. I was the nerdy kid brother. She certainly wouldn't have told Mom and Dad. They were frazzled enough with Dad being in the Navy, Vietnam era and all that. And Mom coping with all four of us kids. They wouldn't have approved of her singing rock music, especially in a band over in San Francisco. They were strict with us. But somehow it didn't take with Martha." He paused. "So, she did run away."

"Yes, to San Francisco, again."

"I'm surprised my dad didn't find her," he said. "He went looking for her over in the Haight, again. He was hoping to find her in that rooming house, but she wasn't there."

"I think she didn't want to be found. I gather she was living with Monk. He was her boyfriend." I took another sip of coffee. "So, you were the kid brother."

"I always think of my brother George as the kid brother. Martha turned eighteen that spring. I was seventeen. Our younger sister, Sarah, was twelve and George was nine. In addition to *Star Trek*, I was into baseball. I remember that the Oakland A's were playing the Kansas City Royals at home the day Martha went missing. Tuesday, June twenty-fourth. It was a night game. The Royals won, six-five."

"Tell me what happened when Martha left."

"It was summer," he said, a faraway look on his face. "We weren't in school, of course. Martha had graduated from high school. Mom was planning our family vacation. Dad was going to take leave in July and we'd go see my grandparents, his family in Minnesota. Martha didn't want to go. I remember her and Mom arguing about it. Mom and Martha argued about a lot of things that year. My parents wanted her to go to college, even if it was just taking a couple of courses at the College of Alameda. But Martha wasn't interested."

Martha hadn't wanted to leave Monk during the family vacation, I guessed. As for continuing her education, she was more interested in her burgeoning career as a singer. She'd kept that hidden from her family.

He continued with his story. "Martha left sometime during the day. Dad was at work, of course. Mom was at some officers' wives function at the officers' club on base. George and I were in the backyard, working in the garden. Mom had left us with a plate of sandwiches and orders to pull weeds. I was looking forward to listening to the baseball game on the radio. Sarah was in the house. She told my folks that Martha said she was going to San Francisco. She walked out of the house at the air station and we never saw her again." He paused and stared into his coffee cup.

"She didn't come home that night. My parents realized that the next morning, when Mom saw that Martha's bed hadn't been slept in. And that some of Martha's things were gone. Mom started calling around, to the friends that she knew of. No luck there. No one Mom talked with had any idea where she was. That same day, Dad went over to the city, to the Haight, looking for her, but he had no luck. Later that day, my parents went to the Alameda Police Department to report Martha missing. I guess they investigated, but everyone assumed she had run away."

He hesitated, a look shadowing his face. "I overheard Mom and Dad talking with the cops when Martha was reported missing. One of the officers said something like, oh, she's probably gone off with her boyfriend, shacked up with some hippie. Then later, when the cops were leaving, that same cop said something about Martha, why should they waste their time looking for some hippie slut." He tightened his jaw and I could tell that it still hurt, more than fifty years later. "It made me so angry to hear that. The hurtful comments from neighbors and relatives, like there was something wrong with my parents because my sister left."

"It never goes away. That feeling of loss." I thought of my own brother's disappearance last year. I found him in a matter of days, but those days had been fraught with worry. I could only imagine what it must feel like to have a loved one vanish for good, never seen again, never knowing for sure what happened.

His next words echoed what I was thinking. "It's really hard, not knowing what happened. You're right, it doesn't go away. Martha's disappearance didn't affect the younger kids as much. But my parents? I don't think they ever got over it. They left it in the hands of the police. Dad got orders to another duty station in San Diego. We packed up and moved again. I remember Mom being upset about leaving Alameda. She said that if Martha came back, she wouldn't know where to find us." He paused. "I suppose if Martha had wanted to find us badly enough, she would have found a way. And still, I think about that phone call. I think that was Martha, calling to let us know she was okay. I just wish she'd said something instead of hanging up."

"What about you? How did you deal with it?"

He took another sip of his cappuccino and set the cup in the saucer. "Funny you should ask. A few years later, when I was a young officer in the Navy, I hired a private investigator. I wanted to see if he could find out anything about Martha. It would have meant a lot to my parents. But he didn't. Not a trace."

"Do you still have a copy of the investigator's report?"

"I do, somewhere. When I get back to San Diego, I'll find it and send it to you."

Martha had disappeared over fifty years ago, so I was guessing the private eye Frank had hired was long gone and his files probably destroyed. Almost sure to be a dead end. Still, I'd like to see the report he'd given to Frank.

He reached for the accordion folder. He tugged at the elastic band and then opened the flap, reaching for a bright purple flash drive. "Photos, as promised. I've digitized a lot of these over the years and I've put a lot of them on this thumb drive. There are several good shots of Martha with the family, taken that year before Martha disappeared."

Pictures spilled out onto the table. Actual photographs had been slipped into plastic protector sheets, while other pictures were photocopies. I sorted through pictures of the Post family in the late 1960s. One photo showed Martha, in a cap and gown at her high school graduation, her parents standing on either side. Martha looked a lot like her mother, I thought, the same blond hair and small features, though Martha's hair, in the style of the times, was worn long and parted in the middle. Her father looked like a ramrod straight military officer, full of what they call military bearing. The next shot showed all four of the Post siblings on a sandy beach, in shorts and T-shirts, barefoot in the shallow water. Frank was on Martha's right, her sister Sarah and brother George on her left.

"You and Martha really looked alike," I said. They did, back then, the same shape of the head, the same cheekbones.

He nodded. "Blue eyes, like my mother. My hair was blond, too, but a bit darker. I've gone completely gray."

"I have photos, too." I'd used my phone to take pictures of Anita's snapshots, the ones that showed Martha as Sunny. When I got back to my office, I'd transferred them to my computer, enlarged several shots, and printed them. I took them from the envelope I'd brought with me and handed them to Frank.

A slow smile spread across his face. "So that's what Martha was up to all those times she went over to San Francisco."

"The band your sister was singing with, the Mad Monks," I said. "The leader was a man named Monk Guidry." I pointed. "He was in his mid-twenties. That's him, playing lead guitar. The woman who had these photos, Anita, was the bass player's girlfriend. She told me that Martha was Monk's girlfriend. And they all thought Sunny was older. When I was talking with Anita a few days ago, she said that they knew Sunny was a Navy brat. That's how I made the connection."

"I'm not surprised." Frank shook his head. "I know one of the things that Martha and my parents used to argue about was boys. Or young men. Martha wasn't interested in dating any of her high school classmates. She wanted to hang out with older guys, like sailors. We lived in officers' quarters on the base, shopped at the commissary and the Navy Exchange, went to dinner at the officers club. There were enlisted men and junior officers everywhere. The base was busy at that time, during Vietnam, and Dad was the executive officer of a unit. She would flirt with the sailors, the enlisted guys in Dad's command, and with the young officers who lived in the bachelor officers quarters. Martha could make herself look older, that's for sure. What about this Monk guy? Is he still around?"

"He went missing, too. In September nineteen sixty-nine. Monk's former girlfriend told everyone that he went to visit relatives and never came back. He was from Lake Charles, Louisiana."

"Louisiana? Lake Charles is a hundred miles or so from Baton Rouge, where my aunt lived. That's the western part of the state. Do you think Martha went to Louisiana with this guy?" He shook his head. "I suppose it's possible. The first time Martha ran away, she went to my aunt's place in Baton Rouge. But if any of our relatives had the slightest inkling that Martha was in Louisiana, they would have notified my parents. They all knew how upset my family was because Martha had disappeared. The extended family knew Martha was missing. There are still cousins scattered all over the country. Dad's family in Minnesota and Mom's family, a lot of them are still in the south."

"I agree, it's a long shot. But I'd still like to check it out."

He sounded dubious as he gave me his mother's family name, Lorimer, and the name of the aunt in Baton Rouge, the one Martha had gone to the first time she ran away.

"Monk had more reasons to stay in the Bay Area than he did to move back to Louisiana," I said. "His musician friends were really surprised when he disappeared. I have no proof that he left the Bay Area. A friend in New Orleans, another investigator, located Monk's sister. She says he never came back to Louisiana."

I took another look through the pictures that Frank had brought with him, hoping that something would catch my eye. Then it did.

It was an outdoor scene, a color shot, faded with time. Frank had enlarged the photo and it was blurry. The picture showed a baseball diamond. Several people were visible in the shot. Martha Post was one of them, in the foreground. She wore jeans and a blue-and-white checked blouse, her blond hair tousled. Next to her was a younger version of Frank Post.

"That's you and Martha," I said, pointing. "Tell me about this picture. When and where was it taken?"

"May of 'sixty-nine," he said with a smile. "Right before Martha graduated from high school. It was a softball game one weekend, a Saturday, some sort of command function. The sailors played against the junior officers. Martha didn't want to go, but Dad insisted that we all had to put in an appearance. Martha sulked through the first inning but then she started to enjoy herself. I'd gotten a new camera for my birthday, so I took lots of pictures."

"You're in this picture, though. Who took it?"

"Mom, I think. That's Dad in the background." He indicated a figure at the periphery. Then his index figure hovered over the image of his older sister. "I really like that shot. Martha looked happy."

She did. She was smiling. Frank was on her left and next to him was a tall young man whose hair looked white-blond in sunlight. On his left, a short stocky guy held a baseball bat.

Two people stood a few paces from Martha's right, not part of the group. But something about their faces made me peer at the photograph. The young man looked relaxed and cheerful, hands tucked into the pockets of his jeans. But the young woman next to him had a frown on her face as she slanted her gaze at Martha. No, not Martha. The focus of her glare was the tall man with blond hair.

I'd seen those faces before. Ann Lombardi and Eddie Baldwin.

"There are some names on the back," Frank said. "Dad's leading chief gave me the names. I made a copy for him and I remember writing them on the back."

I turned over the photo and checked the names listed. The two men standing with Martha and Frank were Bill Higgins and Kelvin Ward. The young couple nearby weren't listed by name. I returned to the images. Ann and Eddie, I was sure of it. And from the look on her face, Ann didn't have much use for Kelvin Ward.

I heard Tessa Lombardi's voice, from our earlier conversation, telling me that Eddie had taken Ann to a softball game on the Navy base.

There was another sailor, she said, and Ann had dated him. But she'd ended the relationship because he'd asked her to do something she didn't want to do. She'd been bothered by the fact that he was at the softball game, and because he'd said something to her. Something unpleasant, according to Tessa.

Kelvin Delbert Ward. I examined the image of the tall sailor with blond hair and remembered what former Navy investigator Lloyd Humphrey told me during our recent meeting. Ward was the possible owner of the footlocker, the sailor who went AWOL while he was under investigation for smuggling drugs from Vietnam to Naval Air Station Alameda, stuffing heroin into candy boxes. At the time, the investigators thought he was transporting them off the base by giving the boxes to girlfriends.

Had Ward asked Ann to do that while they were dating? Had she suspected something wasn't quite right?

I pointed at Ann and Eddie. "Do you know these people? The ones with Martha in this photo?"

Frank shook his head. "Never saw them before, or after. They acted like they were a couple. Why? Is it important?"

"They disappeared in October of that year. They went out on a date and vanished. Your family had moved to San Diego by then, so maybe you didn't hear about it."

Frank stared at the photo. "I did hear about it. One of my high school buddies from Alameda told me about it. He said there was all kinds of talk about the Zodiac killer. That was going on then, all those murders and the letters to the *Chronicle*. You know, when Martha disappeared, and then a couple of weeks later those people were shot in Vallejo. That was supposed to be the Zodiac, too. But no, if that was Martha on the phone, calling in August—" He shook his head. "I just don't know what to think."

"What about the other people? The tall guy next to Martha and the short one holding the bat?"

"Those two guys?" He pointed at the young man holding the bat. "Him I remember, because he hit a couple of homers during the game. And the other one? The tall blond guy, I remember him because he had this cool T-shirt. Someone had drawn a picture of the USS Enterprise on it. Not the Navy ship, the starship from *Star Trek*. Look, you can see it in the picture." I peered at it more closely, squinting as I made out the shape and the letters NCC-1702.

"A *Star Trek* fan," I said.

"Just like me. Like I said, I was really into all things *Star Trek*. I guess this guy was, too. I remember telling him I thought his T-shirt was cool.

He just laughed. Said he was into *Star Trek*, too." Frank paused and tilted his head, as though dredging something else out of his memory. "His shipmates called him Scotty."

"Scotty?" I focused on the figure in the photo. Tall and blond, just like the guy Anita had seen with Gloria at a music festival later that year. The guy Gloria called Scotty.

"Beam me up, Scotty," I said.

Frank grinned. "That's right."

"Would these guys in the picture have known each other?"

"Sure. They were all enlisted men, working in my dad's command. They must have known each other."

Scotty.

Gloria's sailor boyfriend was Kelvin Delbert Ward, the sailor who had gone AWOL in the fall of 1969, as investigators closed in on his drug smuggling activities—and the possible owner of a footlocker containing the bones of two missing people.

# Twenty-Four

I RETURNED TO MY office and made notes on my meeting with Frank Post, speculating about this latest revelation of the links between all four of the missing persons. Were the bones in the footlocker those of Ann and Eddie? Or could they belong to Monk and Sunny? How long would it take to get an identification?

My phone rang. The screen readout said the caller was Nathan Dupree. He worked for Gary at Manville Security and had given me some vital information when I was investigating Cal Brady's death.

"Hey, Nathan, what's up?"

"Hey, Jeri. I got a guy you need to talk to."

I sat back in my chair. "Who? And why?"

"His name's Earl Marshall," Nathan said. "He's an older guy, a friend of my dad. As for the why, could be about those bones you found in that house in Alameda. Gary told me you're looking into that situation."

"Does Earl know something about the bones? Or how they came to be there?"

"Maybe. He's got a tale to tell, anyway. No point in me giving you the hearsay. It's better you have a face-to-face with him."

"I agree. Ask him to call me and we'll set something up."

We disconnected. Then I took another call, this one from a client. After we talked, I made notes on our conversation and settled down to work on a report for another client.

When the phone rang again, caller ID showed a number, no name. I answered and identified myself. A man's voice said, "I'm Earl Marshall. Nathan Dupree gave me your number, said I should call you."

"I spoke with Nathan earlier. He said you have some information for me."

"Yeah, maybe. I was thinking about calling you anyway. I saw on the news that you found those bones in that old house over in Alameda."

"Nathan said you had a tale to tell."

Marshall laughed. "I guess I do. His dad and me, we're buddies. I was over there last night and I mentioned it, and that's when Nathan said I should tell you. Way back when, I worked on the Navy base in Alameda."

"How far is way back when?"

"Back in nineteen sixty-nine."

The same year that those four people had disappeared—Ann and Eddie, Monk and Sunny.

I was intrigued, itching to hear what he had to say. "I'm in the uptown section of Oakland. Can we meet?"

"I'm over at Kaiser right now," he said, mentioning the big medical complex that anchored the area around Broadway and MacArthur. "Had a doctor's appointment and I just finished up. Piedmont Avenue is just a couple of blocks from here. There's a Peet's."

"I'm on my way."

Truth be told, there was a Peet's almost everywhere in the Bay Area. Alfred Peet had come to San Francisco from his native Netherlands, by way of London and Indonesia, and he'd worked in the coffee and tea trade most of his adult life. He'd opened the first Peet's Coffee in Berkeley in 1966 and the Bay Area had been drinking dark roast ever since. There were now over two hundred Peet's coffee bars.

One of them was on Piedmont Avenue, a bustling street lined with all sorts of shops and restaurants, from hole-in-the-wall breakfast and lunch joints, to delis, to high-end expensive destinations. And La Farine, a bakery which made delectable breads and pastries. The Piedmont Theatre showed movies on three screens. On Friday and Saturday nights, the line of post-cinema ice cream seekers was out the door at nearby Fenton's Creamery, which had been dishing up ice cream for over a hundred years. Just thinking about Fenton's made me hunger for a Black and Tan, one of their signature sundaes, with vanilla and toasted almond ice cream scoops drenched in hot fudge and caramel sauce. I would have to content myself with coffee, however.

It was a beautiful day, sunny with a blue sky dotted here and there with clouds. There was just enough chill in the air to remind me that it was October. I made the drive from my office near 27th Street, turning off Broadway onto Piedmont Avenue. I found a spot in the metered lot. I crossed Piedmont at 41st and strolled down the sidewalk. Peet's was on the corner of Glen Avenue. Inside, there were customers sitting at every table, most of them drinking coffee or tea.

One man at a small table to my left was reading a paperback book. He was in his seventies, I guessed, with curly gray hair and a face that looked lived in. He wore faded jeans and a black windbreaker over a red and gray checked shirt.

I walked over to the table. "Earl Marshall?"

"You must be Jeri." He smiled as he set aside the book, lines crinkling around his brown eyes.

I gestured at the counter. "What can I get you? Coffee and something to eat?"

"Plain old black coffee, large. High test. None of that decaf stuff. Nothing to eat, thanks."

"Sure thing." I stepped up to the counter and got his coffee and a latte for myself.

I carried the coffees to the table, pulled out a chair and sat down. "What do you have to tell me?"

"Way back when, like I said, in 'sixty-nine. I was nineteen, but I had a high draft number. Never did get called up. I was going to school part time at the College of Alameda. Doing construction work, hard labor most of it. I was on a job at the Navy base in the summer and fall of that year. And I lived in West Alameda."

"Where?" Had he been one of Gloria's tenants?

He anticipated my question and shook his head. "No, I didn't live at that house. But I almost rented a flat there. As soon as I saw the picture of the house on the news, I recognized it. The woman that owned the place, I remember her. She looked like a hippie, you know, long hair and beads and clothes that looked like something out of a rag bag. Anyway, I wound up living a couple of blocks away, on Pacific Avenue. A buddy of mine had a place and his roommate moved out, so I moved in. There were a lot of sailors living in that part of town, because it's so close to the base. But that's not the main thing I want to tell you."

"It has something to do with the base?"

"Yeah. I thought of it when I heard about those bones on the news. Like I said, I was doing construction work. Just labor and muscle, you know. We were remodeling a building at the base. It was old, probably built during World War Two or maybe the early fifties. The plumbing and electrical were already there and working just fine. We had gutted the interior and were reframing rooms. Making smaller offices out of bigger rooms, that's what it looked like. The work site was near the runways and those enlisted barracks."

"You remember the location that well?" I asked.

"I do. That's because I was on the base last week. There's a few places out there now that serve food. A deli, a couple of breweries and wineries. That's where I was going, with my grandson, taking him out for his birthday. I drove by that building. Or what's left of it. It's being torn down. I said to my grandson, hey, your old grandpa worked on that and now they're tearing it down."

"There has been a lot of work at the old base since it closed." I said. "Apartment construction. And there's a new ferry terminal at Seaplane Lagoon."

"Glad to see them doing that redevelopment over on the base. That's a lot of space that can be used. It said on the news that the bones you found had been buried and dug up." He looked at me, as though seeking confirmation.

I nodded. "That's right."

He sipped his coffee. "That building had a crawl space instead of a concrete slab, so it was up off the ground, maybe four feet or more, with a wooden enclosure around it and some little windows—air holes, really—covered with wire to keep the critters out. Dirt underneath, with a layer of gravel on top. At the back of the building, a little door, about three feet wide, so you could get into the crawl space."

After another swallow of coffee, he continued. "One morning when I got to work, it looked to me like someone had been messing around on the job site. The door that led into the crawl space was open, like somebody had been in there. Then there was this stink. We figured something got in there and died. Sure enough, it was a dead raccoon. One of the crew guys hauled it off but, you know, that stink kept lingering. I wondered if something else was dead in there. So I got a flashlight and got into that crawl space, just a couple of feet."

He shuddered. "I hate enclosed spaces. A couple of feet was more than enough. But it looked to me like there was a spot in one corner where some gravel and dirt had been dug up and heaped over something. I backed out of there and went looking for the foreman. He blew me off. Said I was imagining things. I said, crawl under there yourself and take a look. But he didn't, not as far as I know. The stink went away. Then we were done and we moved on to the next job. I forgot about it until I saw that story on the news, about the bones. And saw that building being torn down. I'm wondering all over again."

So was I. Was the demolition still in progress? It must be, if he'd been on the base last week. "Did you see any signs, indicating what might be built on the site?"

"Yeah, there was a sign. But I didn't look at it, just noticed the demolition work."

And I hadn't even noticed the building or the demolition, when I was on the base visiting Tessa Lombardi at the deli. I need to take a drive over there.

Earl finished his coffee. He said he had to leave and I thanked him as he stood up and left the coffee shop. I sat for a moment longer, staring at the dregs of my latte.

Now I had a plausible scenario. Suppose a killer had a couple of inconvenient bodies, and a convenient work site with an accessible crawl space? It could have been a dark night or an early morning. Dirt and gravel, a shovel, some exertion and maybe some quicklime to speed up decomposition and reduce the stink as the bodies decayed into skeletons. But the killer didn't count on that building being demolished all these years later. The inconvenient bodies would be found again. So the killer retrieved them and hid them somewhere else.

But I found the bones anyway. Why stash them in a footlocker at Gloria's house? Was it simply a temporary solution until a more permanent resting place could be found?

This line of reasoning led me back to what I believed all along. The killer must be someone who was familiar with the house and had access. Someone who knew about the storage room on the ground floor.

I walked to the parking lot and retrieved my car. I didn't go back to the office, though—I headed for Alameda. Coming out of the Tube, I took the route I'd taken on my way to Lombardi's Deli, past the dry dock and the ferry terminal, in through the main gate. I drove up Lexington Street, past the old administration building, and turned right on West Midway.

It was a long block, with a huge hanger on my left. On my right was a row of two-story buildings, the enlisted barracks that had once housed sailors stationed at the base. I counted ten wings in all, extending from a building at the rear. With the lack of housing such a hot-button issue in the Bay Area, I wondered if there were any plans to turn these buildings into apartments. The duplexes that had once served as officers' quarters, on the other side of the base, were being rented to families. But these old barracks were in bad shape. They looked as though they were ready for the wrecker's ball.

I turned right from Midway onto Monarch. The site Earl told me about was tucked behind the barracks and surrounded by a chain link fence. There were several cars and trucks—probably belonging to the work crew—parked on either side of the gate opening onto Monarch Street. I drove past the vehicles and pulled to the curb, a few yards from the corner of fence. In front of me, on the other side of the estuary, huge mechanical cranes towered over container ships berthed at the Port of Oakland.

I got out of my car and walked to the fence. Demolition was still in progress on the building, a rectangle about thirty by forty feet. Opposite me, at the far corner of the site, an excavator was at work on one end of the structure, the bucket at the end of the boom chewing away the wall. I counted a dozen people on the crew, one in the cab of the excavator, several others wielding sledgehammers to break down debris. All of them wore coveralls and hard hats. A large truck was heading from the site out to the street, the bed loaded with window frames and doors.

A few feet to my right, a sign affixed to the fence told me that this redevelopment project was funded by Bertcor, in partnership with the Base Reuse and Community Development Department of the City of Alameda.

Bertcor. The same Bertcor that was buying the houses next to Gloria and planning to turn them into condos.

I took a photo of the sign. The excavator stopped its mechanical roar. In the ensuing silence, I heard a whistle as a train moved through the Oakland railyard.

The workers must be breaking for lunch. A man in a hard hat exited the cab of the excavator. A few of the workers headed out the gate, perhaps headed toward their vehicles, or to Lombardi's Deli, where I'd seen men in hard hats during my earlier visit with Tessa Lombardi. A few of them gathered on a couple of benches set up next to a temporary shed near the gate. Two men retrieved lunch boxes from the shed while three others sat on the bench nearest the driveway.

A car drove onto the site and braked to a stop near the bench. It was a Nissan sedan, old enough to have collected a few dents and scrapes. The paint job had faded to the point where I couldn't tell if the car had originally been dark green or gray. There was also a large rust blotch on the hood, just below the windshield on the passenger side. The driver's side opened and a man got out. He was in his mid-twenties, with blond hair and a thickset torso. He opened the hatch on the sedan and pulled out a cardboard carton, carrying it through the gate to the group of men gathered at the shed.

"Hey, Wes, you got clearance to be on the work site?" The words sounded stern, but the tone was light, as though the man who spoke was joking. He was burly and middle-aged. He removed his hard hat, revealing a balding head.

Wes grinned. "Don't mess with me, man. I got the food." He set down the carton and began pulling out sacks bearing the familiar logo of a local fast food outlet. "Okay, got a double cheeseburger, fries, chocolate shake, for Leo." He handed the bag to the burly guy and turned to a younger man with dark hair and a colorful sleeve tattoo on his left arm. "Double burger, fries, large Coke for Enrique. And for my man Milo, bacon cheeseburger, fries, vanilla shake."

"Thanks, buddy." Milo stuck his hand into the sack. He pulled out a burger, unwrapped it, and took a bite. He looked about thirty, stringy, with ropey muscles on his forearms and a thin mustache.

The new arrival, the man called Wes, wasn't part of the work crew, but he seemed to know them, at least the ones on the bench. He sat down and delved into his own sack, pulling out fries. He squeezed ketchup from several little plastic packets.

Something was nagging at me about Wes. I watched him tear into his burger, wondering what it was. Then I heard Leo ask Milo a question. "Hey, you still playing around on the Mothball Fleet?"

Milo set down his burger and reached for his fries. "Nah, that was years ago. Besides, it's gone."

"What the hell is the Mothball Fleet?" Enrique wiped his mouth with a paper napkin.

Milo chomped on his fries. "Old ships. My Uncle João—he's retired now—he used to work for a government outfit that was babysitting a bunch of old ships, sitting out in Suisun Bay."

"Oh, yeah, out near Martinez. I remember seeing them lined up on the water, whenever I was driving across the bridge. I wondered what they were doing there."

"Navy ships," Milo said. "They were out of service, decommissioned, they call it."

"Put out to pasture. But no pasture, just water." Wes laughed at his own joke, then took a big bite out of his burger.

"Why would they stick them out in the bay?" Enrique asked.

Milo slurped his shake. "The idea was if there was ever any emergency, they'd put them back in service. But it never happened. Kind of a lame idea anyway. It would have taken a hell of a lot of work to make those ships go again. My uncle called it the rusty fleet, because all those ships, man, they were just falling apart. Rust falling into the bay. Lead, old paint, asbestos, all that shit. The enviros were raising a stink about it. So, over the past few years they hauled them off. Sent them to shipyards where they got busted up for scrap."

Leo nodded. "Just like we're knocking down buildings on this base. Making room for something else." He waved a hand at the dilapidated old barracks that lined Midway Avenue. "Like those buildings. They're too far gone for anyone to do anything with them. We'll be tearing them down next."

The younger guy turned to Milo. "So, you used to play around on those ships?"

"Yeah, playing war." Wes laughed.

Milo shrugged. "Not really. It wasn't like that. Uncle João used to take me out there, that's all. And a few times, Wes went with me. We got to go out on the ships to look around."

"It was cool," Wes added. "Like being on a ghost ship. All those empty spaces, places where there used to be sailors and equipment. All kinds of cool places to hide stuff, right, Milo?" He laughed as Milo shot him a look.

I narrowed my eyes, taking a closer look at Wes. In my head, I went over the description that Peggy Slocum had given me of the man who had threatened her when she refused to move out of the apartment. A young guy, in his twenties, she'd said. With muscles and a beer gut. Shaggy, dirty blond hair and blue eyes. I wasn't close enough to see his eyes, but Wes definitely had the hair and the beer gut.

I raised my phone, as though I was going to make a call, and snapped a photo of the men and the car. Just then, Leo looked up from his lunch and noticed me. "Hey, didn't see you standing there. Something I can help you with?"

I slipped the phone into my pocket, ready with a cover story. "I'm an insurance investigator, looking into a car accident that happened on this block a couple of weeks ago. It was a small gray SUV and a red sedan. A collision at that intersection there." I waved a hand at the corner of Midway and Monarch.

Leo frowned. "Two weeks ago, you say? I don't remember seeing anything. Any of you guys see a car accident?" The others shook their heads. "What time of day was this?"

"Late afternoon, around five o'clock."

"Well, that's why," Leo said. "We knock off work around four. But I'm usually here later. I'm the foreman. Once everybody quits for the day, it's pretty quiet around here. Except for the breweries along this stretch."

"That's interesting," I said. "Quiet, you say. But I hear there have been some break-ins and vandalism around here in the evening and at night."

Leo was shaking his head. "Break-ins? No, I never heard anything like that. We haven't had any problems."

"Yeah, we did," Enrique said. "We had a break-in, remember? We got work that morning and it looked like someone had been in that crawl space." He pointed at the building and I saw the space, four feet between the ground and the building floor. "There was a door but it was gone."

"Oh, that." Leo rubbed his chin. "Well, it didn't look like anyone broke in. The lock on the gate hadn't been jimmied. But it looked like somebody had been on the site. There wasn't anything missing, not that we could tell. I was kinda surprised. That kind of thing happens all the time, but here on the base, not so much. Like I said, there's not many people around here at night, unless they're going to one of the pubs. Or that gym a few blocks away. They got people living in the old Navy housing, but that's the other side, not here by the runways."

"That crawl space is creepy," Enrique said. "I don't like going in there. All that dirt, and those feathers that blew under there make me sneeze. I'll bet it was some homeless guy that got in there, trying find a place to sleep."

Milo spoke up. "You're imagining things. The gate was locked and there aren't any gaps in the fence."

I had been keeping an eye on Milo and Wes while the other two men were describing what had happened on the site. Something in their expressions piqued my interest, as though they might be worried. If Milo worked on the site, he might have a key that would give him access. Time enough to dig up bones and a few stray feathers? He'd have needed help to transport them and stash them in the footlocker. His buddy Wes, who looked a lot like the thug who had threatened Peggy Slocum, was a good candidate for that.

I thanked the men and moved toward the intersection, where I took more photos to go with my cover story, making sure I snapped off a shot of the sedan's license plate for good measure. Then I walked back to my car. A sidelong glance showed Milo and Wes, heads bent together as they conversed. I was planning to go back to my office to do some research on Carol Bertram and her company, Bertcor. Maybe if I peeled back the layers of ownership, I'd get some answers.

As I slid behind the driver's seat, my phone rang. I picked up the call.

"It's Lieutenant Chen at the APD. We've identified the bones."

# Twenty-Five

"Ann Lombardi and Eddie Baldwin," Chen said.

I was in his office, after driving across town to the police department. "Dental records?"

He nodded. "That confirmed it. The Lombardi family provided dental records for Ann. And the Navy gave up records for Eddie."

"Plus something else," I said. "That little metal disk that was in the footlocker. I'm guessing it was from Ann's charm bracelet."

"You're right. It was a silver charm that Eddie gave Ann, with a Navy anchor on one side and their initials on the other. Tessa Lombardi identified it. She'd like to have the whole bracelet, if we can find it. By the way, the two skeletons you found in the footlocker are not complete. There are bones missing. Small ones, like fingers and toes. They might still be in the site where the bodies were buried, along with the rest of Ann's bracelet. If we can just find out where that was."

"I might be able to help you there," I said. "I have information, and a theory, about the bones."

Chen leaned forward in his chair. "I'm listening."

"Earlier today, I got a call from a man who worked construction on a building at the Navy base, back in 'sixty-nine. It's near the corner of Midway and Monarch, behind a row of barracks." I relayed the information about the long-ago building remodel and the crawl space underneath. "My source tells me when he looked under the building, it looked like something was covered up. The crawl space is about four feet high. It would be possible to dig a hole to stash two bodies and scoop dirt and gravel over the grave."

"It would have to be a big hole, or wide enough to put the bodies side by side," Chen said. "It would take a few hours, but at night? Maybe. The building is being torn down?"

"Yes. That's why the man contacted me. He saw the news reports about me finding the bones. And he was on the base last week and noticed the demolition work. My theory is that the killer knew the building was being demolished, retrieved the remains, or had someone do it, and put the bones in Gloria's house. Temporarily."

"Then you upset the apple cart by finding the bones," he said. "That's an interesting theory. Do you have anything to back it up?"

"I was on the base when you called," I said. "I wanted to check out the site. I got to talking with some of the work crew. One of them said it looked like someone had gotten into the crawl space. But there's a chain link fence around the site and it's locked at night. There was no sign of forced entry. And as far as I know, it wasn't reported."

"So either they're imagining things, or someone used a key. As for whether it was reported, that's easy enough to find out." Chen turned toward his computer. "Do you have an approximate date?"

"No, but given the pace of the work and when the bones were found, I would guess sometime in the last couple of months."

Chen focused on his computer, fingers moving over the keyboard. "No, I'm not seeing any reports about a possible break-in at a construction site. So more than likely, they just didn't bother."

"Might be worth checking to see if there are any stray bones at the site. Or the rest of Ann's charm bracelet."

Chen made a noncommittal noise, then said, "I'm about to call the police department in Lakewood, Colorado. That's where Eddie was from. If his family still lives there, the local police will do the notification that his remains have been found."

When I returned to my car parked on Oak Street, I got inside and sat for a moment. Two of the missing persons from 1969 had finally been identified, giving the families of Ann Lombardi and Eddie Baldwin some answers. But I still didn't know what had happened to Monk and Sunny.

I pulled out my phone and scrolled through my contacts. Maggie Constable answered my call after two rings. "Hi, Jeri. Do you have news?"

"I do. The bones in the footlocker belong to Ann and Eddie. I just spoke with Lieutenant Chen at APD. They used dental records to make the identification. And that metal disk I saw was a charm that Eddie had given to Ann."

Maggie sighed. "Finally, after all these years. That doesn't make it any easier for the families. They talk about closure. I'm not sure such a thing exists." She paused. "What about the other missing people you told me about, the musician and the singer?"

"Monk and Sunny. Still missing and still no answers. That one is still very much up in the air. They disappeared about the same time. I have the feeling they're connected, because of the house. Because of Monk's relationship with Gloria. And Sunny's connection to the Navy base. There has to be something tying all this together."

"Keep me posted," Maggie said. "I'm definitely writing about this."

"By the way, do you know anything about a couple of property developers named Carol Bertram and Lee Corland. Their names came up."

"Bertram I don't know anything about. But I have heard of Corland. He tried to bribe someone up in Santa Rosa a few years back and it backfired on him."

Which is what I'd heard from Emma, and my uncle. It was time to do more research. I went back to my office, where I returned phone calls and answered emails related to other cases before settling down to check out Carol Bertram and Bertcor, the company that had close ties to Lee Corland. After reading about the company and its CEO, I decided my best bet was to waylay Carol Bertram, at her office or another location. I doubted I could get on her calendar, especially since whoever would be making that appointment would want to know why I was asking for a meeting with the developer. And I had my doubts that Bertram would be all that forthcoming when I posed my questions. Still, I wanted to see her reaction to our coming encounter. Body language and unanswered questions often spoke volumes.

So, ambush, I thought. A technique that usually worked well for me.

According to the Bertcor website, the company's headquarters was located on Market Street, in San Francisco's Financial District, the neighborhood that served as the city's business center. I reached for the phone. After being passed through several people, I found myself on the phone with an eager-to-please administrative assistant who told me Bertram was out of the office. That saved me a trip to San Francisco, at least today. Further probing elicited the information that Bertram was in Oakland and likely to be at that location until four o'clock. She was attending a meeting on waterfront development at a hotel on the Embarcadero.

I had a meeting as well, in downtown Oakland. After that was done, I headed for the waterfront.

The area south of Jack London Square and Fifth Street looked vastly different than it had a few years ago. On this stretch, where the Embarcadero paralleled the I-880 freeway, multi-story apartment buildings had gone up, with units already rented. Others were in various stages of construction. The area, and the nearby cove, were called Brooklyn Basin, named after a long-ago town called Brooklyn that had been incorporated into Oakland. Beyond the busy construction site, a number of low rise hotels backed onto the estuary. The first of these was the site of Carol Bertram's afternoon meeting.

I found a parking space and entered the lobby, where a signboard indicated the location of the waterfront development meeting, with a description that told me the meeting was supposed to be a discussion on the future of the Oakland waterfront. I suspected the answer to that was more buildings going up along the estuary. I moved down the hallway to the designated meeting room and slipped through an open door at the back of the room.

I stood next to a rectangular table that held a coffee and tea setup and a nearly-empty basket containing an assortment of granola bars. To one side was a collection of used mugs on a tray. Between me and the table, a trash can brimmed with wadded-up napkins and wrappers. The room had more rectangular tables set up for the meeting participants, four on each side of a central aisle, with another set up as the head table. Two men and a woman sat there, with one man at the lectern. It sounded like the meeting was wrapping up, I'd arrived just in time. Sure enough, the man finished his spiel and there was a smattering of applause as the people at the tables stood, preparing to leave.

I moved toward the side wall, a better position to scan the room and its occupants. I'd seen several photographs of Bertram online. I spotted her, at the far end of a table close to the front of the room. She had just pushed back her chair and was standing. She had a trim, athletic body in gray slacks and a matching tailored jacket, her peach silk blouse complementing her pale complexion and blond hair. She paused where she was, chatting with a man and a woman who had been at her table. I picked up a discarded brochure and edged closer, eavesdropping as I glanced at the glossy tri-fold advertising a new apartment complex.

"The new ballpark has to be part of that conversation," the man said, referring to the controversial plans by the Oakland A's baseball team to build a waterfront ballpark on the site of the Howard Terminal, located two miles to the north on land owned by the Port of Oakland. It was controversial because a lot of people were against it, including the maritime industry at Oakland, the sixth largest container port in the United States. If the ballpark project went through, it would transform this area. A lot of developers were salivating at the prospect of building more apartments and condos.

"Now that Brooklyn Basin is well on its way," the other woman said, referring to the big project going up on the waterfront.

I heard a buzzing sound. "Excuse me," the man said. He reached into his pocket and hauled out his phone, put it to his ear and moved away.

"I have to go," the other woman said. "Great to see you, Carol."

"I'd better get going myself," Bertram said. "The traffic on the Bay Bridge gets worse as the afternoon wears on." The other woman took her leave as Bertram stood at the end of the table. She gathered up several papers and file folders. She tucked them into a slim leather briefcase and snapped it shut, preparing to leave.

I discarded the brochure I was holding and made my move. "Carol Bertram?"

She looked up, a pleasant, public-face sort of smile on her face. "Yes, that's me."

"My name's Jeri Howard. I have some questions about a project involving your company."

"I have a lot of projects," she said. "Which one are you talking about?"

"It's in Alameda. Your company has been purchasing old Victorian houses on the West End, with plans to convert them into condominiums."

Her smile dimmed a bit and she tilted her head to one side. "Yes, I believe a project like that is in the works. I'm not sure where we are in the process."

"You don't have planning approval. I checked."

"Why would you do that?" she asked. "I mean, what's your interest?"

"My interest is in a particular house, one you haven't bought yet." I gave her Gloria's street address. I wanted to see her reaction. She had a fairly good poker face, but not good enough. There was a little twitch at the corner of her mouth that gave her away.

"I'm sorry," she said, with a smile that didn't extend to her eyes. "I'm not sure what you're asking."

"I've heard of some unusual incentives that were deployed to make sure the tenants moved out of that house, so that it would be empty when it came to time for the conversion. Bribes in one case. Strong-arm tactics in another. What do you know about that?"

"Nothing," she said, her voice and face indignant. "What kind of accusation is this? Who are you?"

"As I say, Jeri Howard." I handed her a business card. "I'm a private investigator."

She looked at the card as though it was toxic. "I've heard your name before. You were involved in that business down by Brooklyn Basin. A developer I know was arrested."

"Yes, for murder." I gave her stare for stare.

She put my card on the table, her mouth tightening. "I don't think I've done anything that would warrant your interest, Ms. Howard. The Alameda project is completely above-board and I expect we'll soon get approval. Now, if you'll excuse me, I have an appointment in the city." She picked up her briefcase and walked toward the door.

"What do you know about a man named Lee Corland?" I asked her retreating back.

She paused briefly, then kept walking. I followed her out of to the hallway, in time to see her enter the ladies room. I went to the lobby and stood where I could see the restroom door, next to a large potted plant that I hoped would hide me from view. A moment later, Bertram came out of the ladies room, holding her phone to her ear. She swept into the lobby and I backed up a bit, hoping she wouldn't see me through the profusion of green leaves. She looked around the lobby, then exited the building. I followed. She turned left at the end of the front sidewalk and walked through the parking lot, dredging a keyring from her bag. Up ahead, a red Audi blinked lights as she unlocked the car. I slipped between two parked cars and watched as she got into the car. She didn't start it, though. She sat for a moment in the driver's seat, making another phone call. A few minutes later, she ended the call. The Audi's engine started.

I backtracked to my own Toyota. I followed Bertram out of the hotel parking lot onto the Embarcadero. She was heading toward Jack London Square. That made sense if, as I'd overheard, she was driving back to San Francisco. She would access the on ramp at Oak and Sixth. She drove past the Brooklyn Basin development, stopping for a red light at Fifth Avenue. When the light changed, she continued on the Embarcadero, crossing the bridge over the channel that links the estuary with Lake Merritt to the east. As I guessed, she turned right on Oak Street. A few blocks later, she made the left onto Sixth Street, which fed onto the freeway.

I kept going on Oak Street, which from this point on was one-way. I went through the intersection at Eighth and Oak as the light flashed to yellow. Behind me, a car sped up and barreled through on the red. I thought it was going to hit my rear bumper, but the driver braked and slowed as we drove past the BART station. Up ahead was the Alameda County Courthouse and several county buildings, the Main Library, and

Lake Merritt itself, actually a tidal lagoon in the middle of downtown Oakland. Another light flashed red at Twelfth and Oak. I stopped and glanced into my rear view mirror. The car that had run the red light earlier was still behind, in the same lane. It was a sedan with a rusty spot on the hood.

The light signal changed to green. I moved through the intersection and switched lanes, from the right lane that had to turn at Fourteenth to the left lane that went straight. So did the car behind me.

Was the driver just going my direction? Or following me?

Past Fourteenth, Oak Street became Lakeside Drive, curving around the lake to my right. There were two lanes here, still one-way, and I stayed in the right lane, because a UPS truck blocked the left lane up ahead. As was usually the case, the lakeside paths were crowded with walkers, enjoying the afternoon sunshine. I dawdled, driving slowly enough that I caught the red light at the next intersection, Madison Street. I checked the rear view mirror again, examining the driver. Male and young. He wore sunglasses and a ball cap pulled low over his brow. Fair hair was visible around the cap.

It was the same Nissan sedan I'd seen at the demolition site in Alameda. The murky gray-green paint job and the rust spot made it easy to identify. The driver was Wes, the guy who had delivered burgers and fries. He was following me. And he wasn't very good at it.

I must have touched a nerve today, talking with the crew at the demolition site. Or was this due to my encounter with Carol Bertram?

I was asking the right questions, making someone uncomfortable.

Past Madison Street, Lakeside became two-way, with one lane in each direction. It dead ended at Harrison Street. I turned right, driving past the busy Grand Street intersection. A few blocks farther on, I turned left on 27th Street. The light turned yellow as I went through the intersection and I watched the sedan run the red light to keep up with me.

I reached the entrance to my office building at 27th and Valdez and pulled into the driveway. I stopped and turned in the driver's seat, hoping to catch a glimpse of my tail. The sedan went past, slowing for a few seconds, just enough time for me to see a large scrape on the passenger side door. Then the car sped up again, through the nearby intersection of 27th and Broadway.

I pulled out my phone and hit the photo icon, calling up the pictures I'd snapped earlier at the work site. I had one shot of Wes and one of the car.

Peggy Slocum told me the young man who had threatened her, telling her she had to move out of her apartment, was in his twenties, with a thickset body and dirty blond hair straggling to his shoulders. And he drove a sedan with a dark paint job and a big ding on the passenger side door. Wes certainly matched that description. So did his car.

I parked and went inside to my office, where I sent a text message to Peggy, attaching photos of Wes and the car. She responded about twenty minutes later, with two words. "That's him."

---

After working in my office for another hour or so, I headed home, stopping first at the Trader Joe's on College Avenue to pick up a few groceries. I parked my Toyota in my driveway and retrieved my groceries from the trunk. Then I heard a voice call my name. I looked up to see Madison, coming down the stairs from the studio apartment above the garage. She joined me on the sidewalk that led to my own front porch.

She had a worried look on her face. "I'm glad to see you. There was a creepy guy here. I saw him about thirty minutes ago, when I got home from class."

"What was he doing?" I asked.

"He was on your porch, like he was trying the door. Then he started climbing the stairs to my apartment. I had just started up the driveway. I called out and asked what he was doing here. He came back down the stairs, then he hemmed and hawed and gave me some story that he was looking for a friend. I told him he must have the wrong address." She shook her head. "He didn't look like a homeless guy, but I didn't like the look of him. There was something about him that rang all my alarm bells."

Mine, too. I fingered the strap of my canvas grocery bag. Was it the guy in the grungy car that had followed me to my office? "What did he look like?"

"He had a ball cap pulled low over his face," Madison said. "So I didn't get a good look at that. His hair must have been short because I didn't see that either."

That didn't sound like Wes, the driver of the sedan that had followed me to my office.

"Height, weight, clothes?"

"Blue jeans and a gray T-shirt. Muscles in the arms, but a skinny build."

It could be Milo, Wes's friend. "What happened after you spoke to him?"

"He hit the street and walked back toward College." She pointed a thumb over her shoulder. "I went up to my balcony to watch him and I took a couple of pictures."

"Great. I want to see them."

"They're not very good," Madison said as she pulled her phone from her pocket. "Blurry. But I think one of them shows part of his face." She accessed the photos. "Here, these two." She handed the phone to me.

I examined the photos in turn, touching the screen to enlarge the images. Both were indeed blurry, taken from a distance while the man was walking away from the house. On the plus side, he had been crossing the street to the sidewalk on the other side. He must have glanced back at the house or checked for oncoming traffic at the moment the pictures were snapped. As a result, the second photograph showed most of his face, but I couldn't make out features. It looked to me like he had dark hair.

"It's good enough," I said. "I'm glad you were able to get pictures. Email those to me. I'll enlarge them and see if I can get more detail."

"I will. I didn't see him get into a car. If I had, I would have taken a picture of that, too. I lost sight of him."

Madison headed back up to her apartment and I stepped onto my porch, keys in hand, and unlocked the door.

My probing into whatever was going on with Gloria's property had definitely brought me under scrutiny. I thought back to Carol Bertram, who'd made a phone call in the lobby of the waterfront hotel, probably alerting someone.

My phone pinged as I was unloading groceries in the kitchen. Madison's email, with the photo attached. I stepped out of the kitchen to the living room, where my laptop sat on an end table. I opened and turned it on, heading for my email program. After downloading the photos to my computer, I opened the image that showed the man's face, enlarging it by degrees, until I could look at the blurry face. Dark hair, yes. A streak of some sort? A shadow?

No, it was a mustache. Dark hair and a thin mustache, on the face of the man called Milo, who had been working on the demolition crew at the old Navy base. Prowling around my house a few hours after I'd visited the site, and shortly after I'd confronted Carol Bertram and my car followed by Milo's buddy Wes.

That was an unpleasant turn of events. How did he know where I lived?

I could think of several scenarios. All the while I'd been investigating people involved in this case, others had investigated me. I'd handed out my business card to various players. It would be easy enough to go from there. Milo and Wes must have noted my car license plate while I was at the demolition site, meaning they saw through my story about investigating a car accident.

But someone else pulled their strings. Was it Carol Bertram? Or Lee Corland?

# Twenty-Six

I LEFT HOME ON Friday morning, heading to downtown Berkeley for a meeting with a new client. By ten o'clock, I was back in my Oakland office, making a pot of coffee to go with the chocolate croissant I'd picked up while I was out. I sat down at my desk and checked the messages on my office phone, returning a few calls. Then I booted up the computer and made notes in the client file. I finished off the croissant and washed the chocolate from my hands.

Fortified with coffee, I was ready to investigate the two men I'd seen yesterday at the demolition site on the old Navy base. One of the photos I'd taken was a clear shot of the license plate on the beat-up car Wes had been driving. I logged onto one of the databases I used and keyed in the letters and numbers.

The car was a Nissan Versa sedan, ten years old, and it was registered to Wesley Chandler. Now that I had a name, I expanded my search. His address was an apartment building on 21st Avenue near Foothill Boulevard, in Oakland's San Antonio neighborhood, southeast of Lake Merritt. He was twenty-six years old, with a spotty work history and two misdemeanor convictions, one for petty theft and another for driving under the influence. His most recent job was listed as maintenance work and his employer was CLB Properties in San Francisco. The same CLB Properties that was owned by Carol Bertram and Bertcor. Somehow I wasn't surprised.

Chandler. That name was familiar. Then I recalled the obituary for Richard Chandler. He had been the third party in a now-dissolved company formed two decades ago by Lee Corland and Carol Bertram. I went looking for the obituary again and read through it. Sure enough, the obit listed a son named Wesley. So, Wes was Carol Bertram's nephew. He'd been working for his aunt, doing some low level intimidation. Keeping it all in the family, I thought again.

I turned my attention to Wes's buddy Milo. I hadn't seen him near a vehicle so I didn't know what he drove. Construction worker? Was he in a union? Or a casual worker? I drummed my fingers on the surface of the desk as I thought about it.

Then it came to me. The Mothball Fleet. Milo had talked about that yesterday, when I eavesdropped on his conversation at the demolition site. He and Wes had gone out on those old ships, he said, courtesy of his uncle, who'd worked with the fleet before he retired.

Most people called it the Mothball Fleet, but the official name was the Suisun Bay Reserve Fleet. Since 1946, old military ships, supposedly ready to be activated, had instead been quietly moldering in Suisun Bay, the tidal estuary at the confluence of the Sacramento and San Joaquin Rivers. The fleet had been anchored on the north side of the bay, on the Solano County shoreline, east of the bridge leading from Martinez to Benicia, visible to drivers on the bridge and the nearby freeway.

Years ago, there had been as many as 340 ships lined up in rows. Milo's uncle had called it the rusty fleet. That was because those ships were rusting away, the detritus going into the bay—harmful chemicals, lead, hazardous paint and asbestos. Over the years some 20 tons of the stuff had washed off the ships and into the water. Which was bad, since Suisun Marsh is the largest saltwater marsh in the western United States, an environmentally sensitive area known for its abundant bird life.

Finally the decision was made to send the ships, way past the end of their useful life, to the scrapyard. Over the past few years, they'd been hauled off, a few at a time, west through the narrow Carquinez Strait into San Pablo Bay, the northernmost reach of San Francisco Bay, then out the Golden Gate to the Pacific Ocean. They sailed down the coasts of California and Mexico and through the Panama Canal to ship-breaking facilities in the Gulf of Mexico. Two such sites had been designated by the Department of Defense to handle the job. One of those was in Brownsville, Texas and the other was near New Orleans. The last of the older ships had left the Bay Area in 2017, leaving just a few riding at anchor in Suisun Bay.

I didn't have a last name for Milo, but he'd mentioned Uncle João. That was Portuguese, a fairly common first name, though uncommon enough to make it stand out on a list of employees. The Maritime Administration, known as MARAD, had charge of the Suisun Bay Reserve Fleet. It took some digging but I finally found what I was looking for. As it happened, it wasn't a directory of employees. It was a tiny article in a local newspaper, about Uncle João's retirement party. His last name was Fonseca.

Was Milo's last name Fonseca? It was. I found him as well. Milo was thirty years old, had graduated from Concord High School in Contra Costa County, and he'd been working construction and demolition jobs for the past twelve years, mostly in the East Bay. He too lived in Oakland. In fact, it looked like Milo and his buddy Wes Chandler were roommates, with the same Oakland address. Had Milo ever worked for other Bertcor projects? His employment history told me he'd done construction and demolition work all over the East Bay. And yes, several of those jobs were for Bertcor.

Wes and Milo—partners in crime?

If, as I theorized, the bones had been buried at that site, Milo could have dug them up. After all, he worked there. He would have access. His buddy Wes worked for Bertcor, the company that was buying up the houses in the West Alameda neighborhood. It looked like his job was intimidating tenants. It was a short step from that to access to Gloria's house. So Wes and Milo hiding the bones, yes. But not on their own. They had to be acting on orders from someone higher up the food chain.

I was staring at my computer screen, thinking, when the phone rang. The caller ID showed the publishing company's number, and it was Lakshmi's voice I heard when I answered. She sounded exasperated. "Jeri, when we were going through Gloria's file boxes, did you see a notebook with a green cover?"

I glanced at the corner of my desk, where the notebook sat atop the copies I'd made of the pages. I'd planned to take another look at the pages, to see if I could glean any more information from the contents.

"Why do you ask?"

"It's Gloria. She called here, insisting that we stop whatever we were doing and go through the boxes we're storing here. She's looking for this green notebook and having a meltdown because she can't find it."

I'll bet she was, given what the notebook revealed about her financial dealings.

"She brought some files with her when she moved into her new apartment," Lakshmi continued. "But she looked through those and can't find this notebook. She thinks it was mixed in with the stuff we found in that closet at the house. There was a pile of loose papers on the floor. I gathered them up and dropped them into one of the boxes to bring over here. Noel and I just looked, but we didn't see a notebook anywhere. Then I thought about you. Did you see it?"

"I have the notebook. I found it yesterday, mixed in with the tenant records, in one of the folders I thought was empty."

"Oh, good. Could you bring it over here, as soon as possible?"

"Lakshmi, we need to talk. And soon."

"We do?" She hesitated. "I don't like the sound of that."

Before I could respond, Noel's voice came on the line. "Jeri, you've got the notebook? Great. Gloria sounded frantic when she called. I know you're as busy as we are, but could you please meet us at Gloria's apartment? I'll call and let her know we're bringing it over."

"Don't tell her that I have it," I warned. "We need to talk, as soon as possible. And I'd rather not do it on the phone. I'll meet you there."

I ended the call, not giving them the chance to argue with me. I slipped the notebook into my bag and reached for my keys.

Noel and Lakshmi were waiting in front of the building, near the glass doors that led into the lobby. He had his phone to his ear, frowning. "I've called Gloria several times. But she's not answering. It goes straight to voice mail." He jabbed the red button on the screen and pocketed the phone. "We'll just have to go up to her room."

He moved toward the glass doors but I forestalled him.

"Let's talk first." I gestured toward the nearby bench and chairs, which were unoccupied. I took a seat on one of the chairs. Noel reluctantly followed suit, sitting on the bench, while Lakshmi perched on the arm.

"It's just as well we came over to see Gloria," Noel said. "Lakshmi and I have been meaning to talk with her about cleaning out the house and getting rid of the rest of her stuff. Which has been delayed because it's a crime scene. But we want to discuss, again, this issue of putting the house on the market. I know she would get a good price, if I can just convince her to do it."

"Good luck with that." Lakshmi shook her head. "She has her mind made up and I don't think you'll be able to shift her. She insists that she has a buyer ready to write her a check. I asked how much that check would be and she told me a number that is way below market. If she goes ahead with this, she's practically giving the house away. She needs that money if she's going to live here and pay the kind of rent this place wants."

"She isn't paying the rent."

Noel's face reflected his consternation. "What? What are you talking about? She paid a big deposit and the first year's rent."

I shook my head. "I checked into Gloria's finances. She's not as solvent as she would have you believe. Which is why she is eager to unload the house as quickly as possible. But there's more to it than that. Someone else paid the deposit and the rent. His name is Lee Corland. He's a real estate developer. In fact, he's the buyer Gloria has been talking about."

Lakshmi frowned. "I knew there was something fishy about this, the way Gloria kept insisting this was a done deal, that she already had a buyer. He's taking advantage of her, trying to get her out of the house."

"I agree that he's taking advantage of her. But she's known him for years. That's one reason she's willing to sell the house directly to him instead of putting it on the open market." There were other reasons, but I didn't want to go into that now. "I've been wondering if they have some sort of arrangement, where Gloria signs the house over to him in exchange for him paying for her current living expenses. Corland has already purchased several houses in her neighborhood and has offers in on several more. He plans to turn them into condos. From what I've been able to find out, he's eager to move ahead with this project."

"I thought Alameda had all sort of rules about that," Noel said. "Multi-unit buildings and condo conversions."

"I checked the municipal code. Condo conversions are permitted, but the developer has to meet various requirements. That includes providing tenants with notice and a copy of the condo conversion plan."

"But there aren't any tenants," Lakshmi said. "They all moved out."

"Exactly. So, no need for Corland to jump through that regulatory hoop. I've talked with all three of Gloria's tenants, the ones who left earlier this year. The guy who moved in June got laid off and moved to Portland to find work. Straightforward reason for him. For the others, a different story. The man who left in July was offered a deal. One year's free rent in a fancy new high rise located south of Market in San Francisco. When I looked into that, I discovered the building is connected to one of Corland's business cronies."

"And the third tenant?" Lakshmi asked.

"Peggy, the woman who lived in the ground floor unit and liked to garden. In August, a man showed up, told her the house was being sold and she had to leave. She said she didn't want to leave, and tried to contact Gloria. She got no response there. However, her garden was vandalized. By then she was the only tenant in the house and was feeling vulnerable. Then the man showed up again and threatened her. That's why she didn't give notice when she moved. She was scared."

Noel was shaking his head. "I can't believe what I'm hearing."

"Corland," Lakshmi said. "I've seen that name before, on the news. He was involved in some dodgy deal in Santa Rosa."

"That's right. He tried to bribe someone in city government to get that deal done, but someone blew the whistle on him. I verified that with my uncle, who worked in the planning department before he retired. I suspect Corland might try to pull some strings here in Alameda to get this condo deal done."

"We have to talk to Gloria now," Noel said. "Before she goes through with this. But where is she?"

Lakshmi got up from her perch on the end of the bench and opened one of the glass doors for a white-haired woman steering a walker.

"Thank you," the woman said. She moved toward the chairs and settled into one of them. "I hope you don't mind me joining you. I'm just waiting for my daughter to pick me up."

"Not at all," Lakshmi said. "I've seen you before. You live down the hall from my husband's aunt, Gloria Rossiter."

"That's right," the woman said. She looked at Noel. "You're her nephew. Are you here to see Gloria? You just missed her."

I stood and jumped into the conversation. "When did she leave? And did she say where she was going?"

"About ten minutes ago," the woman said. "I was in the lobby when she came through. I said hello and she said she had to go out. Over to her house, the one she's selling."

"To look for the notebook," Lakshmi said.

The woman shook her head. "She didn't say anything about that. She said she was meeting the man who is going to buy the house."

"We have to get over there, right now." I pivoted and headed for the parking lot, Noel and Lakshmi at my heels.

"I agree," Noel said. "It's time we had a conversation with this guy."

"Never mind the buyer," Lakshmi said. "What the hell is in that notebook?"

"Records of financial transactions," I said.

She frowned. "And are they legal?"

"I'm not sure. Let's just say I have concerns about those transactions, and what they reveal."

"This guy Corland," Noel said. "You've got concerns about him, too?"

"I do. He has some sort of hold over Gloria. I don't know what it is."

But I had a good idea what was going on, and what had happened in the past. I had to find out if I was right.

Noel's face turned grim as he stopped at the driver's side door of the blue Honda. "If my aunt's in danger, we have to get over there."

"I agree." I unlocked my car and opened the door. "Follow me over there and park down the street, out of sight of the house, so she doesn't see your car. And stay in the car and keep an eye out. Text me if you see anyone approach or go inside the house. I'll talk with Gloria. If the man's not there—"

"Enough talk," Lakshmi pulled a keyring from her pocket and handed it to me. "For Gloria's house. Let's get moving."

# Twenty-Seven

I PULLED TO THE curb at the corner and looked at Gloria's house. Her red Mustang was in the driveway. According to Peggy Slocum, the older man—Lee Corland—who'd visited Gloria drove a silver BMW sedan. I didn't see one parked nearby, though I had to consider the possibility he was already here.

I turned right and drove slowly past the side of the house, its windows revealing nothing. I found a parking space halfway down the block and locked my bag in the trunk, along with the notebook. My phone was on silent mode, set to vibrate if I got a text or a call from Noel and Lakshmi. I looked back down the street and saw their blue Honda slip into a parking space near the corner.

I walked back to the house, phone and car keys in my pocket, Gloria's house key in my hand. I'd go in through the back door, hoping I could slip in through the kitchen, undetected. If Gloria was searching for the notebook, she'd be in her bedroom closet. That must be where she'd hidden the notebook, locked in that compartment in the wall.

The back door was unlocked. Had Gloria left it that way, since she was expecting a visitor? In the kitchen, I stopped, listening. I heard Gloria's voice, no other. Was she alone, talking to herself?

I moved quietly out of the kitchen, past the bathroom, and stood in the doorway, looking into the bedroom. To my left, the pocket doors were open, showing an empty living room. The armoire was where Lakshmi and I had left it, pulled out from the opposite wall. Between the pocket doors and the armoire, the closet door was open. Gloria was inside, at the back, bent over as she looked into the compartment in the wall. It was empty now, as it had been the day I'd found it. She straightened and struck the closet wall with her fist. "God damn it. They're lying to me. Noel and that bitch Lakshmi."

I stepped into the bedroom. "Lying about what?"

Gloria whirled and stared at me. "You. The damn private eye. What are you doing here? How did you get in?"

"The door was unlocked." I shrugged. "That closet was empty when I was here a couple of weeks ago, helping Noel and Lakshmi. I was particularly interested in the compartment. Looks like you kept it locked. What was in it?"

"None of your damn business," she snapped. "Get out of here."

"What are you looking for, Gloria? The notebook?"

She didn't answer. Emotions warred in her face. Then her expression turned to alarm as the floorboards creaked above us. Someone was upstairs. Footsteps came down the stairs. The pocket door leading from the front hallway into the living room opened.

Lee Corland walked into the living room. He stopped near the doorway to the bedroom, his tall, lean figure in a gray business suit that went with his short silver hair. Aloof and unapproachable, a look he'd cultivated for decades. With his pale blue eyes, he gave me stare for stare, but didn't say anything.

Until I spoke. "Beam me up, Scotty."

Surprise flickered in his eyes, if only for a second. There was a touch of annoyance in his voice. "Don't call me that."

"That's what Gloria used to call you back in the day. I understand you were quite the *Star Trek* fan. If you don't care for the name Scotty, I could call you Lee. Or we could go all way back to the beginning, and use your real name, Kelvin Delbert Ward."

Again the flicker of surprise. "You've done your homework."

"It's what I do." I moved toward the armoire. "Gloria is looking for a notebook. She was hoping to find it before you got here."

He frowned and narrowed his gaze. "What notebook?"

"Gloria has been keeping a record of all your financial dealings through the years. It makes interesting reading."

"How did you get it?" Gloria demanded.

He slanted a sideways look at her that told me what he thought of her recordkeeping. "Shut up, Gloria. It doesn't matter how she got it."

"It only matters that I have it. And I've read it. The contents are quite interesting. They show a pattern of money coming into Gloria's hands, courtesy of Kelvin, aka Scotty, and later Lee, whenever you adopted that name." I paused, sizing up his reaction. Nothing so far. I wanted to shake him up, bring something to the surface of that bland facade.

"You were importing drugs from Vietnam to NAS Alameda," I said. "You hid the stuff in candy boxes, ready to be picked up on this end by one of your many girlfriends. Including Gloria. Then the stuff was distributed. You had lots of cash back then. You wanted to launder it. So you gave Gloria the money to buy the house. When you left, you gave her that classic Mustang out in the driveway."

Gloria's eyes widened with alarm. I'd hit the mark.

Lee's face was blank. He watched me like a cat watching a mouse hole, looking for the right moment to pounce. He was good at concealing his thoughts. He'd been very good at hiding himself for decades.

"Back in the summer of 'sixty-nine, things were getting hotter. Someone tipped off the authorities about your drug smuggling scheme. You used to date a local girl named Ann Lombardi. You asked her to pick up one of those candy boxes. She didn't feel comfortable doing it. In fact, she was suspicious, so she ended the relationship. She started dating Eddie Baldwin, your shipmate. Then came that softball game on the base, when you said something nasty to her. It upset her. She told her sister. I'm betting she told Eddie about the incident, or maybe he witnessed it, because he brought her to the game. I think she told him about those candy boxes. He kept an eye on you, until he had enough information to tip off NIS and they started investigating you. Ann and Eddie were liabilities. Before you disappeared to reinvent yourself, you followed them one night when Ann and Eddie went out on a date. What was it? A walk on the beach after the movie? You waylaid them and killed them both."

Gloria stared at him, stunned. Had she known about Ann and Eddie?

"There was a building being remodeled near the barracks on base. You hauled those bodies into the crawl space, dug a hole and buried them. They stayed hidden for decades. And then, because you and your crony Carol Bertram are involved with projects for base redevelopment, you found out that building was being torn down. You knew those bodies would surface. You had Wes and Milo dig up the bones and dump them in that footlocker in the storeroom. Because you've always had the key to Gloria's house. For all intents and purposes you own it. They've identified the bones, by the way. Definitely Ann and Eddie."

"You lied." Gloria spat out the words, disbelief and anger on her face, fighting with the fear that was already there. "You told me it was Monk. The bones in that trunk. You said it was Monk."

"Of course he did," I said. "He let you think those skeletons belong to Monk and Sunny. Because they're dead, too. It happened about the same time. Monk wanted the ring he'd given you, because he was going to give it to Sunny. You wouldn't answer his phone calls, so he came over here. And they wound up dead. Which of you killed them? Or was it both of you?"

"He killed both of them," she screamed, rounding on him. He stepped back, but not far enough. She slashed at him, her fingernails raking a path down the left side of his face. He hadn't been expecting it.

Blood oozed from the wounds as he backed away from her. He pulled a handkerchief from his pocket and stanched the blood. He finally spoke, his voice steady and devoid of feeling. "On the contrary. It was you, Gloria. You and Monk were arguing at the top of the stairs. You pushed him. He hit his head on the way down. While his new girlfriend was wailing over the body, you went downstairs and finished her off with that bottle of wine you were holding. When the bottle broke, the wine went all over the place, stained your clothes. Or was that blood?"

"You're a liar." Gloria spat out the words, leaning toward him. "I didn't push Monk. He slipped on the top of the stairs, I swear it." She glanced at me, appealing for me to believe her story. Then she turned back to Lee. "It was you holding the wine. He was still alive. You hit him with the bottle. It broke. And then you slashed that girl with the broken bottle. You cut her throat. And she bled—" Gloria shuddered. "Right there at the foot of the stairs. You killed them both."

"You two have been lying for so long I'm not sure which of you I believe," I said. "But you're both responsible for their deaths. The police will sort out the details. My guess is Monk came over here with Sunny." I looked at Gloria. "You were already angry with him because he broke off your relationship. And you were jealous of Sunny. Something happened at the top of the stairs and Monk wound up at the bottom. Maybe it was an accident. Maybe the fall killed him. Maybe it was a wine bottle over the head."

Now I fixed Lee with a stare. "But Sunny? No, that was deliberate. Sunny recognized you as Scotty, the sailor who played in that softball game in the spring and chatted about *Star Trek* with her brother. She knew you worked at her father's squadron. She had to die, too."

He examined the blood on his handkerchief, then folded it and returned it to his pocket. "How are you going to prove it?"

"There's bound to be some blood soaked into the cracks between those planks in the hallway in front of the stairs. The forensics are so much better now than they were fifty years ago," I said. "And Gloria, of course. Since she's an eyewitness."

"Gloria won't say anything. Neither will you."

"You're very good at making people disappear. But somehow the bones always come to the surface. What did you do with Monk and Sunny?"

His voice was cold. "I want that notebook. Where is it?"

"In a safe place." Safe, for now. It was in the trunk of my car. If he got hold of my keys, he could retrieve it. But I didn't intend to let him.

I felt a vibration. A text from Noel and Lakshmi? A warning that someone was approaching—or entering—the house?

Sure enough, a movement at the back window caught my eye, someone coming up the back steps. I moved closer to the armoire. Someone was coming through the kitchen, then the hallway past the bathroom.

Wes and Milo, eager to do Lee Corland's bidding.

Wes was the first one into the bedroom, wearing baggy jeans and a swagger, his belly straining his green T-shirt. Behind him was Milo. He didn't look as cocky as Wes. In fact, he didn't look all that happy to be here, as though he realized he might be in too deep. He hung back, a few feet behind his partner.

"You know what to do," Lee told them, stepping back into the living room as though he wanted to steer clear of the action. "I don't want any mistakes this time."

"That's your play?" I said, my voice derisive. "What are you going to do about those people outside who are waiting for me?"

Lee didn't believe me. I could tell from the twist of his unsmiling mouth. Neither did Wes, who upped the ante to a dismissive snort.

My phone vibrated again. Oh, good. Were there more people approaching the house? I had all I could handle right here.

Wes made his move. He walked toward me and cocked his right hand.

I dodged the punch and sidestepped him. Then I slipped behind the empty armoire and pushed. It fell on top of Wes. While he was down, I kicked him. Then I moved toward Milo. He made his decision and ran, back down the hallway to the kitchen.

I turned toward Lee. He appeared to be in good shape but I had forty years on him. He took a step back and his right hand moved to his back. Reaching for a gun? I wasn't going to give him the chance.

The set of fireplace tools still stood this side of the fireplace. I reached for the poker as the rest clattered to the floor. I swung the poker at Lee, hitting him in the knees. He ducked forward, reacting to the impact. I raised the poker and slammed him on the back of the neck. He fell to the floor with a satisfying thud. The gun flew out of his hand. I kicked it away, toward the bay window. Poker in hand, I waited to see if Lee tried to get up. But all the fight had gone out of him. He lay on the floor, looking stunned and disoriented.

Gloria was screaming. The sound registered with me and so did the sounds coming from the foyer. Someone was opening the front door.

Had Milo changed his mind, circling around to come in through the front door? I moved toward the foyer, ready to confront whoever had entered the house.

It was Noel, his face white.

I took a deep breath to calm myself and snapped, "I told you to wait in the car."

# Twenty-Eight

ONLY THEN DID I register the wail of sirens, getting closer.

"Who called the police?" I asked Noel.

His mouth was open but he was having troubling finding his voice. "Lakshmi did," he said finally. "We got out of the car and we were watching the back of the house. When we saw those two guys, she hit 911 and told them they were breaking in and we heard screaming and I just had to—"

Metal clanked against metal. I glanced back as Gloria picked up the fireplace tongs. Lee was still on the floor, stunned by the blow I'd landed with the fireplace poker. She swung the tongs at Lee, who was once again trying to get up from the floor. I wrenched the tongs from her hands and tossed them away.

She huffed at me and turned to Noel for a more sympathetic reaction. Tears trickled down her face as he put his arms around her.

I fixed Lee with a glare, waving the poker. "Don't even try getting up, or I'll lay you out again."

He stared at me, pale blue eyes glinting with fury, the blood from the scratches Gloria had inflicted red against the white mask of his face. Angry, but cornered. He didn't have much fight left.

Wes had pushed clear of the armoire I'd dumped on top of him. He scrambled to his feet and looked at me, still holding the poker, as the sirens went from loud to deafening and stopped outside. He bolted for the kitchen and the back door. I heard a loud voice from the back of the house. "Police!"

I moved quickly to the bedroom window and looked out, gratified to see Wes on the sidewalk below, being handcuffed by a uniformed police officer. I returned to the living room as two officers came through the front door. One of them had been part of the team that responded the day I'd found the bones. Fortunately, she recognized me, too.

"You want to tell me what's going on here?" she asked.

I pointed at Lee. "Call Lieutenant Chen. This is Lee Corland, the man who killed Ann Lombardi and Eddie Baldwin."

"The lieutenant's on his way." She looked at Gloria and Noel. "And who are these people?"

"Gloria Rossiter. She owns the house. This is her great-nephew, Noel Benjamin."

"We got two guys who ran from the house, one with dark hair, the other blond. Know anything about them?"

I nodded. "The blond one is Wes Chandler, the dark-haired one is Milo Fonseca. They dug up the bones and stashed them here in the house."

Lieutenant Chen came through the front door and entered the living room, in time to hear what I said about the bones. He flashed a smile. "I look forward to getting your statement."

I gave him the short version and told him I'd come by his office later, for the long version. All the while, I could hear Gloria talking with another officer, her voice rising and falling as she vehemently denied involvement in anything that might lead to criminal charges. Two other officers hauled Lee to his feet and out the front door. I followed, in time to see him being put into the backseat of a police car. I looked around and saw two more police cars pulled to the curb. Wes was in the backseat of one, Milo in the other.

People crowded the sidewalks, with curious faces as they pointed at the corner house. There hadn't been so much excitement since the day I'd found the bones, two weeks earlier.

Lakshmi was on the front sidewalk, behind the police perimeter, her face anxious. "Where the hell is Noel? And Gloria? What was he thinking, going in there like that? He could have been killed. What is going on?"

"He should be right behind me," I said. I glanced back at the porch. Sure enough, Noel was ushering Gloria through the front door. She moved like a frail old woman as he walked her to the red Mustang. "Looks like Lieutenant Chen has decided to let her go, for now. But this isn't the end of it." I brought Lakshmi up to date.

She stood in silence for a moment, watching as Gloria backed the car into the street and drove away. "Do you think she actually killed someone, Monk, that old boyfriend of hers?"

"It's possible," I said.

"Of course she didn't," Noel protested. He'd walked from the driveway to where we stood on the sidewalk. "It was that man Corland. I can't believe Gloria would have anything to do with—"

"I can," Lakshmi said, her voice cold. She'd finally had enough of Aunt Gloria and she wasn't making nice anymore.

He recoiled. "You're just saying that because you don't like her, you never have."

Before Lakshmi could answer, I jumped in. "You're going to have to sort this out between you. It's a he-said, she-said situation and we may never know exactly what happened to Monk and Sunny."

I made my exit, thinking about that as I walked to my car. Later that afternoon, I sat in Lieutenant Chen's office at the Alameda Police Department. I'd given the police a detailed statement of the events that occurred at Gloria's house. Now he and I were discussing the unanswered questions about the other two missing persons—Monk Guidry and Sunny Post.

Chen wasn't speculating, but I was. "I can see it both ways. Gloria says Lee killed both of them. His story is that Gloria killed Monk by pushing him down the stairs, then she hit him with a wine bottle. An impulsive act on her part? But what were Gloria and Lee doing upstairs with a wine bottle?"

"They were in the apartment he was renting?" Chen theorized.

"My impression was that he was living with her in the downstairs flat at the time. But I'm not sure and I didn't find anything in the tenant records showing me that Gloria rented an apartment to him under his real name or any other name, for that matter. So who do we believe? They both have a long history of lying and reinventing themselves."

Chen had been twirling a pencil in his hands. He tapped it on his desk. "Lee Corland isn't talking. But those two guys he had working for him, Wes Chandler and Milo Fonseca, I have a feeling we'll get something out of them. As for Gloria Rossiter, not sure. She's playing the victim, denying any involvement."

I nodded. "She's involved. It may take some doing to prove it. I think Lee killed Sunny because she recognized him as one of the sailors in her father's command. As for Gloria killing Monk, yes, I could believe that. They had an acrimonious breakup. Gloria was extremely jealous of Sunny. Either way, they were killed in that house. Is there any chance of physical evidence?"

"It's been more than fifty years," Chen said. "I have a team in the house now, looking for evidence. But blood and tissue degrade over time.

Maybe there's something else for the team to find. Where are the bodies? In the foundation of a building somewhere?"

"That would fit the pattern, since Lee disposed of Ann and Eddie's bodies in that crawl space. I'm not sure." I paused as I recalled my earlier Internet search on skeleton remains. The ship. "When I was at the demolition site, eavesdropping, Milo Fonseca was talking with some of his coworkers about the Mothball Fleet."

"All those old ships out at Suisun Bay? They're all gone now, hauled off for salvage. And a good thing, too. They were shedding toxic paint and leaking all kinds of nasty stuff into the bay."

"That's right. Fonseca's uncle worked for the MARAD, the Maritime Administration, that was overseeing the Mothball Fleet. On Thursday, Milo told his coworkers that his uncle took Milo and Wes aboard some of the ships. And Wes commented that the ships had all sorts of places to hide things. Right after I found the bones, I did an Internet search on skeletal remains. I saw a news story about some bones being found on a decommissioned ship that was being salvaged at a yard in New Orleans. It caught my eye because it was odd. And now I'm wondering."

"So am I," Chen said. "I'll contact the New Orleans police department and find out where those bones are now. We'll see where it leads."

---

As it turned out, Monk Guidry went back to Louisiana after all. His bones, anyway. And Sunny's remains went with him.

Milo said it was Wes's idea. The bodies of Monk and Sunny had been buried on the Alameda waterfront, on a stretch of former industrial land off Clement Street. It was about to be developed and Lee was concerned that someone would find the bones. He sent Milo and Wes to dig up and dispose of the remains. This was a year or so before the last of the Mothball Fleet had left Suisun Bay.

Wouldn't it be a laugh, Wes said, if they hid the bones on one of those old ships? So that's what they did, both of them transporting the bones in backpacks, with the unwitting aid of Uncle João.

Something else was mixed in with the bones found on the old ship—one of the matching fleur-de-lis pendants Anita made for them. The other pendant was found lodged in a crack between two floorboards in Gloria's house. Anita identified the pendants from evidence photographs. Dental records, along with DNA samples from Charlene Hebert and Frank Post, did the rest.

At long last, Monk and Sunny were no longer missing.

---

THERE'S NEVER A NEATLY wrapped ending to a case. The loose ends can straggle for weeks, months, even years. The last I heard, Gloria was still under investigation for her part in the deaths of Monk and Sunny. Lee Corland was facing murder charges in the deaths of Ann and Eddie—and possibly those of Monk and Sunny. His financial empire was in disarray, the condo conversion in Alameda was kaput and his business partner Carol Bertram was backpedaling as fast as she could to disassociate herself from Lee and his crimes.

And the Navy still wanted to talk with Kelvin Delbert Ward—aka Lee Corland—about about drug smuggling and going AWOL.

The families had claimed the remains, with Tessa Lombardi holding a memorial service in Alameda for her sister Ann. I wasn't sure what Eddie's family in Colorado had done. Monk's sister was planning a service for her brother, while here in the Bay Area, Liam Ebbets and Anita Ryker held a remembrance for the musician in Point Reyes Station. As for Sunny, Frank Post flew to New Orleans to retrieve his sister's bones.

Dan and I were still on speaking terms with Noel and Lakshmi. From something Dan said, I understood that husband and wife were still bickering about Gloria. Noel wanted to be supportive. Lakshmi was ready to write her off.

And Maggie Constable wrote a hell of a feature about the whole case for the *Chronicle*.

---

A WEEK LATER, I closed my office and headed home. I was on my own this evening. Dan was meeting a friend for dinner in Walnut Creek. I fed the cats, who assured me that they had faced privation since breakfast, despite the level of crunchies in the feeding bowl. Black Bart, in particular, felt that if he caught the tiniest glimpse of the bottom, the food bowl must be empty.

"You are so fat, I don't think you are in danger of starving," I told him as he circled my feet. He looked up at me and meowed in disagreement. Abigail, on the other hand, waited patiently until I put down the small ceramic bowls containing cat food. Then she began to eat, daintily, while her companion inhaled his repast.

That done, I rummaged in the refrigerator for the remains of a casserole I'd made the day before. I put together a salad, heated up a portion of the casserole and poured a glass of chardonnay. Then I put everything on a tray.

Before I carried my dinner out to the back deck, I rummaged through the CDs in a basket, looking for one in particular. There it was, *Court and Spark*. One of my favorites, too, I thought, recalling my conversation with Anita. I put the CD in the player and listened as Joni Mitchell sang, her voice weaving through the tracks.

Out on the deck, I ate my dinner and looked out at the garden. Late October, and the sunny weather had given way to clouds. There was a chill in the air as I finished the casserole and tipped back my glass, savoring the wine. Birds flitted in and out of the trees in the backyard. I heard a buzzing sound and looked up as an Anna's hummingbird swooped in on the beaded glass feeder I'd bought from Anita.

A gardener's work is never done, I thought as I took another sip of wine. The weeds were taking over one of the raised beds. There were pumpkins and acorn squash ready to harvest.

I heard my name being called and looked up to see my tenant, Madison Brady, waving at me from the window of her studio apartment above the garage. I beckoned her to join me. A few minutes later, she climbed the exterior stairs connecting the back yard to the deck.

"Help yourself to wine," I said. "There's a bottle in the fridge. In fact, bring the bottle."

"I will, thanks." She disappeared into the kitchen and returned with bottle and glass, pulling out a chair to join me at the table. "I'm celebrating. I have news."

"What's up?"

"You remember I told you about that project I applied for?"

I nodded. "One of your professors is taking a team of grad students to Thailand."

She grinned. "That's right. Ten city planning students and the professor from UC Berkeley, plus ten students and professors from Chulalongkorn University. It's a sustainable development project in cities on the Gulf of Thailand, south of Bangkok. They notified the Berkeley students today. And I'm one of them!"

"Congratulations!" We clinked glasses. "That is exciting news."

"It's really an honor to be chosen." She swallowed a mouthful of wine. "Thing is, I'm going to be gone for a couple of months. And there's the apartment..."

I waved a hand. "Don't worry about that. We'll work something out."

Madison was paying for her own graduate education, cobbling together funds from previous jobs, grants, and some help from her mother, I knew money was an issue. It was difficult for UC Berkeley students to find places to live. Many of them wound up renting portions of already-crowded apartments or lived farther from campus. That's why I didn't charge market rate rent for the garage apartment. It was worth it to me to have a tenant, someone to be here, looking after the cats and the property when I was absent. That would be the case in a few days. I'd cleared my calendar. Dan and I were heading up to Mendocino.

She was good company, too. We talked a while longer, finishing our wine.

"Still on for cat sitting? Dan and I are off to Mendocino for a few days."

"Of course. When are you leaving?"

"Thursday morning. We'll be back on Monday."

She smiled. "It will be nice to get a kitty fix."

"And nice for us to get away."

Madison's phone rang and she picked up the call, moving away for privacy, down the stairs to the back yard.

I looked out at the garden, then reached for the bottle and topped off my glass. When I finished the last of the wine, I left my dishes in the kitchen and headed down to the garden. As I harvested the squash, it began to rain. I lifted my face to meet it.

THE END

# ACKNOWLEDGMENTS

It began with a house. On my weekly forays to the Farmers Market, I frequently parked near an old Victorian house in Alameda's West End. Someone lived there, I could tell that much. But the house, of the Queen Anne style, was in a state of disrepair. It made me wonder about the stories hidden within those walls. As writers do, I asked myself, "what if?"

What if my Oakland PI Jeri Howard found a footlocker full of old bones in that house?

That was the start of *The Things We Keep*. The journey led me back to the days when the now-closed Naval Air Station Alameda was an active, bustling Navy base. I was stationed there as a Navy junior officer in the early 1980s and it's quite a contrast to see the base now.

Other forays into the past included San Francisco and the Haight-Ashbury neighborhood in the 1960s as well as the killing spree by the Zodiac Killer in the late 1960s. Among the excellent resources I consulted: *Zodiac*, Robert Graysmith; *Season of the Witch*, David Talbot; *Reporter's Note Book*, Duffy Jennings.

Many thanks to Lieutenant Erik Klaus, Investigations Commander of the Alameda Police Department. I also appreciate the input of Carolyn Thomas, who grew up in Alameda and gave me insights on what the city was like back in the 1960s and 1970s. My guitarist brother, Roger Dawson, gave helpful information.

Many thanks to fellow mystery writers D. Z. Church, Heather Haven and Margaret Lucke. In lieu of getting together in person, I have looked forward to our regular Zoom sessions. I appreciate my fellow writers who are always willing to answer questions, who assist me in many ways as I write and complete the journey from idea to publication.

# ABOUT THE AUTHOR

Janet Dawson is the author of 14 books in the series featuring Oakland private investigator Jeri Howard. The first book, *Kindred Crimes*, won the St. Martin's Press/Private Eye Writers of America best first PI novel contest, and was subsequently nominated for three best first awards—the Shamus, the Anthony and the Macavity. *The Things We Keep* is the latest addition to Jeri's list of cases.

She also writes the Jill McLeod historical mysteries. Starting with *Death Rides the Zephyr*, the four books in the series feature Zephyrette Jill McLeod, who solves mysteries in the early 1950s while working aboard the historic train called the California Zephyr.

Her new series featuring geriatric care manager Kay Dexter began with *The Sacrificial Daughter*. She has also written a suspense novel, *What You Wish For*. Her short fiction includes a novella, *But Not Forgotten*, as well as a dozen short stories, including Macavity winner "Voice Mail" and Shamus nominee "Slayer Statute."

She worked as a newspaper reporter in Colorado, and her stint as a U.S. Navy journalist took her to Guam and Florida. As a Navy officer, she was stationed in the San Francisco Bay Area. After leaving the Navy, she worked in the legal field and at the University of California. She is a long-time member of Mystery Writers of America and Sisters in Crime. She enjoys birding, riding on trains, gardening, theatre, music and museums, and thinks afternoon tea is a most civilized English tradition. She loves cats but denies being a crazy cat lady.

Information/newsletter: www.janetdawson.com

www.facebook.com/Mysteries.PrivateEyes.Trains/

# ALSO BY JANET DAWSON

### The Jeri Howard Series
*Kindred Crimes*
*Till The Old Men Die*
*Take A Number*
*Don't Turn Your Back on the Ocean*
*Nobody's Child*
*A Credible Threat*
*Witness to Evil*
*Where the Bodies Are Buried*
*A Killing at the Track*
*Bit Player*
*Cold Trail*
*Water Signs*
*The Devil Close Behind*
*The Things We Keep*

### The Jill McLeod California Zephyr Series
*Death Rides the Zephyr*
*Death Deals a Hand*
*The Ghost in Roomette Four*
*Death Above the Line*

### The Kay Dexter Series
*The Sacrificial Daughter*

### Other Works
*What You Wish For*
*But Not Forgotten*
**Short Stories**—a list can be found at www.janetdawson.com

Printed in Dunstable, United Kingdom